My Cambodian Twin

Annie Caulfield

First published in 2019 by
Martin McNamara
www.anniecaulfield.org

ISBN: 9780368678783

Book cover designed by Woodrow Phoenix

Special Thanks:
Dr Tom Newsom-Davis,
Mr Kevin O'Neill and the many, many kind staff, nurses
and doctors at the Chelsea & Westminster Hospital,
Royal Marsden Hospital, Charing Cross Hospital,
and Royal Trinity Hospice
Janet Fillingham
Woodrow Phoenix
Sarah Daniels
Jo, James & Margaret Caulfield
Emma Harding
Mike Walker
Jon S. Fink
Lisa Stevens
Molly & Jasmine Warwick
Solomon Adebe
Anne-Marie Doulton
Rosanna & Gaye O'Brien
Lenny Henry
Sandi Toksvig
Gordon Kennedy
Catherine Townsend
Lesley Allan
Susannah Kraft Levene
Mary Ward Lowery
and
Sophea Kagna & all of Annie's friends in Cambodia

My Cambodian Twin

SPECIAL THANKS:

Dr Tom Newsom-Davis,
Mr Kevin O'Neill and the many, many kind staff, nurses
and doctors at the Chelsea & Westminster Hospital,
Royal Marsden Hospital, Charing Cross Hospital,
and Royal Trinity Hospice
Janet Fillingham
Woodrow Phoenix
Sarah Daniels
Jo, James & Margaret Caulfield
Emma Harding
Mike Walker
Jon S. Fink
Lisa Stevens
Molly & Jasmine Warwick
Solomon Adebe
Anne-Marie Doulton
Rosanna & Gaye O'Brien
Lenny Henry
Sandi Toksvig
Gordon Kennedy
Catherine Townsend
Lesley Allan
Susannah Kraft Levene
Mary Ward Lowery
and
Sophea Kagna & all of Annie's friends in Cambodia

FOREWORD

My sister Annie started writing this book because she was fascinated and moved by Sophea's story.

After she made her first visits to the country she told me about the vivid colours of Cambodia and about this woman whose life - like that of countless other Cambodians - had been changed forever when the Khmer Rouge soldiers came to power and unleashed four years of genocide and madness.

This is a story of brutality and ballet. Sophea was determined to help heal her damaged fellow countrymen and woman spiritually, through traditional Khmer dance. That was the story Annie was telling.

I loved hearing about Sophea. Although she clearly trusted Annie, the relationship between them was, at times, spiky. This was not the typical hagiography you get from West meeting the East. Here were two outspoken, irritable and funny women; a million miles from the world of "Eat, Pray, Love".

By the time Annie was able to return to Cambodia to complete her travels for this book everything in her life had changed.

She had been diagnosed with inoperable lung cancer.

She had endured months of chemotherapy and radiotherapy. She was in the limbo stage where your body has to recover, and you wait to see what the cancer will do next.

On the day she got her diagnosis, the oncologist, Dr Tom, asked her what was important to her; what did she most want to do with her time.

She said she wanted to go back to Cambodia and to Sophea, and finish telling her story.

Her partner and I think the oncologist, and maybe this is the profession's great skill, had managed to get to the essence of Annie. He didn't say it in words but the message is clear: "You may have a limited time; what is important to you."

And Annie wanted to finish this book.

On that final trip, she sent Dr Tom a photo she took high up in the Dangrek Mountains. It was her way to thank him for helping get her there.

She told me she had 15 years or more. She didn't and she knew it. Well, that's too simple; I think she knew the truth of it, sometimes.

This was the last book that Annie wrote. You might argue that you don't need to know about the author; that the work should speak for itself. But I think what Annie was going through as she wrote it informs so much of this volume.

Within a few days of her return from Cambodia she had her first seizure. The cancer had spread to the brain. She continued writing. The morning after brain surgery she was sat up in her hospital bed, demanding her laptop.

She was so relieved that her brain was still her brain, that she was still 'herself'. Thrilled to be propped up in bed and writing; full of funny stories about her drug induced hallucinations and the other people in the ward. She already had new ideas and was making notes, planning what she would write after she had finished this book.

She knew it was a cliché, but she felt very 'look at the trees - look at the sky'; a gleeful smile on her face.

For me this book is about those joyful moments in life. About recognising, creating and enjoying those small moments. That whether it's the Khmer Rouge or cancer, these forces of evil can't stop us from trying to make life a little bit better, trying to help and heal as Sophea does, by teaching kids to dance, or by doing something well.

Annie barely mentions her cancer in the book, She does tell Sophea but it's a few lines and she then dismisses it. But the fact of her cancer and that she was writing with an increasingly pessimistic prognosis is there, on the pages.

There is joy and wonder at life, but I can also hear her fears and her thoughts on the big life/death questions.

She would have written about cancer, afterwards, if she had come through.

After coming home from Cambodia that last time, Annie died 11 and half months later. She continued working right up until a few weeks before her death.

'Be useful, be busy and try and do whatever you do well.'

That's what I learnt from my big sister.

And I can hear her voice now, adding: 'Jesus Jo, would you at least tell them that the book is also very funny and interesting?".

It is.

Jo Caulfield

Thank you to John Rovira and Jennie Sykes, without whose inspiration, kindness and support this book would not exist

— Annie Caulfield

INTRODUCTION BY ANNIE CAULFIELD

WHY is it so irritating when friends say; "Oh you must meet so and so, they're so interesting, you'll really like them."?

Perhaps it's not irritating to you, perhaps you are not a curmudgeonly soul who 'really likes' only a handful of people. I prefer to find people for myself and decide about them for myself. Then again, I did really like the people who were telling me about the interesting woman they'd encountered, on the other side of the world.

There was the first difficulty with this interesting new person. I couldn't just cross London and have a cup of tea with her. I'd have to go to Cambodia.

Then my friends seemed to lose their minds completely; "She has this amazing story, this amazing thing she wants to do, you could write a great book about her. And you'd love Cambodia."

Could I? Would I? Why were they doing this to me? Now they'd be hurt if I didn't at least hear what they knew of Sophea and promise to think about this book I could be writing.

Then I'd have to invent an excuse because the truth itself might seem too much like an excuse. How would it sound if I told them I'd been thinking about not travel writing anymore? The world was full of adventurers and bloggers – why keep adding to the noise? Why not stay home and write stories about the many things and people already in my mind, and not properly examined, perhaps because I kept moving around so much. There was always some new place over the fence that needed looking into, distantly located things to learn and ponder. But I didn't want to write those lives of others stories any more; it seemed, like travelling, a way to avoid myself.

But maybe just one more journey? If I didn't inhale?

When I started looking for books about Cambodia, I discovered there were very few about the present day. Books by Cambodians were, understandably, pulled back to or haunted by the recent past – the horrors of the Khmer Rouge regime in the 1970s. But the books by foreigners were sentimental, orientalist evocations of ancient days. Or they were full of analysis of Cambodian history that tried to make a case that there was something peculiar to Cambodians. This is why, in this small country, one part of the population had massacred two million of the others – because they were not like the rest of us. I knew this kind of writing – for decades people had written about my home, Northern Ireland, this way. But the dozens of people in my family back there were like everyone else. They just happened to be in a bitter and angry situation. From left wing playwrights at the Royal Court to right wing political pundits, the Northern Irish were dismissed as a people who'd become somehow different. A London upbringing had evaporated most of my accent but I only had to mention where my family were from, and I was answering the same old questions about our unfathomable ways, our intransigent hatreds and casual violence. Actually, we did all manner of other stuff, all the time.

There was killing in Northern Ireland but no massacres. There were some poisonous leaders but no all powerful Pol Pot. But small countries full of hate and violence have one thing in common. When it's all over, you have to wonder, who were those people? In this sparsely populated place how many of the killers did I know, do I still pass in the street? How well do people really recover, forgive, forget? And in Cambodia? What was left behind alongside those piled skulls we'd seen in The Killing Fields.

It would be hard to begin to know, unless I knew someone there who had lived through it all. My friends urged me that Cambodian dancer Sophea was just that person.

When I got past being irritated with them for telling me who I might like and what I might want to write about, I realised there must be qualities in Sophea that had inspired them to this point of fanaticism. Not something these quiet, diligent business people were susceptible to.

Although I found little to read about present day Cambodia that didn't feel stuck on the one note — that there was something intrinsically wrong with the place — I knew I didn't want to annoy the world with some tale of my gadding about the country having hilarious and deeply moving adventures among foreigners. If I was going to abandon my half formed resolution to stay home and stop picking at the world for curious yarns and strange customs, I needed a story that told me something about all of life – because it does increasingly seem to me, wherever you go, the details are different but people are the same.

CHAPTER 1: MIRROR MIRROR

One person at our table had lived through the twentieth century's second most efficient genocide; the other one had not.

On the surface there were dozens of obvious differences between us, but my childhood lived as a child and Sophea's lived under the brutal Khmer Rouge regime – that would be the one to notice on deeper acquaintance. So why had Sophea just said: "It's interesting Annie. I have realised that we are very alike."

She said this and returned to picking daintily through the dishes on our table, as if her words were so clearly true there was no need for discussion.

Let's start with those surface differences. Lithe as a willow wand, up, down and sideways, Sophea was about half my size. She was always perfectly groomed, from her manicured toes to the white magnolia flower she'd absent-mindedly tucked into the braid of her long black hair. If I'd picked up a wind-fallen flower to try any such casual self-adornment I'd have ended up with a bee-stung head. Or would look as though the flower had just been thrown down on me by a spiteful tree lizard, because to tree lizards there was just something about my face...

Even without trying any ambitious flower-on-head manoeuvres, I looked like a giant, sunburnt, comical beast Sophea was leading around the streets to show her friends and ask: should she keep it, or would it break the furniture?

Sophea put a flower in her hair with the same confident carelessness she showed in explaining how something had happened to her "… because I'm very beautiful." In the matter-of-fact way someone else might say: "…because I'm very tall."

Sophea was never just dressed; every day, a fetching outfit and accessories had been assembled. Sophea didn't walk into a room, she presented herself to it. A professional performer, she was used to being watched and admired. In turn, the performing had polished her compelling appearance. The rigours of what she did meant that food just disappeared into her fine bones and gravity hadn't yet dared to make grabs at her face.

Sophea was a dancer. She'd achieved this against all personal odds. And the style of dance she performed, Khmer Classical Ballet, had almost, at several points in history, vanished from the face of the earth.

Sophea's involvement with dancing, and indeed the face of the earth, had nearly been cut short in 1975 by the Khmer Rouge regime. During the regime's killing of people deemed enemies of the state, 190 ballet dancers were put to death.

Sophea was seven years old when the slaughter of dancers happened. She'd been hoping to begin training. Seven was the ideal age, as her bones would still have a malleable softness to achieve perfect form. The dance school was for rich and royal children, but she was pleading with her very ordinary parents, she'd do anything… Her father was a chef and her mother a clerk in a tobacco factory – they just managed. Very bright Sophea was already at a costly primary school; now her dream of ballet-dancing was breaking their hearts.

If they'd had more money and influence, Sophea might have been among the privileged, dressed in a silk costume, refining a hand gesture, when Pol Pot's troops came through the dance studio door, full of homicidal rage. But here she was, decades later, having survived and achieved astonishing things.

How could she think we were "very alike"?

Little hands darting around the table, Sophea was urging me to help her finish the lunch. It was hot and airless in the storefront restaurant; I didn't really feel like eating, couldn't eat as much as Sophea at the best of times.

We were the same age, there was that, both fifty, but then... I had nagged at my parents for ballet lessons when I was seven years old, but it had been a whim, not a passion. The moment I realised the process didn't go from nought to twirling in a swan costume on pointed toes, I was bored. I went home in tears, and anyway, my friend Susan Fogden had a new pink bicycle, a bicycle would really be much better for me… Our lower-middle-class home had a contentment, occasionally strained financially by children full of whims, but so much of what we needed was free – education, health care, school lunches…. Outside our house the most dangerous thing was the North Circular Road.

There was also contentment in Sophea's family home, with her gentle, creative father and efficient, ambitious mother; her younger brother and sister. Their Buddhist faith centred the household. Respectable, minding their own business, they were only strained by the cost of Sophea's schooling and the perfect blue and white uniforms the school required. Their house was in a quiet side street, safe to play in, safe for walking to school. But then.

The chic, corrupt ruling class of Cambodia had been very greedy with what they'd acquired from France post-independence, while the countryside peasants were struggling hard. The peasants to the North were under escalating threat from the war in Vietnam. American planes hunting Vietnamese Communist fighters incinerated Cambodian homes, crops and families. In the forests, grief-stricken, destitute, angry and susceptible to the worst of promise-makers, Cambodia's peasantry became Communist fighters. These black-shirted Khmer Rouge, half-starved, half-crazy with hate, were taking Cambodia for themselves. In Phnom Penh, American-backed government troops fought to hold the city.

Every day, fewer children came to school. Sophea, so delighted with her lessons and smart uniform, insisted on crossing the city as normal, despite parental anxiety about the bombs and shells beginning to fall.

"I lied to my parents. I said everyone was still attending, I mustn't get behind or they'd have wasted their money. Then one morning I went and the whole school was shelled. I went to my teacher's home. I said she could still teach us in her house but she started crying. She said I mustn't cross the city any more until the shelling stopped."

The shelling did stop. The government troops seemed to vanish overnight. Many simply burnt their uniforms and disappeared into the general population, knowing that the moment was close when the Khmer Rouge would strut through Phnom Penh.

The arrival of the young Khmer Rouge soldiers was greeted with ambivalence. For a few hours, the city people thought they could relax, the war was over; life would get back to normal. But then, along with most of the bewildered population of Phnom Penh, Sophea's family was told they had to leave the city immediately. The Americans were going to bomb it and everyone was in mortal danger. People had to grab enough supplies for three days and head into the countryside. In three days they could come home, safe to celebrate the Khmer Rouge triumph.

Sophea's father bought a handcart to transport their belongings. They'd head along the Tonle Sap lake to a fishing village where he had cousins, only half a day's distance but far enough for safety. Sophea wanted to take her books and the school uniforms that she kept so proudly spick and span. Her father said it was silly to take them; they'd be back in three days. They needed to carry food, bedding, cooking pots, mosquito nets, medicines.... Besides, her six-year-old brother and three-year-old sister were too small to walk all the way out of the city; the handcart was for them. Enraged, Sophea hid her uniforms inside her bedding.

Brother and sister perched on the handcart while Sophea walked behind with her mother, pushing a little, but mostly still sulking that pots and these candy-sucking infants had taken priority over her belongings. Then Sophea grew curious about the young men in black with guns who were watching them all the way. She thought they could offer to help people like her father, pulling the cart like an ox – but they weren't offering to help anyone. Not even the very old people struggling with bundles, or the families with no cart and too

many small children to carry.
On the edge of the city her mother said; "Don't look."
But Sophea was already looking at a burnt-out service taxi, swollen bodies spilling out of it. A rear wheel of the taxi was in the air, pushed upward by the bloat of a body on the ground beneath.From side roads more and more people joined the stumbling procession from the city.
"When we stopped for a moment's rest my father would talk to these strangers, asking them questions. This wasn't like him; he was a very shy man."
There was an expression in her father's face that Sophea didn't recognise when a gang of soldiers on the road told him the family couldn't go to his relatives. They had to follow everyone else to a camp by the lakeside.
The new expression disappeared quickly. Sophea's father forced a cheeriness with his family, urging them onward as he hauled his cart where he was told.
"I was going to say, looking back, that it was the first time I'd seen him frightened but I can see it now and it was more as if he felt stupid. As if he was realising these soldiers were lying, that everything was a big lie and we were tricked. You know, the kind of shocked face when you realise you've been really stupid?"
At the crowded camp, Sophea helped her parents to arrange the bedding and make a fire. Her baby sister slept. Sophea's brother, six-year-old Sann, went with some of his friends to wash at the lake's edge. Sophea grumbled; Sann wouldn't be washing, he'd be splashing and playing and in her opinion he was quite old enough to help with the work as well…
An hour later the boys came back, Sann wasn't with them. The boys said a woman in Khmer Rouge uniform had introduced herself as Sann's aunt, his mother's sister, and taken him to collect a gift for the family.
Sophea looked at her mother for confirmation. Yes, it was true, she didn't have a sister.
They searched the camp and the riverbanks. They begged every Khmer Rouge they saw for information. Halfway through the following day they still hadn't found Sann, and the soldiers were telling them they had to move on, further away from Phnom Penh.
"I started shouting at my father. He should tell the soldiers it had been four days now, couldn't they count? They should let us go home, maybe Sann was already home… That was when my father spotted the school uniforms hidden inside my bedding. He grabbed my shoulders and shook me; 'You idiot, what did I tell you?'
"He snatched the uniforms and threw them into the ditch behind us. He told me never to talk about my uniforms or my fancy school again. I didn't know his face. He never hurt me or spoke like that. Even when I started crying he spoke roughly to me and told me to help my mother pack up."
They moved on along the lake, on beyond any world that seemed familiar or

sane. The city was weeks behind them, then months, then years behind them. They moved from lake fishing for the Khmer Rouge, to growing an endless rotation of crops in remote districts, where food was rationed, medical care was non-existent and they couldn't wash properly, or sleep enough to think straight.

"You know how time is long when you are a child? So when I say 'a year' now, it was a longer time for me then. It was forever. At first I tried to make myself dream about good things when I fell asleep. After that I think there were no dreams, asleep or awake, my thinking was just black."

It was four years before they could go home again, the shreds of themselves, still looking for Sann.

This had happened to Sophea between the ages of seven and eleven. This woman sitting opposite me in her favourite Siem Reap restaurant -'cheap but high quality'- refining the cutlery shine with a paper napkin, claiming we had things in common.

There was only our age in common, and we each had one younger brother and sister. Neither of mine had disappeared. When my brother was six he'd shaved all my dolls and I'd very much wanted him to disappear. I kept pushing him into wardrobes hoping he'd accidentally go to Narnia and never come back. He was always still there, spitting in the bottom of the wardrobe, plotting his next crime against me.

There wasn't simply a vast difference in experience between Sophea and me; we perceived the whole of life in different ways.

Sophea believed in gods, spirits and reincarnation. She had a Buddhist altar taking up half her living room. When she meditated, she told me, she could take her mind and soul away from the earth. She could look down from far above.

I could imagine what her real life had been like. But I knew I wouldn't catch even a fleeting heel of her beliefs. This magical, flying-soul Sophea left me staring blankly at her. Not wanting to give offence, I'd ask questions but the answers too would flit past me like elves. Sophea could leave her troubles for another plane. I knew I'd be fixed in my plodding scepticism whatever befell me.

At some long-ago rock festival, I'd avoided the inevitable rain by ducking into the tent of a hippy fortune-teller. She gave me a small crystal to hold; then she grasped it, eyes closed. She opened them, shook her head and gave me my money back. She said she couldn't see anything about me in her crystal because I had no spiritual life. Good, I'd thought as I indignantly pocketed my money and went out into the rain again, I'm glad the crystal can see that I'm no fool…

Possibly because I did get tangled into thinking that a crystal could see I didn't believe in it, there might be a tiny opening in my mind for an unearthly thought to squeeze through – but not a whole religious system. And certainly not anything involving sitting still for so long I hallucinated, choking on incense, waiting for spirit lift-off. I wasn't interested in dragging around behind Sophea hoping she'd provide Eastern enlightenment. I was curious about her complicated matrix of beliefs because I was curious about her and her tangled, still tangling, life. Growing out of the Khmer Rouge horror, her life suggested remarkable things, good things, about mere human beings.

Sophea was interested in me because she had a story she wanted to tell and she was on a mission that she hoped would change her life, possibly several lives.

We'd been pottering around Siem Reap province together for about ten days now, getting to know each other, wondering if the whole bizarre expedition could work out.

Sophea wasn't easy to know. Never mind her life on other spiritual planes; just on the plain ordinary earth where I grunted around, she lived on several planes, in shifting shapes of her character.

Some holidaying friends, able to afford the trillion-star hotel where Sophea gave performances for a select, respectful audience, had spent time with her and passed on her story. She wanted it told; she hoped we'd make a little money to help her set up a dance school for poor children at her local pagoda.

"I must teach because soon I'll be too old. If I teach the dance to ordinary children, then they can teach it too, then it lives for people who are not royal people or rich people. It's the good I can put into the world, or what is the point of me?"

I first arrived to meet her at the hotel, my notebook in hand, thinking she'd be delighted, but she looked at me coldly, notebook in her hand.

"Your friends say you are good, but we must make a decision about how the money will be divided. And if you can write down some names of things you have written. I will ask the manager here who I trust, she can check on you so I know you are suitable. This is my life, you understand. I must be sure about you."

I started writing in her notebook. She was right, of course, who the hell was I to march in and take her past to market?

Then she said; "I remember you emailed me in French, perhaps we should speak French?"

Proud of myself, I switched languages; of course, French was fine.

She stared a moment. "Speak English. Please, write the name of where you are staying and I will call on you on Wednesday morning."

Wednesday was two days away. I lay awake that night in my cheap guesthouse, alternately annoyed and anxious. I'd economised wisely, by not taking an air-conditioned room, in Cambodia's hot, humid off-season. Still, people from all over the world poured through Siem Reap; there was plenty to see and do.

On Wednesday morning, Sophea was almost an hour late. Was she not coming? Was this gamesmanship? When she appeared I half-expected her to be brandishing legal documents But she just said, charming and bashful:

"I am very sorry to be difficult. I am nervous. This could be my only chance. I am of course very pleased you have come so far to meet me."

The wary aggression seldom re-appeared. I saw her chatty, funny, always a little regal but very trusting with her memories, ideas, dreams, regrets and, sometimes, I was trusted to be around when she kicked off her strappy shoes and relaxed at home.

Sophea lived two or three miles from the ancient forests and ruins of Angkor, past Siem Reap town, with its hub of luxury hotels. The luxury could be modern – glass-walled, feng shiu-ed minimalism, a lotus blossom on every pillow. Or there was a liveried recapturing of the colonial era in refurbished palaces, with vintage Rolls-Royces parked beside manicured grounds, to transport visitors in an amusing style. Among these grand hotels were cute terraced cafes, with views of magnolia trees, bougainvillea and gilded pagodas, flashed with the orange comings and goings of Buddhist monks.

Then there were red dirt side streets full of tumble-down shops, hostels, and meandering backpackers. The air was dense with traffic fumes, but suddenly there'd be a waft of perfume from the creamy jasmine growing over a garden wall. Down the dirt tracks the buildings changed from concrete and stone to weather-beaten wood. There were farmyard animals milling around, gaunt-faced men on bicycles and children sitting listlessly, while thin women pounded washing in tubs.

Out beyond this, in the clean air at the edges of the countryside, Sophea had a patch of land and a small rectangular house.

The two-roomed house was surprisingly untidy, apart from the very large, carefully maintained area where Sophea had her Buddhist altar. There were clothes everywhere, there were suitcases, boxed kitchen appliances, magazines, musical instruments, a tool kit, lengths of silk, a bicycle… So we did have that in common – housekeeping by the maelstrom technique.

Sophea spent a good deal of her time outside, working in the large garden that was tellingly full of food plants and fruit trees. This was another Sophea, the one who took a machete to her long hedge of lemon grass to donate some to a neighbour, while giving advice on the best plants to cure a child's toothache. Out here she was one of the rural women, barefoot and laughing loud at some local gossip. A kind, helpful woman, without an air or a grace.

Then I found the sum of Sophea. She had a dozen hens in a run behind the house. The hens all had glitter painted toenails.

"I was bored with them." She laughed when I spotted it. "A hen is not pretty to look at like a peacock."

Yes, there was some part of her that should have had peacocks on a lawn, not hens in scrub grass. But she didn't mind. Life was life. She slipped between worlds.

I could see I amused her and we'd progressed a long way from that spiky first encounter. But I couldn't fathom what she was seeing to make her announce over lunch that we were alike. Perhaps she was picking up impressions of me from some dimension I couldn't access or believe in.

Our quiet lunch was disturbed. We both glanced across and flickered a scowl as a clump of Asian tourists installed themselves at the next table, making the small hot restaurant feel startled. They moved furnishings, shouted between themselves and were soon noisily destroying a table full of food.

"Typical." Sophea continued scowling.

"Typical Chinese?" As soon as I said it I knew I'd guessed wrong – the sounds weren't right, the faces weren't Chinese.

"Vietnamese." Sophea confirmed. "Typical behaviour. My father calls these people 'born on a boat'. They shout like that between fish boats, you see?"

I was sure, despite their loud boatiness, that they could hear her.

Sophea loathed the Chinese and Vietnamese in equal measure. Thais and Koreans formed a sort of second tier of enemies, with Europeans in swimsuits forming a rear-guard of humanity that Sophea couldn't tolerate.

We often met for coffee on the terrace of a little hotel near her home. It was quiet in the mornings, cool and pretty beside the oval swimming pool. Unlike the hotel where Sophea danced, non-resident customers didn't need to have any special permission to broach the grounds and drinks were not the price of a small car. We'd chat peacefully but if we didn't watch the time it would be the hour for pre-lunch swimming; hotel guests would amble to the pool beside us, remove bathrobes and sarongs, revealing thighs, chests – great walls of naked hairy flesh towering around Sophea.

"Let's go, let's go, I don't know where to look." She'd hiss, and we'd have to flee the flesh.

Sophea had little dresses with short skirts she'd wear once in a while and her dance costumes had tight and revealing moments, but there was something about the daylight brazenness of a western swimming costume that made her flutter from her perch like a startled papal dove.

There was less strange comedy in her feelings about the Chinese and Vietnamese.

During the late days of the Khmer Rouge regime, propaganda urged the Cambodians to fear the invading Vietnamese as capable of anything – rape, torture, even cannibalism. But as the Vietnamese defeated the Khmer Rouge, it became clear that they were a lot less prone to this kind of thing than the Cambodians had been led to believe. Although a threat throughout history, in 1979 the Vietnamese had rescued the Cambodians from their own leaders. The Vietnamese withdrew their military forces in 1989 but they retained enormous economic power and political influence in Cambodia. Opposition leaders accused the Cambodian government of being Vietnamese puppets, of heading up an occupation in disguise. The government called the opposition dangerous racists….

Then there were the Chinese. Chinese Cambodians, populous and prosperous in Phnom Penh in the Seventies, had been targets for genocide. Long established as merchants and civil servants, intermarrying and intermingling, they were denounced as impure Cambodians. Yet Pol Pot was one of several Khmer Rouge leaders with a mixed Cambodian-Chinese ancestry. Not to mention his educated upper-class origins, seemingly forgotten as he purged the country of the privileged, the educated…. To add to the double-think of all this – Chinese communists had backed the Khmer Rouge. Pol Pot's regime traded the tonnage of rice produced by Khmer children, like young Sophea, for Chinese armaments.

Sophea was haunted by many things, one being that when she was eleven, she'd been put on a list of attractive, virgin girls who were going to be sent to brothels for the Chinese military, to be traded along with the rice.

"Some officers came and looked at me, wrote something down. I was told later it was for this list. I don't know for sure but I can believe it. It was the kind of thing they did."

Her innocence had been the saving of her a few months after this list rumour, when her family was able to make its way back to the battered wreck of Phnom Penh, a city with no power, running with sewage, rats and stray dogs. They had to live in what had once been a suburban office block, while Vietnamese soldiers kept them out of the city centre. The soldiers told all the returning Phnom Penh citizens this was for their own safety; they were clearing the city of landmines, unexploded bombs and suspected booby traps. They also wanted to prevent looting. Not being allowed into their own city infuriated the Cambodians. Especially as they suspected the Vietnamese were themselves looting anything the Khmer Rouge hadn't already run away with. Children, however, could sneak into the guarded sectors. The soldiers would shout, threaten and even take aim at them but seldom fired. Getting in wasn't difficult; the children were more concerned not to be caught coming out and have their looted goods confiscated. Nimble and smart, Sophea would scramble through the city in search of something useful for her ragged, empty-handed family.

On one raid, she was overjoyed to find a store of prahok, the fermented fish paste that flavours Cambodian food, making dishes something of an acquired taste if too liberally applied. prahok smells as if a kipper, stuffed with stilton, has been left under a dead dog in the sun for at least eight years. Eleven-year-old Sophea piled the batch of sealed prahok jars into a cloth bundle and carried it on her head, using one hand to balance the pile. As she clambered out of the rubble, she slipped and dropped her bundle. It wasn't until she put the bundle back on her head that she realised a jar had broken, seeping stink through the cloth, into her hair and skin. When a Vietnamese soldier shouted at her, telling her to give him the bundle, she saw his face change as she

approached. He waved her and her stink to go away, quickly.
On other forays she found cooking pots, bowls and spoons and once a store of make-up.
"My sister and me put on lipstick, nail varnish and eye shadow. My mother found us and shouted at us that we were still children, it wasn't for us and couldn't we see how silly we looked, like some kind of monsters in our dirty clothes, our hair cut with knives? My mother took the make-up away and sold it for rice to some soldiers who wanted it for their girlfriends."
About a week later, feeling every building in walking distance had been picked clean, Sophea ventured far beyond the other kids. She walked for several hours. In a bomb-blasted tailor's shop she discovered a bale of beautiful blue canvas fabric. As the fabric was too heavy to carry, Sophea used some broken crockery to cut off lengths that she wound round herself, or piled on her head. She was hurrying, anxious that she was so far away from everyone else and wouldn't be able to get home before dark. As she was walking out of the doorway a big scruffy soldier stood in the way and pushed her back inside. The material on her head fell. The soldier looked at her. He pulled at her clothes.
"I thought he wanted the fabric I had wrapped round me under my shirt. When I was young I had a mind as stubborn as a stone. I decided I wanted this fabric and I would keep it, and if I'd decided something, that is what I would do. I stepped back, looking for a way to go past him but suddenly he gave me another big push onto the ground and made a sign with his hand across his throat. He said; 'Keep quiet or I kill you.'
"He wasn't Vietnamese. There were some Cambodians who ran away but then came back fighting for the Vietnamese. He was one of those, supposed to be saving us.
"I was lying on my back on the ground, very frightened now. He stood over me, leg on either side and started to unbuckle his pants.
"I screamed, 'what are you doing? Why do you want make pee pee on me? Don't make pee pee on me! That's disgusting!' He dropped to his knees and was going to put his hand on my mouth but I started crying out in Pali, the royal language, the language for prayers; 'Help me, help me!'
"He was shocked. He didn't put his hand on my mouth. He looked at me and then got to his feet and did up his pants. He told me; 'Get out.'
"He looked so sad, so ashamed, I even knew I could pick up the fabric I dropped and he wouldn't stop me.
"He just watched me and when I got to the door he was still looking with his face like a sad animal. He said. 'Don't tell anyone.'
"I didn't understand why he had tried to do such a disgusting thing. I was a child so I said; 'I hope you die soon.'
"I was angry about the fabric too. I knew I couldn't get the rest of it. I couldn't go back to that district at all now.

"My mother was pleased with the fabric but I told her I wouldn't get more because this mad soldier had tried to make pee pee on me. She made me explain what I meant. She didn't tell me what he'd really been doing, she just said; 'Ah, don't tell that story to anyone else, it's not good.' I didn't understand what happened until years and years later, when I was married." Sophea smiled awkwardly.

"You can imagine there was a lot of confusion on my wedding night." Her smile went as she disappeared to some steely place behind it. "If you rape a girl, you can make a girl hurt all her life. Men don't understand, it's over for them, but the woman feels it all her life. I was lucky. If I'd been raped I'd have never got over it. I feel Buddha protected me, to stop me having a bad mind. I'd have done something, lots of bad things, because of it, and never got over it."

She lightened up again, laughed; "Seriously, even with my husband the first time I thought, what is this? Here's another one wants to make pee pee on me?"

I'd been about eight or nine years old when I'd been told why men would be taking their trousers off around girls. I remembered squealing on the swings with my friend, Susan Fogden, when a teenager imparted these facts of life. I rushed home, startling my mother over the washing-up, demanding confirmation of the ridiculous facts. She'd confirmed them, but said it was something to forget about until I was grown up, as it was only for making babies when you were married – my Catholic household wasn't such a far leap of propriety from Sophea's. Perhaps that's another reason why we could be alike?

I'd also experimented with make-up when I was too young. Like Sophea's mother, mine had told me I looked silly. But she didn't sell the make-up for food; she put it in her dressing table drawer, promising she'd keep it for me until I was older.

Actually, now I remember it, I think, probably under the malign influence of Susan Fogden, who had a bra when she was ten, so was obviously on a slippery slope, I'd acquired the collection of small make-up items on a shoplifting spree. There was a craze for shoplifting in our school and no one we knew had been caught, so we kept on.

Shoplifting eye-shadow in Hendon chemists was a very like-for-like experience with looting for survival in gun-guarded, war-shattered Phnom Penh. Yes, I could see that if I wrote my life story, Sophea would read it and reel from the pages, not knowing which of us it was about.

A pack of British teenagers lumbered into the restaurant. They looked sweaty, dirty, and weren't wearing enough of their faded, rucksack-wrinkled clothes. They were wondering loudly to each other if the place served beer, hauling two tables together without asking the waitress and generally behaving like creatures reared on watercraft.

I noticed that Sophea had devoured every grain of our food. With the Vietnamese to one side and the British bellowing to the other, hearing our own conversation was going to be impossible.
I said; "Let's have dessert somewhere else."
Sophea smiled at me.
"I knew you'd say that." She tipped her fake Prada sunglasses down onto her nose "I told you. We're very alike. We are both very bad-tempered people."
Ah. There was that.

CHAPTER 2: TRAVEL WITH YOUR EYES CLOSED

"We were sent to the countryside, to strangers. They were called 'old' people because they were from the country and we were 'new', from the city. The Khmer Rouge did this to so many people. We stayed with these countryside people maybe one month. They gave us food, taught us fishing, how to grow vegetables. But my father already knows these things. The main thing they did was steal everything, all our clothes, everything. I fought the children for my clothes and bedding but they were stronger. Anyway some soldiers came and told everyone they had to make their clothes dyed black. It is from a bark, this dye. Imagine, a whole country dressed in black."

Then Sophea's family were moved on by the soldiers, to a village purpose-built for the 'new' people.

"Nearly one hundred families. Small bamboo and straw houses, like dog kennels. My father was sent far away to look after cows. My mother was out for hours digging ditches. I stayed in the house with my sister. We had very little food, only rice soup. They sent my mother to dig further away, so she has to walk in the night for two hours to see us. She talks and talks, telling me about my grandparents, her childhood, like she is making me into a book. She goes away while it is still dark. We are like this for a year, getting thinner, wondering how this can be happening to us. We don't know what is happening. Everyone in black, everyone so tired, not understanding why someone from outside is not noticing the situation."

Sophea clasped her hands together. Today, I noticed, her fingers were covered with silver jewellery. She went on with her story that conjured The Killing Fields. I'd seen this film when it opened in 1984 and more or less forgotten about Cambodia since. There was an occasional news story about land mine clearance. Cambodia had been full of land mines; presumably there was some connection between all this clearance and the increase in tourism. The punk song Holiday in Cambodia was no longer a sarcastic proposition. In preparation for my journey, I had been reading Khmer Rouge survivor memoirs. In some ways they were all the same: the shock of being herded from the city to the country; glimpses of increasingly gory horror – fear, hunger, hard rural labour and murdered relatives. They were the same because the regime had tried to destroy individuality and had a process for doing that. They were not the same because individuality didn't disappear, whatever was done to people.

Records of what happened back then were destroyed by the perpetrators after their defeat, but they couldn't destroy everything. Cambodian filmmaker Rithy Panhhas collected archives of footage where black clad people dig and scurry about in massive earthworks. It's become difficult to know what half this work was about – perhaps for irrigation channels, for troop-carrying roads... Grey, scratchy blurs of aunts, fathers, daughters... The late Seventies. The Russian-backed North Vietnamese had to be kept out of Cambodia, in case they spread on into Thailand and beyond. So America, Britain and their allies did worse than do nothing about the Chinese-backed Khmer Rouge situation: they gave covert assistance. They had certainly noticed.

Sophea had a pink hooded sweatshirt with rabbit ears that no one her age should get away with, but she did. She put it on as the generous air-conditioning in the cafe we'd chosen became overwhelming. Her jewelled hands made little fists under the slightly too long cuffs and she began talking again.

"One day, I am with the small children, trying to stop them crying, but how can I when they are hungry? The soldiers bring home my mother; she is sick, too sick. She cannot stand up. They throw her inside the house. One says: 'She is stupid. She poison herself. She does it on purpose. She is stupid.'

"I shake my mother: she is confused and cannot speak. I run after the soldiers, I beg them, please get a message to my father to come, please. One soldier says my mother will die, there is no point. The other is different; he asks me about my father and says he will drive in the jeep to collect him because I have a face that is pretty. He touches my face and I don't like it but I say nothing because I want my father. The soldier says: 'when I bring back your father you can give me a present.'

"I am a child, I don't understand but I don't know how I can give him a present when we have a bare hut and only enough food for ourselves. But he brought my father who gave mother honeycomb and water to get rid of the poison. He tells me he is surprised they fetch him. I tell him what the soldier said, and he looks very angry."

Sometimes, when Sophea went back in her life, she took me into the moment, in the present tense. Other times it could be tiredness, or agitation that made her start a slight tangle in her three languages. Khmer has no tenses, so knowing when a thing happened depends on context.

It was increasingly obvious as I travelled around the country that a language with no tenses was appropriate. The past was so strongly in the present.

"My mother is getting better. She is sorry; yes, she did poison herself because she can't stand anymore. Her son is lost, she can hardly even move she is so tired. She cries and holds my father. He tells her she has two children who still need her. She must get better and stay strong.

"In a few days the soldier came to ask if my mother was better. My father says she is not, although this isn't true.

"Then we have some luck, in a way: a different soldier came and told my father to go, the other soldier made a mistake getting him and had been sent to the front line. But then he said my mother has wasted working days so I must go to work now too, to make up for the time my mother wasted. My sister will be put with a central nursery.

"My mother is still weak but we go to chop down grass and brush to make land for planting. My mother says she is so sorry she tried to leave us."

Sophea picked up a paper napkin from the drinks tray and blew her nose daintily.

"I have to stop talking about this for one moment. It makes me cry a little bit." Frowning, she put a knuckle to the corner of her eye. "Usually I don't cry, I make myself not to cry. Sometimes in a film I can't help it but my husband says I am like a stone." Oh yes. This husband. Dead perhaps. The missing in Cambodia could often be presumed dead.

"I will tell you more about my mother soon Let's talk about dancing, then I will be strong enough for more about my mother."

Perhaps she thought she'd explained the husband, but we'd agreed to talk about what she wanted to talk about, and the dancing was always the easiest option.

Sophea had told me the tradition she'd been trained in was vanishing: "For the young it is all discotheque. This is not Khmer. But the dance will bring blessings and harmony for Cambodia. There is no harmony if we lose the traditional dance."

Although it was unusual to see a genuine performance of this ancient, sacred dancing, Khmer ballet, anyone visiting Cambodia would know what the dancers looked like. They featured repeatedly on the wall carvings in the famous temples and palaces of Angkor.

The ancient kings of Angkor kept hundreds of dancers, known as Apsaras – celestial dancers – cosseted in privilege. The performances were for the kings' delight but their purpose was also religious – to thank, celebrate and channel the gods of Angkor.

Over the centuries, the dancers had come to look more demure than the bare-breasted figures on the Angkor walls. Now their intricate costumes were layered like fairy armour and as much part of spectacle as the ethereal movements themselves.

At the Royal Palace in Phnom Penh there was still the official royal troupe and a museum of dance costume – didn't this preserve the tradition?

"They have their school, they have what papers and history have survived but it is in the control of the government. The dance should be for Buddha, not for the government. What can I do? To them I am poor, I am just a worm. The royal family and the government, their friends. Every government is a friend for the royal family, you understand, even the Khmer Rouge. I want to dance without worrying who I work with, I want to do this in peace. For the Buddha and the ancestral spirits."

There were dinner shows around the tourist spots of Cambodia where visitors could see troupes of Apsara dancers. Pretty enough, in silk trousers with bangles jangling by the dozen; feet and hands upturned to uncanny angles. Sophea dismissed their dancing as 'not pure, just for money shows'. Increasingly, big sparkling troupes from Thailand were coming in to perform in Cambodia. Another heart-breaker for Sophea was that the true celestial dance, full of religious meaning, was confused with these skilful but superficial shows.

A know-nothing, I'd been charmed by the commercial performances.

Then I saw Sophea dance.

One of the most female females I'd ever come across, she performed in a finely jewelled costume, silk swooped hither and nipped in at a tiny waist. A high gilded headdress completed her look of an expensive souvenir doll. I was confused when I saw her step onto a stage in this costume; she'd told me she always played the male role, but here she was, looking like a sparkly distillation of girlness.

The instant the dance began, by some disconcerting shape-shift, she became her male role – a charming, slightly roguish prince. No heaviness was added to her movements, no pantomime boy thigh-slapping; she just conjured herself into a man.

In another dance, where she had to mimic flight, she seemed to get away from the earth while very clearly having her bangled feet fixed to the ground. The twists and trills of gesture in this dance had been performed around Angkor since before 800 A.D. For five centuries, the kings of Angkor ruled with extravagant ceremony, but then the kings began retreating from constant battles with the neighbouring kingdoms of Siam. They built a more easily secured capital in the district of Phnom Penh. This didn't keep them safe. From another direction, the Vietnamese empires encroached on the kings' territory, culture and economy. By the time the French arrived, in the late nineteenth century, the Angkor dynasty had faded so much it welcomed the protection of France. Extravagant religious and cultural traditions shrank down to the immediate court of Phnom Penh. Among the fashionable upper classes, French ways were adopted; rice bowls swapped for baked goods; folk arts replaced by an obsession with cinema.

In the 1960s, artistically inclined King Sihanouk put money and energy into his enthusiasm for Cambodia's classical dance. It revived as a chic entertainment, for a while. In 1974, political events overwhelmed King Sihanouk's elegant interests and hobbies. Pol Pot's incoming regime took particular exception to artists, musicians, dancers… Yet Sihanouk and many of the royal family survived as useful figureheads for the regime. While teachers and doctors were seen as a threat to the egalitarian, agrarian regime and executed, a hereditary king was fine.

The king had remained in his palace when, after the years suffering far from home and then months scavenging in the rubble at the edges of the city, Sophea's family returned to Phnom Penh, such as it was after the Khmer Rouge, and such as they were.

Their former home, a traditional wooden house, was gone – not even the ashes left on the site.

Her parents found work in a tobacco factory and a small apartment to rent. Sophea went back to school; just an ordinary one because the fancy school never re-opened.

"It was lucky there were teachers from abroad. I had lessons in English and French. I knew those were important."

The foreign teachers, connected to one of the few a charity projects that had returned to Cambodia, gave them books and pens.

"My mother grabbed these when she saw them. 'Where did I get them?' She went with me to the school to check with the teacher because she was scared I had got in a habit of stealing and couldn't stop. She told me: 'Those were special times, the Buddha forgives what we did but now you have to remember that stealing is a wrong thing.'"

Sophea made a contemptuous face. "I think there are young people now who didn't have the Khmer Rouge and didn't learn that stealing is a wrong thing. Too many like that."

On schooldays, twelve-year-old Sophea passed a museum courtyard where a handful of girls were being taught ballet. The dancers were paying the teacher, newly returned from Paris, a great deal of money. They were the daughters of returning royalty and new ministers.

"Everything was ugly and broken but they were there doing this beautiful dancing I hadn't seen since I was a very small child. They looked like a dream."

Whenever she could, Sophea stopped to watch lessons and rehearsals. In her small room at home she tried to copy the moves. She began imitating as she watched at the edge of the courtyard. One evening the teacher strode across to her and told her to go away. Sophea begged to be allowed to watch; she'd keep still, keep hidden even, if she could just watch.

The teacher quickly established that Sophea was a nobody with no money and, at twelve, really quite old to start the intense physical conditioning required.

"But you see, I was very beautiful, with a face they needed to dance the male roles, the face of an Indian prince. And she could see from my imitations I had a rhythm, I understood the music."

The dance teacher went to see her parents. In return for Sophea working as her servant at the weekends – cleaning her apartment, massaging her stiffening limbs, washing and pressing her clothes – Sophea could join the lessons.

Sophea did it all: skivvying, running to school, running to dance lessons, practising in the night until her parents forced her to sleep.

She became the male role star of the little dance class.

"After three years the teacher called me and said; 'You are good but you are just beginning. There are some scholarships to the School of Arts. It is possible you will pass, just possible.'

"Oh there was so much to study, the stories of the dances, the meanings, then I would need costumes… Even with a scholarship there would be such expense. But my parents came to see a show at the end of three years and my mother was crying, she had never seen me dance before. 'You have something in you from your ancestors, I see it now. You must get your scholarship, we will make costumes, we will manage, this is part of you.'

"I knew about my ancestors from what my mother had told me in the night in that dog-kennel house. My dancing made my mother happy but only for a short time. I think this happened to many people, the Khmer Rouge years made them not right in the mind. A child can recover but not a grown person."

Sophea looked close to tears again. She reached for the paper napkin, held it to her face and smiled.

"You see Annie, I am not stone."

I was desperate to ask about this husband who had called her a stone but Sophea had rallied; she clutched the paper napkin more tightly and held an expression of great dignity.

"This is a secret, Annie. I tell very few people but my great grandmother was the wife of King Norodom and a dancer who travelled the world."

I had a funny feeling. Sophea had such a regal manner but I was from Ireland, where dubious tales of secret regal ancestry abounded.

"It's a secret because when King Norodom died in 1904 my great grandmother was allowed to go home to her village. She was just eighteen and she married a very ordinary shopkeeper. We lost our connection and who would believe me now?" Sophea changed tone, shrugged: "So here I am, living like a worm and getting old."

I had so many questions, and creeping doubts, but if I asked the wrong question or tried to control Sophea, impressionistic way of telling me about herself, she could walk away. I was being told a great deal but sensed I was still on probation. It was almost midday. I asked the easiest question:

"Shall we have lunch?"

"Good idea. And I have another idea because I must stop talking for a while Would you like to see a guru, a Buddhist guru who I trust very much?"
Well rub me down with an old Beatles album, this was what I was supposed to be after in the East wasn't it? Enlightenment, etcetera – of course I'd like it.
"It is very far in the forest."
Even better. I might lose sight of western tourists for an hour or so. I might even go home, annoying my Buddhism-dabbling friends with a smug vision of oneness with trees and buffaloes and whatnot.

After a lunch of several dishes for Sophea and one for me, we had to call at a large modern mall. South East Asian modern looks twenty years ahead of European modern; people were selling things that hovered, flew, glistened digitally, were voice-activated, retina-secured... And I didn't understand any of them.
In the fairly comprehensible supermarket section, Sophea bought brightly packaged boxes of expensive biscuits.
"The guru has children, these are for his children."
I wondered what I should take as a gift.
"You can help me pay for this. He lives a simple life like a farmer in the countryside. Sometimes I worry another guru will put black magic on him for not being greedy and asking for money. Maybe we will take some soft drinks..."
She loaded a dozen juice cartons into our trolley, then a party bag of sweets the size of a toddler and we were ready to take a tuk tuk out of town.
We rattled through the sharp green of rice fields with their seaweedy harbour smell, then into a forest scattered with wood-smoke scented villages. The guru lived above a noisy yard of animals and children, in a traditional wooden stilt house. His pale, unlined face looked to be that of a twenty year old, but Sophea had said he was nearly forty. Photographs on the wall showed the guru when he was very young, shaven-headed and wearing the orange robes of a monk; now, he wore loose grey cotton trousers and a white shirt, although the shaven head remained. He sat cross-legged in a dense copse of incense sticks, in front of a statue of a seated Buddha.
Sophea and I had to place our gifts on a platter beside the guru. Then, as she spoke to him in Khmer, he nodded occasionally. He sprayed his hands with perfume, lit an incense stick, chewed a betel nut and closed his eyes.
"Wait." Sophea whispered and bowed her head.
After a few minutes, the guru began to speak. Sophea translated:
"He says he has travelled to England in his mind. He sees all the people sleeping and it is raining."
It would be mid-morning in England. But it would inevitably be raining.
"He says England is an island near another island."

Some expression must have crossed my face.

"Remember he is here in the countryside, he is someone with poor education."

I felt a little ashamed of whatever my expression had been. The guru had a gentle, sweet presence – the sort of person, if you got to know him, you would tell your troubles to.

Sophea said Cambodia was full of people who did black magic; this guru had once taken a bad spell off her.

"What was the spell?"

"That I would not be lucky. It is paid for by another dancer, jealous I am too beautiful. But maybe you are here as my good luck because he took the spell away."

No pressure then.

The guru was speaking again in his soft voice.

"He says our project will succeed but you will need to come to Cambodia for two years, not all the time, over a two-year time, go and come."

That would make sense. Then he said something that made me feel a little strange.

"He says he sees a girl child in your house."

A few years ago, after expensive fertility treatment, I'd had a miscarriage. Last chance: gone. My partner and I had called the baby by a girl's name, although we didn't know, we'd just had a feeling. But the girl chid had never been born.

I explained this to Sophea. She passed the story on to the guru who looked steadily at me as he spoke and waited for Sophea to give me the English version.

"He says he is sorry for your story. Perhaps the spirit of the girl is still in your house."

Fortunately, I had picked up a paper napkin from the cafe table and put it in my pocket in case the dust from the road got in my eyes.

"You shouldn't cry for her, her spirit likes to be in your house."

The guru stood up and made the hands together bow as we left. He said something else to Sophea.

"He is very good." Sophea said as we went down the wooden steps to the waiting tuk tuk. "I am sorry he made you sad."

"I'm fine." I said, trying not to think about girl child spirits any more.

"When we go back we can go to the mall to talk, where they have the cappuccino you like, and the good ice cream I like."

True, their cappuccino cafe was a blessing as my guest house, cute and full of endearingly eccentric staff as it was, did only manage very weak instant coffee.

"I am happy I decided to tell you my story." Sophea said. "He says he sees your home very quickly, very clearly. This means you are a person with a clean soul, a good person."

It felt like time travel to crash from the quiet countryside with buffalo wallowing in ponds and crumbling mud roads, back to the bright flash of the mall, where chatty salesmen were now demonstrating some new kind of liquidiser with many, many attachments, and where pretty girls skipped around another stand demonstrating phone apps that maybe could liquidise food as well; perhaps the liquidisers could make calls...

Modern life was complicated enough; I didn't need mystical, ancient things addling my mind as well. By the time I sat down in the cafe I was looking for ways to dismiss the guru.

I had it – Sophea had phoned in advance to see if he could receive us but really she'd been giving him clues. Had she? All she knew was that I didn't have children. Perhaps at some point I'd said: "We tried but it didn't work out because my partner and I were both forty when we met..."

Perhaps. I couldn't remember.

Like any good fortune teller, the guru had taken the clues, made guesses from them, watched my face.

He'd had his eyes closed.

And I liked the spirit in the house notion more than a bad memory that we didn't talk about in our house any more.

Sophea was ready to face her memories again: "He makes me feel strong. I can tell you more about my mother."

Settling herself behind a mound of ice cream, she began.

As people returned to Phnom Penh, Sophea's family noticed how many had not returned. Still there was some hope of her brother coming back, perhaps taken care of by another family – these things happened.

"But years went by and nothing. I never forgot my brother but I had school, I had my dancing. I cared about myself and not my mother who was not right in her mind again. One evening, when I thought she was at the market, she was carried home by some people who lived near the river. She had no mind and she tried to drown herself. Again my father had to make her well again. He wanted me to look after her and stop school so he could work. I refused. In the end a cousin who had no immediate family left alive moved in to help and my mother was a little better. My father forgives me. He says it is better if I get education and go away from Cambodia. It is still bad. Khmer Rouge are still living in the forest on the border, perhaps they come back." Sophea sighed deeply. "If I had looked after my mother then maybe my karma would not be so bad."

I was confused: "But she got better?"

"That time. She went back to work. My father started a small business selling snack food. All the time we watched my mother, scared she would get sick again. But then, after ten years, ten years imagine, a monk who was a neighbour's friend came to our home. Everyone knew we had lost a son, so the neighbour sent the monk to us. He had been far away hiding as a fisherman; on his journey back home he stayed in a village where people talked about a woman who is one time Khmer Rouge, who kept children in her house to do work for her who are not her children. The children did cleaning, grew vegetables, they collected coconuts that she sold for juice and they collected juice from palms that she fermented for palm wine and they went diving in the river for fish.... She has lots of business, all done by children she took in Khmer Rouge times. They say she took ones she thought were cute. The monk was angry, people will be mourning these children who are still living.

"My father straight away wanted to go with the monk. He says he has a strong feeling that Sann is with this woman. His feeling was so strong he let my mother come with him and the monk. My parents didn't like to leave me and my sister but it was far and at the edge of a place where the people are still very dangerous. My father and mother travelled to the village by boat on the Mekong then by rickshaw. They ask questions and are taken to where Sann is working in a field, away from the house of the woman who took him. My mother knows Sann immediately. She knows his face even though he is nearly sixteen now and he has big muscles and roughness from all the work. She also knows him by a mark on his foot he had since a baby.

"The monk cut my brother and my mother and put their blood in water then they had to wait. My mother was so scared. The drops of blood come towards each other. This shows they are related."

My sceptical self was returning. What was this blood test?

Blood is thicker than water. That's why any drops of blood – yours and mine and the man walking past in the street will be drawn to each other. But in the old culture of Sophea's parents, the blood in water mattered as much as the evidence of their own eyes.

I asked Sophea what would have happened if the blood test had gone wrong?

"I don't know. It is the monk who wants it. So he knows my parents are right. Also my brother is a bit confused. My mother looked so different, all thin and darker. Even her voice had changed. Scratchy."

The woman told Sann and all the children she kept in her Fagin's den that they were orphans. Once the blood test was done Sann started to cry.

"He wants to go with my parents right away. He is scared of the woman. In the beginning the woman had a husband and he was quite kind but he died. There was an older boy in the children she had taken so she wanted to use him for a husband. The boy ran away. That boy is brave. Sann is afraid now he is getting older she will try him like a husband. He has been thinking to run away but he is not brave like the other boy."

They left with Sann immediately, terrified that the woman would come after them and stop them leaving.

"They are scared in the rickshaw, scared on the boat. Someone sent from the woman will stop them. My mother holds Sann all the time. But it's OK, they get home to Phnom Penh. He calls me by my aunt's name. He remembers my face, and an older girl who played with him, he just confuses the name. He remembers there was another sister, a baby. Imagine what an experience."

How could I imagine? This had been 1985. Back in London we'd seen The Killing Fields; we thought the war was over.

While Sophea was telling me her brother's story, Sydney Schanberg, the American journalist featured in The Killing Fields, was giving video-link evidence in the corrupt and chaotically protracted trials of the five indicted members of the Khmer Rouge leadership. This was 2014. By 2015 only two of these indicted were given life sentences. Three had died. The trials, begun in 2006, frequently suspended, cost the UN well over two hundred million dollars.

Sophea went on: "For a time we are scared that somehow the woman will send someone to hurt us... The Khmer Rouge people, they just changed their uniform, you know, but they stayed in Cambodia. But we are OK. My brother and my parents are ... glued."

Sann went to work in his father's snack business; they expanded it and took on a larger property. Sann married and had three children.

Sophea was scraping the last of brightly coloured ice cream from her bowl. I'd been writing, hardly touched my coffee, but somehow she had managed to talk and deal with large, lurid scoops of raspberry and pistachio.

"We will go to Phnom Penh and you can meet my family, but my brother doesn't talk very much about these Khmer Rouge times. As a young man he started to cry if we asked him. He just says the woman is horrible and he cries. Even today he is very nervous, very anxious."

She turned her empty ice cream bowl round, looking into it as if it were a crystal ball predicting what I would say next.

"Would you like more ice cream?"

I drank down my cold coffee and was very surprised when she said: "No thank you. I feel tired. I think many things happen for your heart and mine today. Tomorrow we talk more, perhaps talk about where we will go. Maybe from here it is better to go to Battambang. There is temple there where I studied meditation, where a monk knows very much about the spirit part of dancing." She smiled. "Also there is much to see there, old buildings and the bamboo train. I never went on the train, so we can enjoy that."

Outside the mall she telephoned a neighbour who worked as a tuk tuk driver. She offered to drop me off but I felt like walk; my guest house wasn't far. A walk might settle some of the weird thumps my heart had taken that afternoon.

There was a wat, a temple, along the road. I thought I might wander in, just in case something else might happen to wobble my scepticism into the peace of definite answers about how the universe all ran. Wouldn't that make life

so easy?
Two young, orange-robed monks were standing to the side of the wat entrance smoking, laughing. Then they were picked up by two other monks arriving in a tuk tuk, shouting some sort of "hurry up" greeting. I suddenly didn't feel there'd be any answers in their building. Why did I want them anyway? I'd never wanted them before. It was just something about the nonsense people back home filled you with about the mystical and spiritual to be found in the East. Was it the warm climate and the attractive robes that made all this look better? Well not to me; I wasn't going to travel East and lose my common sense. Or why hadn't I gone rabbi-bothering in Hendon? Why I had I fled in yelling, disbelieving horror at twelve years of age from the grey routines of the Catholicism I was reared in? No no no, keep walking away from that wat.

Any painter looking to be inspired for a picture of hell could try the car repair workshop at the entrance to the alley leading to my Siem Reap guest house. Hot, oily men surrounded by brazier fires, blazed acetylene torches at vehicles; they were yelling, playing loud music, while behind them women boiled steaming god-knows-what in pots, or fried things sparking fat at all angles. But then, in fifty yards, the alley was quiet; there were lush trees and a couple of children playing football. In the guesthouse garden there were more trees and staff dozing in hammocks around the straw-roofed restaurant. Good idea. I needed to lie down too. And to remember how I thought when I was at home. Something that didn't involve mind flying, wasn't it?

CHAPTER 3: WHAT NOT TO DO IN THE TEMPLES

There'd been some two-in-the-morning incident on the landing involving a cat falling from the tree overhanging the corridor balcony. The cat scrabbled around, broke a vase and was tackled with high-pitched shouts from Kiri, the assistant manager. I'd put my head out to check Kiri wasn't in danger, that some kind of lethal Cambodian supercat didn't have him by the throat.

"Sorry, madam, cat." He beamed at me, brandishing a scrawny, tawny creature as he went down the wooden stairs at a house-shaking trot. He was a stocky man but not as heavy as the tread made him sound. With a smile as thin as the doors and walls I went back to bed. Now, at 6.30 am, Kiri was tapping at my door, whispering: "Madam, madam."

Cambodia is courteous and not casual. Everyone's name is prefixed by 'Bong' – Mr, Miss, Madam – and even westernised Cambodians find first name use uncomfortable with anyone slightly older or in a position of responsibility. I didn't like being 'madam' but right then I didn't care what Kiri called me, as long as he did it elsewhere.

I hauled some clothes on.

Kiri was smiling but his eyes were anxious.

"Ponleak driver downstairs."

Ponleak, the tuk tuk driver, was an hour and a half early.

"Problem his son."

Kiri and Ponleak were both around thirty years old, close friends, both working all hours at the guesthouse. As a general do-everything, in Kiri's case, and as one of the drivers who waited hopefully in the alley outside, in Ponleak's.

Tall for a Cambodian, handsome and sweet-natured, Ponleak was standing in the front garden with its fringe of balcony-overhanging trees.

"Madam." The minute he started speaking I could see he was frustrated by his limited English and pushed close to tears by his life. "No work today." He looked behind me to Kiri, sharp with English, for help.

"His son in hospital very bad, he take his daughter to village now for school." I could see a little figure on the seats of the tuk tuk. Ponleak's village was twenty minutes out of town, mostly down dirt tracks. If he'd had to rush his wife and five-year-old boy into hospital, now he was heading back so the six-year-old girl could make it to school, then presumably he'd go back to the hospital again, all without sleep.... Poor Ponleak.

He was talking to Kiri in Khmer.

"He will call Bong Sophea later, she tell you news."

Kiri discreetly looked back at the guesthouse entrance, as if he'd heard something, as soon as he realised I was looking in my pockets for cash. I pushed some petrol money at Ponleak. He'd diverted from his busyness to speak to me. I had a little local phone now and Ponleak had the number; if this situation was too complicated for him to explain, couldn't he have simply called Kiri?

Ponleak was saying; "Sorry, madam, sorry."

"No, no, look out for your son."

Ponleak worked and worked. It didn't seem to get him far beyond survival. Visiting me in person was a plea not to lose his job.

He said something else, Kiri translated.

"Son Is sick for stomach, is not breathing good."

Ponleak nodded at me, his face barely holding neutral. He hurried back to the tuk tuk where his little girl was stirring awake.

In a while I'd call Sophea. She'd become very fond of mild-mannered Ponleak, often sending him home with eggs and vegetables for the family, including him in our travel plans whenever she could.

"You chose a good driver, he is very honest."

We had been planning to leave for the city of Battambang the next day but when I called Sophea she said:

"I don't think these are good days for leaving Siem Reap. You will be upset if poor Mr Ponleak calls to say his son is dead and we are far. Also the hospital is free but he will still need money, you should stay near to give him work."

It sometimes seemed Sophea thought 'Poor Mr Ponleak' was the driver's full name. I hadn't leapt immediately to the dark conclusion that the boy might die but statistically, among poor Cambodians... We would wait. We had plenty to do, recording Sophea's story, meeting people, trying to get away from the overdeveloped malls and hotels of Siem Reap and see what lay in the cracks between shiny buildings.

A few hours later, flaunting her stamina, Sophea arrived on her bicycle. She took a short rest and a glass of fruit juice but barely showed a fleck of perspiration or gave a whisper of panting. It was undoubtedly for my benefit that she suggested: "It's so hot. I think we will go to the Baray, get some air."

Kiri urged Sophea to park her bicycle on the guesthouse terrace, where he could keep an eye on it. While Ponleak seemed at ease, almost brotherly, with

Sophea, Kiri's whole stocky form seemed to tense with fright that he wouldn't please her, the visiting queen. Funny because she'd pronounced him: "Nice but typical Cambodian man, very tough, not sweet like our poor Mr Ponleak."

Perhaps if she'd seen the ache in Kiri over Ponleak's problems she wouldn't have swished past him like that.

We set off into our day with a driver called Kim, from the queue outside the guesthouse, older and far more sure of himself than Ponleak. Also, as I told Sophea, he had the manic laugh of serial killer.

"Really? It is a horrible laugh but… Oh that is your sort of joke. But still, I think he is not trustworthy. I should have brought the driver from near my house, he is a nice boy like Ponleak. You made a good choice of driver, Ponleak is not very high intelligence but he is hardworking and I trust him. This murderer Kim we will keep for today only."

I hadn't done any interviewing, psychometric testing, or even really chosen Ponleak. In the irritating days while I was waiting for Sophea to decide I was a fit and proper person, Ponleak had approached me quietly in the garden restaurant of the guest house and offered to drive me. I'd liked his quietness – tuk tuk drivers were usually, and really needed to be, a lot more brash and pushy to get work.

I didn't think Sophea was right about Ponleak's 'not very high intelligence'. I suspected shyness held him back a great deal, but the way he made an almost physical effort to overcome it, to get money for his children: that emerged as a specialness of character for me. And as a slow thinker myself, I was all for his pace of mind; we did get there in the end.

There were routine tours visitors followed around the temples of Angkor Wat. Ponleak, with help from Kiri, had listed them, with prices. I agreed to the one that seemed to take up the most time and cover the most ground. If Sophea decided I wasn't good enough for her, at least I'd have seen some of the things that millions of people came to Cambodia to see.

Starting before five, when not even Mr Kiri was up showing off with cats or any of the other mysterious facets of his work, Ponleak and I set out on our tour.

The usual frenzy of Siem Reap was a little dampened at five in the morning but vehicles still crawled around and shadowy figures pushed carts past the ever-lit mall fronts or stood huddled around small bonfires. As we turned out toward the forests for the sunrise experience I began to get excited, this would be beautiful, spiritual…

There was a Wacky Races skedaddle of cars, mopeds and tuk tuks along the road to Angkor Wat. It had just stopped raining – rainy season, low season; why were there so many of us racing?

Transport swerved, squeaked, juddered to a halt. Bleary eyed, we flung ourselves into a charge at the one crossing over the wide moat that kept us from the outer walls of the temples.

A phalanx of security guards blocked the tourist assault, checking sharply that everyone had bought the expensive temple passes. Meanwhile panic was rising as the first hints of pink and gold tinged the sky. European, Korean, Japanese, Chinese, Australian… Everyone started pointing cameras as we staggered toward the towers of Angkor.

The sun began to streak the sky with definite light; the temples were silhouetted as perfectly as shadow-puppet scenery.

The stream of people, all moving in a bewildered, too-early-in-the-morning way toward the Angkor towers, shifted in mood from Wacky Races comedy to something more reminiscent of the film Close Encounters: the humans gathering amazed, drawn to a strange and wondrous high thing.

The moth cocoon whirls of the Angkor towers crowned a three-tiered edifice of sandstone slab walls, carved in intricate detail commemorating battles on sea and land, myths and legends, or daily life at court hundreds of years ago. In niches, on the sides of pillars – all around – were carvings of bare-breasted royal dancers, thousands of them, captured mid-step, mid-gesture and tilt of the head.

Thousands of carvings, hundreds of years old, and a sky ripening blue, half a world away from home – I should have been awed, thinking great thoughts, not scowling at the flustered onward, onward crowd around me. Not thinking how many more photos of Angkor Wat in the sunrise does the world need anyway? Why didn't they just buy the blasted cliché on a postcard? I should have had more profound feelings than rising hysteria as one coach party of frenzied Chinese pensioners, all talking at once, met another talking and talking septuagenarian Chinese coach party surging the opposite way in a narrow stone stairway, with me somehow in the middle, fighting an urge to shout something obscenely British about the benefits of forming an orderly queue. Then I was glad I'd kept quiet, not nationally aligned, as I stood at the entrance to an inner courtyard and a gang of young Brits lumbered out of the dawn, scruffy and stale beer scented, one braying in a cigarette hoarse voice; "Yeah it's great, let's get this done, man, then crash."

I forced myself to walk around a little more but there was nothing to be done about my tourist's disappointment in tourism. I walked back along the flagstones to the entrance, turning a couple of times to look again and register that Angkor Wat was stunning, a wonder of the world. I walked further, and as the sun began to lift the night rain from the ground, Angkor shimmered there in a low mist, emerging against deep green forest, the promise of an ancient, extraordinary, fairy-tale city. A fairy-tale city from the proper, non-Disney tradition. A tale with egomaniacal rulers, beautiful maidens held captive, swords dripping the blood of enemies and whips lashing at tower building serfs who weren't working hard enough.

There'd probably never been a good time for Cambodians who weren't in charge. Under the trees across the road, Ponleak was waiting among dozens of other drivers. He habitually wore a faded black baseball cap; he tipped it back as he scrambled from reclining on his tuk tuk seats to jump to attention for me.

A few other early-returning passengers were being greeted with affable deference by their drivers. There were different styles to this; Ponleak's was nervously watchful.

"Good sunrise, Madam?"

"Beautiful." I told him. Who wouldn't think so? No matter how grouchy and – there really needed to be a new word for this common form of misanthropy, tourists despising other tourists – for now let's say pretentious. Hardly fair to inflict that on Ponleak.

Ponleak smiled awkwardly; he knew the next phase of the temple-viewing routine:

"Breakfast, madam?"

He pointed to the cluster of little kiosks and vans serving breakfasts to all nations. With sudden efficiency of movement I was beside the one with strong coffee and croissants. I looked back to see if Ponleak wanted anything but he was bent over his motorbike, frowning, adjusting.

Through the trees, I could see there were low wood and bamboo restaurant buildings, tables and chairs being set outside some, others still shuttered, waiting for the lunchtime trade.

In a while, Ponleak stood up and was discreetly watching for me to move; there was a tour itinerary to get through and I was dawdling, but how could he tell a customer to hurry up? Annoy me and there might not be another sir or madam all the low-season day.

I slugged back my coffee and smiled at him. Smiling a lot, I'd learnt within hours, was very important in Cambodia. My default expression – sulking disapproval of the universe – was all wrong in a country where it's considered bad manners to show anything other than a pleasant-faced acceptance of fate.

Pleasant-faced, Ponleak wedged his bike helmet over his cap: "Bayon temple now, madam."

I climbed into the tuk tuk and we sped away from the refreshment enclave. At that moment there was no reason to notice, particularly, that one of the long, low restaurants among the trees was called Chez Sophea. It was a very common name here. At that moment there was no reason to imagine that I would soon know Ponleak well enough to have an ache of anxiety for his son. Not helped by Sophea immediately talking about the child's possible death. Sophea, who was a lot more connected with the restaurant in the forest than she cared to be.

Days on from this, waiting for news from Ponleak, Sophea and I walked the edge of the Western Baray, a huge stretch of water, just outside Siem Reap. The road where we'd stopped was on a dam across the Baray, with market stalls and women in conical straw hats selling fried ants and beetles from trays. They joked up to me and I was sure I could have choked down these deep fried insect snacks but I had a wimpish horror of street food, however many legs it had.

"If I get sick we're in trouble."

"Yes, yes," Sophea elegantly waved the women away. "You are not strong for this."

Down on the water's edge there were piles of inner tubes and makeshift wooden and cloth shelters. The shores of the Baray were used as a beach as well as a place of work. Fishermen in narrow wooden boats ventured out with their nets. In other months they might carry visitors out to the middle of the Baray to see a ruined island temple, almost completely submerged in this wet season.

The impressive eight-kilometre stretch of water was man-made in the time of the Angkor empire to provide an irrigation reservoir. The reservoirs hadn't been dug out by ancient labour; the sides, one of which we stood on, had been built up to catch and hold rainwater. There was also an Eastern Baray, dry now, and archaeological evidence of others further afield, but this one remained as the legacy of smart kings, or smart kings' engineers.

We watched some boys splashing in inner tubes get shouted at by fishermen for coming too close to their nets. We breathed the clean air off the water.

I took out my camera and filmed the fishermen and boy dispute. Sophea watched me with interest.

"That makes film? I thought it was just a camera."

She looked at what I'd filmed and said: "That's quite high-quality."

We watched fishermen hang nets on a frame to dry, we watched a group of middle-aged white tourists brave the insect snacks, men, to a man, laughing and pronouncing them 'not bad'. Of course someone said: "Tastes like chicken."

Sophea told me they tasted of salt and chillies.

Some local children came up from the beach and bought the snacks for real, gleefully brandishing little bags at their friends.

"You wanted one like this." Sophea said suddenly, holding her arm in front of me, indicating her pristine white cotton shirt. I did, and there was a long, long stretch of market stalls at the roadside.

We browsed and found white shirts. Meanwhile Sophea had, as if by accident, wandered into the racks of pretty cotton sundresses. She held up two the same. "These are my size but blue or red?"

I thought the blue.

"I can't decide. Let me think." She put them down beside my selected shirts. The stallholder woman said something to her; Sophea smiled.

"What about some scarves for gifts?" Sophea suggested. My mother was scarf crazy; I found one she'd like. Now this was on the pile.

Every time I'd asked the woman prices, she named figures far higher than I was prepared to pay. That was the game.

So, not nine dollars for the shirts, I'd pay five. Not five dollars for the scarf, two…

The woman held up the dresses and spoke to Sophea.

"She says two dresses for seven dollars." Sophea took the dresses away from the woman and put them back on the counter. "But I don't need two, I must decide."

The woman then held up my three shirts. "Three twelve dollars." She held up the scarf: "Three". She bundled the two dresses into the pile and announced: "Total twenty two."

"But she has put the dresses with your things." Sophea made a half-gesture to retrieve the dresses.

"No, let me." I said. "But tell her everything for twenty dollars. "

They talked for a moment then the woman agreed.

"Oh that is so kind." Sophea took her bag of dresses as if the gift was an astounding surprise.

Part of me wanted to let her know that I knew she'd been as crafty as a child but I didn't. I didn't even give her a knowing look, just smiled and said: "My pleasure."

I'd been too slow to offer to buy her a gift so Sophea made sure there was a gift. It was seven dollars. And something learned about the way she thought.

Lunch, always important to Sophea, was fresh fish and rice at the side of the Baray. We lingered in the slight breeze.

"I think maybe sometime you can film me dancing, show it to people."

"It would be very amateur on this camera."

"As an example, then documentary makers are interested and come back. People are interested in documentaries all the time."

There was such a crack of desperation in her that needed to get away from the stress of dwindling dance income and fear of the clock ticking. I'd film her dancing, try my best for her.

Then she said: "Even if nothing happens and we have no success I will like the film. I have never seen how I look all around, you know, only in the mirror."

Her phone rang. It was Ponleak. His boy was still sick but the doctors thought he could go home in about a week.

"I have told Ponleak to collect you in the morning. Bring your camera, I have a very good idea for filming."

Sophea got up from the table. She had a show at the hotel that evening and needed to prepare. We took a long parting look out over the green Baray water and she smiled: "Thank you for coming here. The film will be exciting"

Sophea turned away and her smile vanished: "We must go. Oh look at this driver, I don't like him."
Kim was having a flirty-seeming conversation with an ant-tray woman, lolling against his tuk tuk, laughing his psychopath's cackle – but it wasn't behaviour deserving of Sophea's ferocious scowl and sharp words with him.
I began to wonder if Sophea the Buddhist didn't have the edge on me when it came to irritability. And sometimes I felt she considered that, like poor Mr Ponleak, I was probably not of very high intelligence.

In the morning, when we set out with an exhausted but slightly less shredded-looking Ponleak, she told me:
"Of course there's no problem filming at the temples. I am from this place, and you are my guest."
I took her word for it – sure, no problem, there would be no hassle from the notoriously corrupt and officious Apsara Authority, the government department who policed and administered the Angkor site.

We left Ponleak, telling him to rest: we'd be a couple of hours. We walked across the grass to the giant stone Buddha faces of the Bayon temple. Bayon was full of narrow stairs, low walkways, sudden cloisters and seemed a striking setting for our little film sample. It was appropriate too, because Sophea used the name Pragna Barmey as a professional dance name; most celestial dancers took on the name of a famous ancient dancer and Pragna Barmey had been the favourite dancer and wife of Khmer king and enthusiastic Buddhist, Jayavarman V11, who had built Bayon.
After decades of coffer-draining battles with surrounding empires, victorious Jayavarman V11 decided to build bigger, better, than the previous builder king, Suryavarman 11, who had constructed Angkor Wat. Jayavarman V11 ordered up the walled city of Angkor Thom, a mile or so from his ancestor's architectural triumph. The city's houses, shops, barracks, stables and constructions for ordinary mortals would have been made from wood, straw and bamboo, and have rotted away. What remains are fortifications and temples.
If you wondered what manner of a man Jayavarman V11 might have been, the Bayon temple has 216 gigantic stone faces of Avaloketshvara, Buddha of All compassion, on 54 towers, each one the face of the king himself.
We walked below the giant handsome faces, trying to find a well-lit, quiet spot. We discovered a small sunny courtyard, with a cloistered walkway on three sides, the foundations of a giant face at the fourth, and large smooth stones underfoot.
In her small backpack Sophea had the basics of her dance costume. I asked her to explain them on film, as much as modesty permitted, while she dressed, and to explain why we were in the Bayon temple.

She put on the sampot, a long piece of stiff silk that went around her, through the legs and was pulled fast with a carved silver belt to make pantaloons. There were different coloured silks for different days of the week. Sunday – red; Monday – bright yellow; Tuesday – green; Wednesday – purple; Thursday – dark blue; Friday – light blue; Saturday – black. Today was a light blue day.

There was a short-sleeved, tapered silk jacket: "We don't have bare breasts like the statues, the fashion is change. I am glad about that." Sophea smiled sweetly, completely at ease with the camera.

There were layers of hollow silver bracelets to fasten around wrists and ankles, for decoration and to make pretty, time-keeping sounds.

She hadn't bought the headdress, Mokot; it was too heavy and hot, and far too valuable to drag about town for my amateur film.

I concentrated on holding my little camera steady while Sophea described the training. She began by explaining how her strangely concave back was the result of years of stretching for perfect posture, the teacher digging her long nails into Sophea's shoulders, sometimes drawing blood to get the perfect shape from her determined-not-to-cry student.

Sophea showed the backward arch of her hands and feet, how the natural shape of the body had to be changed for the Khmer ballet, the bones distorted. Every spare moment, she had to push back her fingers, pull her toes upward – the shape was there now but she still rehearsed the shaping every day to keep flexible.

She explained that her costume and her outward turned legs indicated she was playing a male role – real male dancers only played clowns, monkeys and monsters, never the elegant heroes.

Hands moving in and out of gestures, she told what some of them meant: a beckoning, the dancer taking flight, offering a flower, indicating grief or fear. She began a walking dance, shifting to a flying dance… The control of every millimetre from head to toe was breath-taking. Around the cloister I heard occasional voices of American, French and unknown language tourists passing by. Some paused to watch Sophea. I heard shutters click – what a pleasant surprise to find a tiny barefoot woman in traditional costume dancing exquisitely on the flagstones.

Then there'd be peace, tourists had left us, Sophea dancing to no music but the song of birds.

I thought we would move on to explaining some of the stories in the dance, many from the Ramayana tales, some from later Khmer legend. Sophea had her own ideas for a ballet based on scenes from the Buddha's life that would be instructional for children. She began talking so compellingly about all this ..... But my memory card ran out; we had to take a moment's break.

As we went over to our bags, five young men with walkie-talkies barged through the entrance and surrounded us. They wore assorted styles of uniform, but all wore the badge of the Apsara Authority. One of the men had a camera for some reason. Maybe to take a picture of us master criminals if we tried to flee.

Sophea just tutted and said: "Oh typical."

If anyone knew the time to be scared of young men in uniform and when to be simply inconvenienced by them, she would know. So, taking her cue, I wasn't unduly perturbed. Also, they were not armed and all smaller than me; I could risk being very grand and English.

I drew myself up so they could see – look, six inches on a couple of you: "Is there a problem here?" And because I knew, I just knew: "This is only a film for me, a souvenir."

"No filming," the one with the camera yapped.

The young man in the centre, who appeared to be their leader, glared at him and said something to Sophea in Khmer. Sophea's response was calm, pleasant. He argued with her; she was a little less calm. Suddenly she let fly a long tirade. All I understood was that twice she said 'sexy dancing' and whenever she drew breath the one with the camera said something smirky, the leader would glare at him, open his mouth to speak – but Sophea would go on spitting words at them. Then they didn't interrupt, just stared.

Suddenly, Sophea stopped talking and looked at me.

"I tell them you are my friend. This is not commercial film. They say film crew must pay, I ask them where is the crew? One girl is a crew? They are too stupid."

She turned to them. "One girl is not a film crew do you know that? No, they know nothing." She turned back to me. "This is the place for sacred dance but no one comes except tourist shows, not real Khmer ballet just the same clothes doing sexy dancing for big money, they don't know what the real dance is, they don't know their own culture."

Two men at the back started whispering, there was a flicker of distress across the leader's face. I felt he had no idea what to do, which wasn't very intimidating. I could risk a little cheekiness. I asked him; "So what's happening, are we going to prison?"

Sophea scoffed an answer for me.

"We don't need prison because already we are in a prison; Apsara Authority has made the temples into a prison."

Despite his mortified expression the leader spoke, a little firmer this time.

"Oh really." Sophea switched to French for the translation. "They want us to leave because they don't believe we will stop filming if they go away."

Now a sixth uniformed youth appeared: just curious. I think.

The leader said: "Yes. Go away please. You have to go outside."

I was about to become indignant about the twenty dollar temple day-pass I'd coughed up for, and to reiterate the personal use defence, but Sophea plonked herself on a low wall:

"I won't go outside dressed like this so I will stay here forever."

Now I could see the camera boy, talking to the leader, gesturing to my camera. Could they confiscate my camera, the memory card? Well, that wasn't going to happen. And I didn't think an eternal sit-in was the best solution either.

"Sirs," I said, bossy and tall-looking as I could be: "She has to get changed so you can't stand there like that, you have to go away now."

As if slowly putting a gun back in its holster I showed them I was zipping my camera into my bag.

The uniformed boys hadn't moved.

"Sir, are you leaving?" I asked the lead one. The big pompous voice I'd found echoed back from the stones.

He looked at me for a moment, then, clearly deciding we were both too mad to deal with further, he turned, and shooed the others away.

As she changed into jeans and folded up her finery, Sophea was incandescent with rage against the Apsara Authority, their greed as an organisation and the personal greed of these boys who thought they might get some money to turn a blind eye. The Apsara people were oppressing their own people, they were supposed to guard the heritage but didn't know the heritage...

Just down the road were the famous, creeper-draped ruins of Ta Prohm. Everyone liked to have their photograph taken at the spot where Lara Croft had vanished underground. I'd done it myself. To film Lara Croft in the ruins must have cost a pretty penny, so any whiff of commercial filming and the Apsara Authority would be looking for fat fees. But it was just us, not Angelina Jolie and a Hollywood entourage.

As she zipped her bag, Sophea had shifted from anger to abject misery. Not helped by her putting on the little pink sweatshirt, with the rabbit-eared hood, rabbit ears drooping.

I carried her bag as we went outside. She straightened up, took the hood down, put on sunglasses and began looking haughty. If any of those boys were around, she wouldn't let them see… We'd just drive away, sneering back at them.

Unfortunately for the tone of our getaway, we couldn't find Ponleak among the tuk tuks outside the temple. He wouldn't have expected us back so soon. We tried our phones; neither had a signal. It could have been the trees and high Buddha faces blocking the signals, but perhaps the Apsara Authority had their own very high tariff provider for use in their territory.

Sophea was swearing in alternating languages. I told her to sit in the shade, she was tired; I'd find Ponleak.

"What if you are lost too? No, we stay together."

Then, from the temple jaunt with him when I was still a mere tourist rather than a menace to the state of Cambodia, I remembered where Ponleak might be. Across some grassland, at the far end of the Elephant Terrace there was a tree-shaded clutch of small restaurants, souvenir stalls and a big tuk tuk park. Ponleak would be where tour driving routine led him. Or not.

We passed the long stone terrace, carved with all manner of animals as well as an elephant parade, once the base for the king's grand entrance hall, now clambered by larky backpackers.

The rainy-season sky was hanging dark and low, a breath crushing duvet. It grew hotter and hotter as we straggled the fifteen-minute walk and Sophea raged about the lack of care for the real traditional arts, the silly commercialised Khmer dances, the sexy videos and films that pop stars shot among the ruins, how dare the Apsara Authority use that name, what a joke, how very dare they all – her great grandmother had been a wife of king Norodom but now no one knew anything....

If we got to the end of the walk and found I was wrong about Ponleak's likely hiding place, I hoped our phones would start working again so we could track him down. I also hoped she'd change the subject soon because the hot walk was shifting me from compassion to irritation worthy of, well, Sophea. She'd said filming would be fine but she'd known damn well it wouldn't be… And why go on about great grandmothers married to kings when it meant nothing? I had just enough intelligence to read and I'd done some research the previous evening. Kings' ex-wives were ten a penny, hundreds a penny.

When the kings first came to Cambodia as invaders from southern India, they brought the sacred dancers of Vishnu with them. As the invaders settled, eventually converting to Buddhism and building vast temple complexes, there was a need for dancers, many dancers. These had to be recruited and trained from local girls, a good chance for poor people to offload daughters into an elegant life. These virgin gifts to the king lived sumptuously, needed no dowry and were considered his wives. Although many went on to a sacred, virginal old age in the palace grounds with a small pension, some might catch the King's eye and he'd make them a mistress-wife. Possibly, although this was no day to discuss it with Sophea, one could say that there had always been some 'sexy dancers'. Of course, the old sexiness was exclusive to the king – any other man touching the dancers could be killed. The king's mistress dancers had their moment of glory, then they were retired back to live among the virgins when the king's fancy moved on. Some of these young retiree dancers had illegitimate offspring, raised in the palace grounds and given some kind of court or military position at adulthood. So, the country was full of illegitimate royals, going back centuries.

Sophea's great grandmother had been one among King Norodom's many dancers. When Norodom died, the ballet went out of fashion, the rules loosened and many of the young ones went home to live ordinary lives, make real, ordinary marriages as Sophea's great grandmother had. The ballet was in Sophea's blood, but not royalty.

The connection was precious to her, though. Quibbling about it, even in my own boiled grumpy head, was just me turning shamefully mean in the sun. "I don't see Ponleak. Really you are wrong to start walking. We should have waited at the temple." Sophea complained. Maybe she was right. I'd sit her somewhere in the shade and roam back through the forests till I found Ponleak, as this was all my fault…

What if Ponleak hadn't been able to phone us but had to dash to the hospital because his son had taken a turn for the worse, and we were upsetting ourselves over nonsense? I was just on the hot-headed edge of snapping this at Sophea when there, our knight on a shining tuk tuk, Mr Ponleak roared out of the shade trees, a grin on his face.

We were saved. So we should probably have lunch.

We went into a little bamboo café serving all manner of local food that Sophea and Ponleak approved of and I could eat without whimpering. They had a long discussion about the iniquities of the Apsara Authority, the government and the ignorant youth of today. Once every drop had been squeezed from this, Ponleak gave us an update on his son, who was much improved, impatient to get home and ride his bicycle round the village. Then he and Sophea switched back to talking politics with such urgency and focus that Sophea had to promise me she'd explain fully later on. I'd never heard Ponleak say so much, or look so angry. I supposed diverting to a topic other than his son was a channel for his fears…

After lunch, Ponleak dropped us off and sped on his way to pick up supplies for his wife, drop them at the hospital, then he'd go to his village, collect his daughter, drive back for us, then return to the hospital….

The children's hospital was free, set up years ago by a dynamic Swiss doctor, but the feeding and bathing of the children was left to relatives. And of course, only parents could do the anxious watching. The initial fear for Ponleak's little boy had been meningitis but that had been ruled out.

Sophea passed on the rest of the story Ponleak had told her over lunch. The boy had a mild poisoning, caused by bad water in the village.

Twenty minutes from shiny central Siem Reap, Ponleak's village was a collection of ramshackle buildings beside what looked like an open-cast mine. These massive diggings were to become a luxury housing complex; some water pipes had been damaged a month ago.

"They say it was an accident, they say it was repaired." Sophea said. "But they want these scruffy villagers to leave, so…."

In Siem Reap and Phnom Penh, lucrative land deals meant ruthless treatment of tenant communities in the path of shiny hotels, offices or villas for the rich.

For now, Ponleak had his small rented house, along the road from a charity school where he determinedly took his daughter every day. In future they would boil the water, or he'd bring it in canisters from the school pump which had its own clean system.

The intense political discussion over lunch hadn't been unrelated to his son's plight at all. Sophea had been letting him talk, gathering all the facts for me, her mean companion who sneered at her secrets.

"I am so sorry I had such a bad temper earlier," she said.

"Me too."

She tucked her arm through mine and told me, if I didn't mind a little walk, she wanted to show me the Terrace of the Leper King, another part of the Angkor Thom complex. The story was that one of kings of Angkor had been eaten away with leprosy, so these walls and a strange sexless statue were said by some to commemorate him and what he lacked. A less lurid, more accepted theory held that this statue represented Yama, the god of death, and the terrace was the edge of the royal crematorium.

What Sophea liked were the tiers of dancer carvings, some beautifully defined, some chipped away by time or attempted looting, usually by the French colonialists. She pointed to one with a thin face and narrow body; "I like this one, my look, you see."

I realised that all the carvings of dancers were different; they were portraits, not generic decorative girl carvings. Each one had been a real girl dancing among these stones over a thousand years ago.

We wandered to the small Buddhist temple of Preah Neak Poan. A pretty, quiet place that had once run with fountains and streams, used for ritual purification. Presumably back then water was something to trust.

Sitting in a dark corner at the heart of the temple was an astoundingly small old lady – really as small as child – with the shaved head and white robes of a religious widow. Her face was gentle as a sigh. She spoke to Sophea in a soft, thin voice.

"Sit sit." Sophea told me.

I scrambled to the ground.

The old lady was selling prayer bracelets of entwined yellow and orange nylon yarn.

"You should take her prayer. She is a very sweet lady and seventy-seven years old."

I put a dollar in the basket beside the lady. She nodded at me, whispering a blessing, as she tied the yarn around my wrist. Then she made a pulling gesture at the loose ends of yarn.

"She takes bad luck out of you, out through the ends of the threads."

The old lady flicked her hand to the ground, dashing away my bad luck.

She looked at me intently with age-paled eyes; she whispered more words that sounded prayer-like, then she squeezed both my hands in hers.

"Akun," she said. Thank you.

Sophea gave the old lady money and took a yarn blessing too.

After her threads were cleansed of badness, Sophea smiled at me: "I know you don't believe in this, but it will be nice for us to look at the thread and

say to ourselves 'I have a good friend and we make good work together.'"
As we were leaving Sophea turned back, handed the woman a local note and asked a question. The old woman nodded and closed her eyes.
"She will pray now for the sick boy."
We walked out to the entrance and Ponleak was waiting there, with his daughter, Maly, pretty as an angel in a yellow cotton dress. With a smile, Ponleak said something to Sophea.
"He says he is glad to see we are not arrested."
We continued to be cheerful as the tuk tuk rattled up to the back gates of Sophea's hotel. We were collecting her friend and neighbour, Chenda, who had a job in the kitchens.
Chenda was also the person Sophea prayed with: "She is so helpful to me. She knows much, much more about prayer and meditation. When she speaks to the Buddha, the Buddha answers."
I didn't know what to think about that, but Chenda seemed to glow with a serenity that I knew didn't come from easy living. She might have been fifty but looked a lot older. She surely had her Khmer Rouge past sorrows but, among present difficulties, her only daughter was in a refuge in Phnom Penh, hiding from a violent husband. A month ago, the husband had turned up at Chenda's door hammering, crashing in, looking for his runaway wife. Sophea had rallied male neighbours to drive the brute off. Sophea had also found the kitchen job for Chenda; it was helping her save up to visit her daughter and perhaps give the daughter a little pocket money for a new life.
"We will stop at the market for some fish and all have dinner at my house. I think that will be nice," Sophea said when we'd settled Chenda into her seat. Maly, as if with some radar for the best woman among us, cuddled against Chenda immediately.
Dinner at Sophea's house was helpful to Ponleak; she could load him up with food and fruit to take over to the hospital later.
When we arrived at the house, Ponleak wanted to fix a couple of broken fence panels but Sophea wouldn't hear of it. We were ushered inside and we watched as Chenda and Sophea bowed to the Buddha's altar and lit incense. Maly held her hands together in prayer and bowed her head but Ponleak waited it out as godlessly as I did. Then Sophea switched on electric fans and found cushions for us to be comfortable on the tiled floor. Clearing a space in all the clutter was something we had to figure out for ourselves.
It seemed to take Sophea ten minutes to cook a delicious meal of vegetables, fish and rice on a two-ring burner, while Chenda handed round cold sodas and organised a picnic-like table setting on the floor, smiling and humming to herself as she went.
To round off the feast, Sophea had slices of fresh mango from the garden and a bar of plain chocolate from the fridge. Excited, Maly took a square of chocolate then spat it out as if she'd start vomiting. She had to be consoled

with more mango and a packet of tissues decorated in pictures of cartoon animals which Chenda produced from her sleeve.

Ponleak's phone rang. He frowned and stepped outside.

I didn't need to look at the others. Perhaps it was nothing.

I helped Sophea clear the dishes and pack up leftovers for the hospital. Chenda made the cartoon animal tissues into squeaking finger puppets to entertain Maly.

Out in the dark Ponleak was quiet now, listening.

I showed Chenda and Maly the footage of Sophea's illicit dancing at the Bayon. It had come out quite well. Perhaps we'd film some more in the grounds of the little Buddhist monastery behind her house where she wanted to start her school. Perhaps…

Ponleak came in all smiles.

"Not one week. Tomorrow, my boy."

There was talk in Khmer. Ponleak looked looser, lighter. It was late now though, time for him to get to the hospital where his wife had been sleeping by her child's bed and preparing food on a stove in a car park.

At the gate, Sophea asked Ponleak something. He swayed his motorbike from side to side. There was a small slosh of liquid sound. Sophea nodded and waved us goodnight.

We bumped along the maze of small dirt roads to the centre of Siem Reap. In the middle of a deserted stretch of unlit back streets we slowed to a halt. Ponleak's motorbike had run out of its little slosh of petrol.

Maly and I got down to help push, while Ponleak resignedly began hauling the motorbike and cart along to the next petrol station or, more likely on his budget, a woman with a roadside stall full of bottles selling cheap smuggled fuel.

Strong as his muscles suggested, Ponleak got a momentum going while Maly and I struggled to keep up, Maly shifting from a trot to a run. Our pushing was probably of minimal help anyway, so I let go of the tuk tuk – we'd just walk. Ponleak seemed to go even faster, leaving us about fifty yards behind. I wasn't that worried. The lights of a Siem Reap main street were up ahead – we were only ten minutes from a frappachino. But it was very dark where I walked with Maly. I forced myself not think about thieves and snakes. I started to whistle a happy tune and Maly tried to copy me. We were fine until a huge barking dog came out of nowhere. Any dog bigger than my shoes terrifies me. But I was the grown-up here. Maly jumped for me to lift her up. I looked for Ponleak – far, far ahead. I swung round so that Maly was away from the dog and tried get my rucksack free to shove in its mouth or something… But the dog was on a chain, just barking, couldn't get us. I took big strides away from its noise all the same, carrying Maly on my hip. I began the whistling lessons again but she didn't join in; she was watching Ponleak, getting tearful. I called out to him; he didn't hear me. Finally I yelled loud enough for him to hear and wait.

He was sweat from his head to his dust covered trainers. He squeezed Maly's hand then pointed to the crossroads just ahead.

"Petrol two minute."

I hoisted Maly higher on my hip and made a real effort to help push the tuk tuk.

As we came out of the side road darkness, a group of Europeans were drinking at a corner café and watched us with surprise. Their surprise or some release of I'm-going-to-be-eaten-by-a-killer-dog tension made me laugh. Then Maly laughed because we were with her dad again and there was laughing. Hysteria took over both of us, we were laughing the way tired children do, until they're sick.

Ponleak pulled up to a petrol stand; he turned to me, beginning to speak but stopped, bewildered by the laughing. He bustled on, getting me home and himself and Maly to the hospital.

Early the next evening, Ponleak came to my guest house with Maly. Once he'd dropped Sophea and I at our destination, he'd collect his wife and son to go home.

"Ponleak has something he wanted me to ask you." Sophea said, after Ponleak assured us his son was now very well. "When you ran out of petrol you were laughing and laughing, why were you laughing?"

I told her about the dog, how scared I'd been, so the laughing had been some sort of hysteria... Sophea pursed her lips and held up her little hand to stop me.

"I can't tell him this, he will feel bad you were scared. And I will be ashamed of you."

She spoke to Ponleak in Khmer.

"I told him that things go on in your head no one can understand."

"Like voices in my head?"

"That kind of thing."

We both started laughing.

Ponleak watched us. Hating to miss out, Kiri scurried over: "What happen? What is funny?"

Ponleak spoke to Kiri and Sophea laughed more.

"Ponleak says he thought it was a foreign thing he doesn't understand but it is both of us."

Kiri grinning, said: "Not just both. All women. All." Then his grin dropped away. "You go Battambang?"

"In a few days."

He looked at Sophea, then at me, more stony serious than I'd seen him.

"Excuse me." He grabbed a discarded leaflet advertising trips to the nearby lake. He scrawled on it and handed it to Sophea. "Please be careful. This is telephone for my brother who is police there"

Sophea took it with polite thanks. What was wrong with Battambang? Ponleak was nodding, talking in Khmer, pleased we had the number. Sophea shoved the paper into her bag as we walked to the tuk tuk.

"He says there are bad people in Battambang, bad people. But everywhere the same. To him we are just women. He has no idea what I did as a child. A woman child. He means well but pay no attention."

No, not worried by that at all, I told myself.

Sophea had more serious concerns than Kiri's concern: "I make a mistake with my dress I think. My sister send it from Paris. It is pretty but it is short. I feel embarrass."

It was quite a short broiderie anglaise shift dress, but not shockingly so. I assured her it looked great.

"Yes, it is OK. I look young so I can wear it. And if I get change we will be late, no? "

I thought so. Sophea sighed, still not getting into the tuk tuk.

"My sister is lucky. When she is twenty-five she meets a French man and goes to live in Paris. She is happy. When I am twenty-five I do the same and it is not good. Not good. But we don't talk about it now. We go out for fun. The dress is nice, no?"

CHAPTER 4: CLOWN TEARS

I saw a formally dressed, middle-aged Indian man, looking as pleasantly surprised as I was to be having such a good time. No one, not even the large school excursion of Cambodian eight year olds, or the family groups of tourists were having as much of a good time as Sophea. Acrobats twirled on high ropes and she gasped; jugglers threw, balancers balanced and Sophea whispered her awe, and I thought her huge intake of breath when a human pyramid formed would choke her on the spot.

The show wasn't simply a display of circus skills; the young performers had built a story into the extraordinary action; it was more a piece of very physical theatre. The strongest element was an impish clown, a snub-faced teenager with a flawless sense of what face to make when, and a leaning, back-flipping, shuddering, teetering physical control that made every double-take, pretend fright and ill-fated prank draw raucous joy from the audience. If Stan Laurel, Lee Evans and Tommy Cooper, somehow, had a Cambodian lovechild, it would have been this kid, Srei.

The antics and story were accompanied by a young band, Dengue Fever, playing a mix of traditional and modern instruments and wearing a confection of costume borrowed from Duran Duran and the cast of The King and I. I also had the recurring accompaniment of Sophea's applause, laughter and commentary, explaining what was going on in an excited whisper – not just to translate the dialogue sections for me, it was a child-like glee in the plot twists: "Oh no, that one's stolen all the money and they think he's their friend...

In the story, devised by the performers, villains were hounding a dysfunctional family. In a magical dream sequence, the lights became like starlight, a girl twirled on a high rope and the music became eerie. Soothed by their dream, the family stopped bickering and helped each other with frenetic juggling and trapeze-ing. Rallying together, the family found love, happiness – and the bad characters were thoroughly punished. Not wishful thinking, or anything like that at all.

Flower petals showered from the roof of the Big Top, as bright-painted young acrobats, clowns, jugglers and musicians came to take a final bow. As the solitary Indian man applauded, I knew I must have the same expression on my face: he looked charmed and surprised at how much he'd genuinely enjoyed himself.

Sophea was on her feet, clapping as if she was trying to shatter her hands.

There was a tannoy announcement: "Thank you for coming. If anyone would like a photograph with our performers, here they are!"

The children in the audience all scampered down into the ring, some waving their phones for photographs, some dragging parents with cameras – way ahead of the pack was Sophea, looking ready to elbow a child in the face if they got in her way. She was calling over her shoulder for me to: "Hurry, get picture!"

Sophea stood among bare-chested, tattooed youths, the silk-clad female jugglers and the fine-feathered members of Dengue Fever like a little doll they'd found. One of the Dengue Fever ensemble handed me a phone, asking me to take a picture of him with Sophea. He looked as thoroughly delighted with her as she was with him.

I was joined by Dara, the remarkable thirty year old who was in charge of developing and fundraising for all this – Phare, a circus and arts enterprise helping vulnerable children and teenagers.

"Bong Sophea had nothing like this as a child, I expect. Even when I was a child, all the entertainers were killed or they didn't hurry to come back. All I remember is a traditional medicine man who would go round the villages with a cart selling cures from bark and leaves. He played music and had a monkey in trousers who danced. Oh no..."

There was a massive shaking of the tent around us.

"Rain! I have arranged for you to use another small office tent but we should go before the way is all mud."

Dara, in his smart chinos and impeccably ironed shirt, charming in confident English, gave the impression of being a foreign-educated rich kid but he was largely educated by himself, or local scholarships. From a career in the hotel trade, he'd begun volunteering over the weekend at Phare's base in his home town of Battambang. Then, when they were given funding to develop the art school and performance centre into a self-sustaining social enterprise, young had been so impressive around the place, he was given the job. He loved his work with a passion, he hounded the wealthy to invest, he encouraged every street kid the project rescued and he refused to have the organisation called a charity: "We are a social enterprise. Social enterprise expands; charity suffocates...." His speech on the subject was a heck of a lot longer but you get the idea.

I knew Dara because the manager of Sophea's hotel had introduced him as a person of interest, not only for the organisation he represented but for his own personality. As another European businessman later said to me:

"He's one of those people you just think, where did you come from? And you just know he'll end up a millionaire, a president, something like that."

Part of the effect Kiri had come from his affable tirelessness, and the impression he could give you that you were the person he was most happy to have met, ever. Although of course, he had made me promise to write some articles, generate publicity and send information packs to suitable 'partner organisations'.

Dara had arranged tickets for Sophea and me to see the show and invited us to meet the performers.

"Bong Sophea can translate of course, but I will need to sit with you: they have to be protected. I have selected the clown for you, as I know from the internet you write much comedy. But you can speak to anyone you like, of course."

As it turned out, Sophea, face still glowing joyfully, wouldn't take up Dara's offer of a meeting, but did accept his loan of an umbrella as the hot, rainy season downpour was now at water cannon force. Someone wise turned out the fairy lights stringing the outside of the big top and the trees, and the large electric floodlights, but in the faint glow of solar lamps I could still watch Sophea elegantly pick her way across a plank walkway to find transport at the road. She'd left me behind because:

"I don't want to break the images. I don't think their real lives are so magical."

She was right.

Srei, the twenty-five-year-old clown, all mischievous glee in the ring, told me his father had been a violent alcoholic. When Srei was five, he saw his mother taking a suitcase to a taxi; she was abandoning him and his four older brothers. Srei ran out and clung to her, screaming, until she had to take him with her, or the father would be woken. Srei had never seen his father or the four siblings again. He'd made a few attempts lately to find the brothers but not a trace. Not a trace.

While Kiri translated, Srei watched him respectfully. Then he'd look at me, sweat melting his lurid clown make-up, and talk again, hesitantly, earnestly.

His mother scraped a living selling rice porridge at the roadsides of Battambang, but there were days when depression kept her in bed and Srei had to take over. He also collected plastic bottles and tins to sell; anything to help out financially. His mother seemed to get better and she remarried, had a new baby. Srei was delighted to have a little brother, but things soon went wrong again. First the stepfather left saying he was looking for work in Phnom Penh. Then his mother became mentally unstable – shouting, breaking things in the house. She told Srei she was leaving to find work in Thailand. This time Srei couldn't grab her and scream to come with her because he was holding his mother's crying baby. He couldn't make her take the baby because he didn't trust her not to harm it. Twelve-year-old Srei was alone and had to take his stepbrother on the street to beg for milk.

At this point, Kiri covered his face, I thought he was going to cry.

"Sorry, sorry," he said. "I have two babies so it makes me... I have heard his story before but not that he had to take the baby outside and beg."

He spoke to Srei in Khmer, Srei nodded and went on talking. Life improved: he found help with a charity for children. When he was there he heard about Phare. With his brother on his back, he went to take a look. The Phare people were so helpful and welcoming... They let him join art classes while his brother was looked after in a nursery. Things seemed so promising but then his mother and stepfather turned up, insisting Srei and the baby come to live with them.

Kiri asked Srei to wait while he explained something to me: "The foreign charities often don't like to interfere in families because the Cambodian parents can go to the authorities and accuse the foreigners of kidnap....Srei?"

Srei looked very agitated. Suddenly he wanted to leave.

"We are coming to a part of his past he doesn't like, it makes him ashamed. Maybe that's enough."

I couldn't bear the wretched look on the cheeky little clown face. I was getting ready to go while Dara spoke softly, persuasively, to Srei who nodded and took a seat again, bowing to me.

He'd run away to live on the streets, living with a gang, sniffing glue and drinking. He stole all the time, that's what they did in the gang. The easiest targets were women. Srei and his friend would be on a motorbike and just drive past, grab... This Khmer woman wouldn't give her handbag so his friend pulled, dragged her all along the street, must have hurt her very bad. She had very little money in her purse. She was dressed like a rich lady but there were a few riel only. And a comb. I saw her face was cut, scraped...."

Srei stopped again. The rain shook the little tent. Perhaps Srei wanted to leave now? No, he could finish his story.

Srei didn't want to live the gang way anymore; he ran to Phare for help. They let him stay in their compound for children at risk. They helped him go to a detox facility and get his body strong. He trained in the circus arts and now he performs everywhere; he'd travelled and he loved it. He also helped a group visiting detox centres to encourage patients to stay strong. If Srei saw a beggar on the street he gave them money that he knew they would spend on alcohol or drugs, but he wasn't afraid to tell them how they could change. He didn't care if the beggar was in a gang who would attack him; he wanted to tell people on the streets his message.

Despite his cute manner, there was a tough-guy air about Srei; it was very easy to picture him in a street gang.

I had also asked Dara to tell Srei that I wasn't just awed by his courage, I had worked in comedy for several thousand years and thought Srei was as funny as anyone topping bills in London.

As Dara explained what I was saying, Srei was on the verge of turning into a song title as tears filled his clown-painted eyes. Saying goodbye, I went to bow to him and he gave me an emotional, double-handed, knuckle-crushing grasp of a handshake.

When I asked to take photos of him, Srei was back in clown mode – posing and pulling faces. He bounced off into the night, delighted with himself. I noticed he wore his jeans hanging mid-thigh-low in the illogical American gangster style fashionable the world over.

Kiri thanked me in advance for the publicity I'd get them, adding: "But I hope you haven't caused me trouble. I may have to tell some small lies that you wanted to interview more performers but didn't have time."

"I'd be happy to interview more."

"The thing is really they would all like to be interviewed. They are so vulnerable these performers. They get jealous and scared if one gets something and they don't. They think they are out of favour, they'll be left out, left behind. The psychology of them is fragile. They all have such bad stories. Orphans, trafficked as sex slaves into Thailand, raped by parents... The psychology of what happened here in the Seventies is passing down through generations. But our mission at Phare is to stop it. It is tricky but look at our success already."

The word 'tricky' reminded me of someone. "I wonder if Bong Sophea could do some work teaching at Phare?"

After the tiniest of beats Dara smiled engagingly.

"That seems a good idea. You are going to Battambang aren't you? Our home base? I can introduce you to our founders and you can discuss it with them."

Perhaps Kiri was a little saved-by-the-rain-drenched-bell of two teenagers coming in, jeans hanging low. They talked fast and distraught at Kiri.

He pulled on an anorak. "Oh Bong Annie, I am so sorry. I would talk more but this rain... The space where the air-conditioners are is flooding, the pump has just broken, so we must all help with buckets."

At the tent entrance, he called for a tuk tuk to cross the mud and collect me, then he sprinted away to do something that I'm sure wasn't part of his job-description, but Kiri would pitch in to do anything.

As good as his word, up in Battambang, Kiri introduced me to the Phare founders. An educational charity had taught these men art skills when they were children in a refugee camp in Thailand. In the early nineties they crossed the border homeward to Battambang and set up a small art school that soon expanded. By 1998 they worked with trainers from Cirque de Soleil to develop the circus side, because they noticed the most distressed, damaged children were full of physical agitation; if they could channel and control that energy...

When I asked Det, the circus founder, about traditional ballet he said:" My difficulty with traditional dance and circus is that they can harm the children's bodies. I believe in our traditions. We use traditional music and design. If you look at the carvings on the walls of Angkor, there are circus performers carved there. We introduce as much tradition as possible but we are interested in how dance and movement can help the children psychologically. We want them to relax, so we teach them warm ups and massage techniques and stretching, so their bodies are healthy and protected. You see the Chinese and Moscow circus? The performers move in unnatural ways. Like ballet, traditional European ballet too. Very unnatural. These things are not for us." I had thought I might have found a place for Sophea but it wasn't going to be that easy.

CHAPTER 5: MEANWHILE, DEEP IN THE FOREST...

Sophea was hoping to teach her dance and guide me through the geography of her past, actual and spiritual, but it seemed impossible for us to just get going.

The first obstacle was Henri, Sophea's husband. If there was a word describing a stage beyond roué, Henri would be the Frenchman it was made for.

In a wood-cabin restaurant, facing across the grass to the towers of Angkor Wat, Henri roamed at ten in the morning, glass of beer in hand, sweat-marked pink shirt unbuttoned over a very round belly, while giving out in fragments of Khmer to a couple of scuttling elderly female staff.

I remembered a film set in Cambodia, City of Ghosts, where Gerard Depardieu played this sort of character – except his character was funny, and content. Henri's colossal alcoholic unhappiness was something he blamed on Sophea. Sometimes she felt he was right.

"It is my bad karma. I married him but I don't love him."

Henri seemed quite hail fellow well met with me, at first, inviting me to sit in the restaurant, take a little coffee... He sent Ponleak off on an errand.

"I tell him Ponleak is a good boy. Henri is always fighting with remok drivers. If he works for Henri, it is good for both."

The Cambodian term for the motorbike and cart transport remok had been almost overwhelmed by the Thai term, tuk tuk. Stubbornly remembering to say remok was something Henri and Sophea had in common.

Henri stood over me, as if staring, but:

"I see nothing." Henri pointed at his tinted spectacles.

Seventy years old now, Henri had developed cataracts. He said he'd already burnt himself trying to cook in the gas-bottle kitchen at the rear of the restaurant. He'd fallen over things several times. But watching him move around, "see nothing" was obviously an exaggeration.

Behind the small kitchen area a bead curtain shielded a rumpled bed and trunks spewing clothes. A plastic water barrel fed a basic shower, a hand basin and the bowl where restaurant dishes were washed. The toilet was across a path, shared with all the cafes in the area. This was Henri's life, alone in the forests of Angkor, with no one but the passing Apsara Authority guards for company at night. Them and the tribal forest people slipping through the trees on unmarked paths.

"We are separated for many years now. He left our flat in the town and came here. He says he is poor because of me but my land is from my sister in Paris; I only took a small salary from him for helping to make this restaurant. I stayed with him as long as possible but he is not good. And now he is old and alone, I am sorry for him."

I'd heard from the hotel manager that everyone felt Sophea hadn't left the marriage a moment too soon.

"I know I am right when I left but just for now I have to cook for him because he thinks these village women don't cook well enough. It's ok for customers but he says he cannot eat their food. Really he is scared. When he phones me he starts crying. I am so sorry Annie. I cannot go far outside with you while he is like this."

Henri was saying something to me in French; I didn't understand it. I don't know if it was his accent or the beer breakfast that made him sound strange, but I could only smile at him in response, apologising that my French wasn't great. He looked disdainfully disappointed.

"She said you speak French. You are a writer, no?"

Did he think I couldn't be a real writer with poor-quality French? Perhaps this was something all French people thought. Perhaps I'd misread Henri's tone and he was only curious. No, there was definitely something challenging in his question. Well, I was inclined to challenge the timing of his weeping down the phone in fear of self-incineration. It seemed more likely his fear was that Sophea might be having fun. Besides, I'm sure I would be burning myself if I declared the sun over the yard-arm at ten in the morning.

In hesitant French, I started explaining what I was writing but Sophea stepped in, asking if I was hungry; she was cooking for Henri so she might as well cook for me.

"You can take late breakfast early lunch, and poor mister Ponleak is always hungry."

Henri glared at her, muttered something incomprehensible and went to sit at a vast desk by the rear wall. He had a cash register and a computer back there. He turned on the latter, loud, and we could all listen to a football match in French. Half the Angkor forest could listen. Although only Henri, who saw nothing, could watch. Perhaps the volume was to compensate for his lack of a picture but I suspected.... Well I suspected many things but mainly that he

was expressing his annoyance at Sophea for bringing me along.
I was unconcerned; I could tune out Henri's noise and stare at the walls and towers of Angkor Wat a few hundred yards in front of me. Maybe it wasn't so bad for Henri living out here, communing with history and nature.
Ponleak came back with a big bag of clean laundry. Nervous of whatever it was Henri was shouting at them, the elderly helpers took out red gingham tablecloths and napkins. They began laying the tables, while Sophea, ushering Ponleak to sit down, served a fish and rice meal she seemed to have cooked in seconds. Then she followed the old ladies around the tables, giving them quiet, urgent instructions. When this was done she smiled at me apologetically.
"He is in a very bad temper now from drinking. But this stupid Buddhism of mine, I cannot leave him old and sick. Thursday he goes to Phnom Penh for the operation and he has a friend there, no need for him to be scared. One time he had friends here – archaeologists, designer for hotels, many French and American people. They used to drink and talk with him but they went home. Or he had arguments with them. Henri, he will not go home. He wants to die in Cambodia and I am to do the ceremony for him. He has two sisters in France but he will not go home because of me."
Now holding a glass of Ricard and a half-smoked cigarette, Henri swayed over to us talking crossly to Sophea. All I could make out in his French was: "...it's all right for now but not when the customers arrive."
Ponleak didn't speak French but Henri's disparaging glance at him was clear enough. Ponleak carried on eating, a little faster, pretending not to know Henri had been talking about him.
Had Henri envisaged some left-bank bohemian type of restaurant? Full of French artistic types in heated philosophical discussion – not tuk tuk drivers, village women, English creatures pretending they were writers and a wife who.. What? How had they reached this place?

Back in her mid-twenties, Sophea was performing an occasional dance show and quite enjoying a job she'd found, waitressing at a new international hotel in Phnom Penh. In what spare time she had, she took an English class, always making an effort to practise on hotel guests, as well as constantly polishing her French. She was restless, though; she felt life must hold more for her – there was a big world out there she wanted to see, and speak to.
Sophea's mother continued to be physically and mentally fragile. The slightest thing made her anxious. Being anxious in Cambodia at that time wasn't entirely irrational. In 1991 the countryside was thick with unexploded ordinance, and Khmer Rouge rebels determined that their day was not done. The Vietnamese had withdrawn. America and its allies in the UN, many of them reluctant allies under a financial thumb, didn't want a communist-leaning government in Cambodia. They were orchestrating a coalition for

Cambodia that would include the royal family and perhaps some of the more co-operative Khmer Rouge. Their justification for this was that it would put an end to rebellion. More and more reeking mass execution graves were opened and torture centres exposed in the newspapers, while the Americans shook hands with men known to be in Pol Pot's inner circle. Meanwhile Pol Pot and the rest of his inner circle lurked in rustic comfort on the Thai border, fighting factions who objected to them, raiding terrified villagers for supplies and being covertly armed and trained by the SAS and CIA.

Sophea's demure, fragile mother wouldn't have known the ruthless political games that were perpetuating her country's distress. She saw her family stumbling to its feet in a wretched, criminal-infested city, where only the politicians and foreigners set foot in new hotels or restored luxury homes. Perhaps if the family had more money, they'd all have fled.

Back then, Henri was assisting a man called Albert Le Bonheur, a conservationist from the Musee Guimet in Paris, who wanted to record and save as much as he could of Khmer culture. Henri and Albert got talking to Sophea at the hotel and asked if she would accompany them on a tour of the Royal Palace to help interpret a mural of the Ramayana.

"They said it was because in talking with me they discover I am a dancer and know these stories, but really it was because Henri fell in love with me on sight. Although it is Mr Albert who said I look like the sculpture of Pragma Barmey, wife of King Jayavarman the seventh.

"Quite quickly Mr Albert came with Henri to speak to my father. Mr Albert is a very clever man who even speaks Khmer. Unfortunately he died in '96. In any case..."

Sophea had mixed feelings. Henri was twenty years older and not, by anyone's standards, handsome. But he was clearly gentle, adoring and a way for her to see Europe.

"Already when I was young I thought was not right to marry when I didn't love him. But my father and mother both thought a foreigner was better. They pushed me to go so much I thought maybe they preferred my brother and my little sister. That they don't love me."

Sophea prayed a great deal but instead of finding peace for the idea of marriage she had a premonition: "I feel if I go to Paris I will never see my mother again."

A colleague of Henri and Mr Albert, Veronique, was returning to Paris; she came to measure Sophea to buy a trousseau of western-style clothes that would wait for her when she arrived in France.

"She showed me pictures in magazines, very nice, and we decide what style of dresses. Remember, I have so little. My best outfit is the costume I wear for work and my dance clothes that I made myself."

The marriage went ahead, a Khmer ceremony.

"Very traditional. My mother was very happy but my heart was broken as I

am scared it is the last time I see her."
The honeymoon was a working holiday for Henri. Along with Albert and a woman named Veronique – "A different Veronique, this one is an archaeologist. I think what is this? Are all women in France called Veronique? But it was her name."
They took a boat from Phnom Penh to Siem Reap. Henri was enjoying it, photographing the villages along the banks, but Sophea was nervous because the boat looked old and she couldn't swim. In addition, they had three armed men with them, guards that Albert had hired because they were heading through territory where Khmer Rouge loyalists hid out.
"I am so scared. It is my honeymoon and we cross land with mines. They think it is a big adventure and I think we will get killed."
They reached the sacred mountain of Phnom Krom. We are supposed to continue to Prasat Preah Vihar. Very old, but the guards refuse. Too dangerous. Only Phom Krom and Ankor. Albert and Veronique took notes while Henri took photographs of the ruined towers on the mountains, the remains of a tenth century temple. As well as being afraid, Sophea felt increasingly lonely. At this stage her French wasn't great and Henri kept talking archaeology with the other two.
When they moved on to Angkor Wat and Sophea's state of mind changed.
"I feel happy. I feel I know it, my home in a previous life. We stayed there four days in a private house of someone Veronique knew. I find out there are planes to Phnom Penh. Being in Angkor Wat makes me strong. I told Henri we should take the plane, and I refused to go back in the boat, it's too dangerous. He was very angry but I refused."
Henry relented and he paid for himself and Sophea to make a very expensive plane journey. He also had to pay bribes in Phnom Penh for a visa to get Sophea into Vietnam where there was a French embassy. He found there were more bribes to pay at the Vietnamese border; then there was a less expensive legitimate French visa and tickets for a flight to Paris. Sophea was no bargain. And no passive, grateful little oriental maid. But Henri was in love.
"While we waited in Saigon, Henri wanted to be a husband to me. I told you before, I thought he wants to make pee pee. I know it seems stupid, I was twenty five and do not know sex but always my family kept me in a very innocent life. I push him and go out of the room. But then I remember what my mother said: 'To make children your husband must touch you and you must keep quiet.' I wanted children so I did what Henri wanted. I didn't like it but I let him do it. In the night Henri started to cry. He asked me why I don't love him? I told a lie, I told him I did love him. I told him I was just confused about things because I never had a boyfriend before – this part was true. I was ready to say anything because I wanted him not to cry and be weak like that."

It was September when they reached Paris. Henri thought this would be a good time to arrive, with a mild enough temperature for Sophea but she still found it cold. That Paris was so bright and clean amazed her – no dirt roads, no broken buildings, no piles of rubbish in every eye-line... She thought it was beautiful but the people had no expression. To her they seemed very hard to read. Inscrutable occidentals.

Henri rented an apartment from some friends in Belleville and worked in the museum. He found some other Khmer exiles so Sophea wouldn't be lonely; through them she was introduced a classical ballet troupe, formed of Cambodian exiles, who hired her as a performer and teacher. They gave quite grand performances, even danced for Chirac when he was mayor of Paris.

A big audience didn't make her nervous: "When I am dancing, I just look for God in front of me. I imagine God is there so I am not bothered by cameras or crowds."

There were offers for her to enter beauty contests. She was tempted by the money and the notion that Miss France would be a Cambodian. But the bathing suit section was out of the question.

"The main reason I don't mind my life in Paris too much is because I can dance. Then my sister phoned to say my mother is very sick. I called to the doctor in Cambodia; I tell him whatever my mother needs, I will pay. Thirty minutes, only thirty minutes after this, my sister called again to say my mother is dead. I am like a puppet if you drop it. I start to cry and I feel like I will never stop. I can't work in the house, I can't dance, I just stay in the bed crying. I can't help it."

This went on for months, until a despairing Henri took her to stay with his elderly parents who lived by the sea, just outside Nice. These kindly people walked with Sophea on the beach, or went to the mountains with her, collecting flowers and spring water. She began to regain her physical strength at least. One night, she dreamt of her mother. Her mother's head was shaved and she was dressed all in white, like a widow or holy woman in a pagoda.

"She touches my head. She says: 'Daughter, don't cry anymore.'"

The kindness of Henri's family and the sense that her mother wanted her to stop mourning made Sophea feel better. And best of all, Henri bought her a ticket to go home to her family.

"He says he is ashamed because he should have done this earlier. It was true what he told me, that a ticket was too much on his small salary, but he could borrow from friends. Really, he was scared I would not come back. I promised to come back. If he has done all this for me, I have to promise. But... I went home and I didn't want to leave Cambodia again. My father, my brother and sister, everything I know is there. But I have promised."

Sophea told me the main problem with Henri wasn't the age difference, or the alarms and excursions in the bedroom – it was that Europeans and

Cambodians didn't think the same. This gulf of difference was something she hadn't understood until it was too late.

According to Sophea, Cambodians kept things inside, forgave a lot and then suddenly exploded. Europeans were too emotionally demonstrative, shouted insults in public and then just forgot it happened. This sort of behaviour was all shockingly offensive to Cambodians. She understood my suggestion that she was talking about Henri, not all Europeans but, very tactfully and courteously, she argued that we all had a fraction of these traits.

"Even though I keep my promise and come back to Henri, he is changed. He starts to drink and shout at me in front of his friends. I think, never mind, I still have dancing. But the leader of the troupe tells me they don't need me. I am away for months, I let them down, they don't know where I am, so they replaced me. She is liar. I talk to other dancers, they told her about my mother but she still replaced me.

"A friend of Henri is sorry for me when she hears him shout at me that I am ungrateful and selfish. She takes me to meet a very old Cambodian dance teacher who ran away to Paris to hide from Pol Pot. I go to her to practise and she teaches me to use the dance like a prayer."

Henri kept on with his pattern of verbally abusive outbursts, followed by sober begging for forgiveness.

"He says it is my fault, I break his heart. This is true, I think. But when we got married my mind was young, I didn't understand how I hurt him."

It looked as though there could be a fresh start. In 1994, Henri found a job helping UNESCO researchers in the Angkor Wat district. The pay was tiny but Sophea helped out, starting a small business selling rattan boxes, mats and teapot holders to the handful of tourists. Henri did a little guiding because he knew the temples as well as any European at this stage. Then Sophea found a musician to work with and gave dance displays for paying customers inside the Bayon temple. Obviously, this was before bureaucracy sent uniformed boys to squelch such enterprise.

As tourism increased, Henri and Sophea noticed visitors bringing in picnics and local children making good money with coolers of soft drinks for sale. They realised they were both great cooks, enjoyed cooking. After several protracted meetings with the Ministry of Tourism, they were given a piece of land to rent and allowed to build a restaurant. It was made from straw and bamboo, in keeping with the forest, serving Khmer and French dishes.

"We are the first, it is our idea. Then other restaurants come, but it was our idea."

One of their early customers was the architect designing a luxury hotel in what had once been the grounds of King Sihanouk's Siem Reap palace. That's why Sophea consented to do her dance in the private library at the hotel, because the architect, although foreign, respected that this was sacred dance, not just entertainment.

For a long time Sophea and Henri made a good team and the restaurant, Chez Sophea, flourished. Gradually though, the cheaper establishments around them became more popular. And Henri's drunken insulting of any customers he deemed to be ruffians didn't help the ambiance. One evening, after years of tolerating his public insults, Sophea had her Cambodian explosion.

"He tells a French customer I think I am a queen but I am like a prostitute but a prostitute who won't make sexy, so I am useless. I throw a tray of food at him. I run away. Next day he apologises but it is over. He can have the restaurant by himself."

Sometimes I felt sorry for Henri and his broken heart, the defeated drunk man, lost in an exotic land; a man from a Graham Greene novel. Then I'd remember what he'd shouted at Sophea, in public.

"We get to be a little bit like friends now. I left him in 2006, long time ago. I want it to be finished but he is very alone in Cambodia. He says it is because he loves Angkor Wat but I think he is ashamed to go home. He also wants to punish me. But I am punished."

All the back-story Sophea had told me over coffees, lunches and ice creams, in fragments, interrupted for tears and changes to easier subjects, filled my head as I went to the computer desk to thank Henri for the meals Sophea had told him I didn't have to pay for. He grunted and picked up what seemed to be the second Ricard of the day. I bowed Cambodian-style, hands together respectfully, but Henri was watching, or looking blindly, at the football.

Sophea would go out with me for a few hours to take in some of the temples further afield, but not so far she couldn't be back in time to cook Henri's evening meal.

As we walked to Ponleak's tuk tuk, Henri came to the restaurant entrance, glass in hand. Ponleak stopped to make a bow.

Sophea said: "Don't worry Ponleak, get in, go."

I'd thought her glance back at Henri would be angry but she looked sad for him.

CHAPTER 6: LOOKING FOR WORDS

The road to Battambang was such slow going Dara and I had time to set the world to rights and if Dara hadn't fallen asleep, we might have taken on several other planets as well. Of course he fell asleep. As arranged, he had picked me up at eight sharp, after taking a taxi for the three-hour drive from his home in Battambang to Siem Reap.

"I hadn't realised you were doubling back. I thought you were setting out from Siem Reap too."

Dara smiled wide.

"I have to make sure you write a lot about the circus so if you are my captive... Also, we had a big meeting there last night. Soon the circus will need a new home because the landlords want the Siem Reap site back. In the beginning it was just waste ground but now, with land prices rocketing, they want it back. I expect we'll have to move to the edge of town, so we need to keep up our popularity so people will come. Anyway, what can I tell you about Battambang?"

In the guesthouse dining room the night before, I had been watching the news with Kiri. Dara told me that the shocking pictures we'd seen were from quite near Battambang.

"People go to Thailand to make money. You will see in Battambang, big cars, new motos but sometimes, that."

That had been pictures of the Thai police driving two gigantic truck-loads of Cambodian illegal workers to the border and tipping them out. They held guns on them, yelling at them not to try it again and tipped them into the road like gravel.

"It's such hypocrisy." Dara said.

"The Thai people don't like to do many of the low-class jobs like cleaning and building that the illegal Cambodians do. Their construction and housework – it is all Cambodians. Exploited Cambodians. Or gangs from Thailand promise them this sort of work and they put them in prostitution, drug dealing. Our organisation has had to rescue many people from this."

I told Dara the mistreatment and exploitation of illegal immigrants was something Europeans and Americans were pretty good at too. Daraknew this, of course he knew. Dara sat up at night reading the Huffington Post and watching Daily Show clips on YouTube. A citizen of the world, Dara saw no reason why Cambodia had to stay as it was. But perception of the country as a basket case might be half the problem.

He asked me if I 'd read a book he'd seen backpackers and NGO volunteers engrossed in – with a title implying Cambodians were inevitably doomed. I had read it and it seemed fine at first, lots of detail about the ancient history, recent history... Then the racist thesis of the book had begun to emerge that there was something inherently wrong with Cambodians, that they were passive, childlike and easily enslaved. This author wasn't alone; PHD writers and cultural essayists felt Cambodia's conservative form of Buddhism, the easily cultivated land – something – made them a pushover for anything. I had assumed their recurring misery had emerged from French colonialism, a ruthlessly exploitative royal family or America using them for target practice with bombs and napalm. But no, according to these writers, what was wrong with Cambodians was themselves. How else had the Khmer Rouge happened?

The Khmer Rouge had promised liberation and survival for frightened, starving and frequently uneducated rural people. By the time those people realised that they were involved in the killing of two million of their countrymen and might be next, it was far too late.

Now Cambodians were down but of course Kiri was right: tomorrow they could be a democratic Singapore. That was how history worked. I told about Northern Ireland, the home country my parents had to leave because it seemed a place where Catholics would always be second-class citizens, a place enduring a seemingly endless civil war. People pontificated a great deal about what was wrong with the Northern Irish, why we had an inherent basket-casery... Then our basket-casery was over. The country was flourishing, troubled only by the influx of tourists wanting to see where Game of Thrones was filmed.

The more Dara and I talked about this, the more we couldn't think of a country that hadn't once been down, or once been the aggressor somewhere. We decided, on the potholed and half-flooded road to Battambang, was that the solution lay in a comfortable life. If everyone felt they were living well...

Dara didn't doubt that the seemingly impossible could happen; breezily, he continued:

"Well, I shouldn't have happened. My mother is poor, husband killed by Khmer Rouge and she can hardly read. Next week I fly to Switzerland with a group of our acrobats on tour. There I will meet with the directors of multinationals seeking investment for our permanent home. Things happen."

I suggested he go into politics. "Oh no, not here. I do think about it but I think I have done more good with Phare. Good I can walk around and see. If I move on it will be to make big money and be a Bill Gates type." He shrugged. "If I fail I'll be proud of my circus work and my sons. I am only just thirty and already ahead."

He showed me pictures of his two little boys.

"Beautiful, aren't they. Maybe it will take another generation but we must give them at least half a step forward."

By the time we finished touring the home base of Phare, where people somersaulted, made music, painted, learnt social skills, computer animation, as well as basic literacy, I was a transmitter beacon of positive thinking. What the founders, three men orphaned by the Khmer Rouge, had achieved would certainly make it easy for Dara to believe anything might happen.

Phare not only taught skills and self-respect to children and teenagers at risk, they had an advice centre for women who were victims of domestic violence. All over town they'd put up illustrated posters showing women what they didn't have to put up with and giving them phone numbers to call.

"This campaign is slow and such a widespread problem. Because people don't know it is a problem. They think it's how real men behave," one of the founders told me. "There is even a book, Chbab Strey, required reading for girls in schools until 2007 but still most schools use it. It's a story in the form of a mother talking to her daughter, telling her to obey the man in everything. Even when the man is wrong or drunk he is superior to the woman, who must be quiet and patient. Seriously, that extreme. And now the women are standing up for themselves more and alcohol is cheaper, domestic violence is worse than in the times girls were taught this book. And women still feel, in their hearts, they brought the beating on themselves. "

The founders of Phare, friends since their traumatic childhood, were very different types. One was quiet and practical, building an extension to one of the classrooms himself and not giving interviews. The man who spoke to me about domestic violence was Svay Bandoul, an artist showing in several galleries around the world, as well as teaching at Phare and developing a gallery in Battambang. The third, Det, the gymnast and showman, lived in a castle-like house beside the Phare centre.

The house had cost him everything he earned, and the interest on a hefty bank loan – his salary wasn't very grand. Dara assured me the house was a personal project, possibly a little reckless, but it was the man's own money. All Phare books were transparent and available for foreign investor scrutiny. "There is so much corruption in Cambodia, we are belt and braces with money. Two belts and lots of braces." Dara gave the house a final, weary look. "It causes him so much anxiety to pay for this. I couldn't do it."

The huge house made sense to me, some manifestation of a refugee's insecurity, the more solid and immovable he could make his house...

The founders of Phare were all a little bewildered by their own happiness. I asked if they managed to put the past out of their minds.
"Yes and no," Svay said. "But if I wake up and feel a bit sad, that maybe I would like to sleep more and not work, I remember the days when I couldn't find my parents, had no food..." He smiled. "So maybe it's good. Khmer Rouge childhood helps you get up in the morning."
I suggested there might be better motivators.
"Yes," he smiled again. "But it's what I have."

Dara checked me in to a hotel near the city centre. The heavily carved, tropical-hardwood furniture in the foyer was a lumpen expression of one of the country's miseries. Since the time of the Khmer Rouge so much profit had been made from forests, with no regard for the people who had lived there for hundreds of years. Not only were forest communities driven out of their ancestral homes, they believed their souls had been destroyed. They were supposed to protect ancient tree spirits as part of their road to paradise. Assurances of financial compensation meant nothing. Anyhow, the compensation promised to the forest dwellers seldom materialised. There were protests that always seemed to end in ruthless police charges. Journalists reporting these stories had met with accidents. The leader of Cambodia's opposition, Sam Rainsy, made vociferous speeches about the land clearances – but he wasn't allowed to live in Cambodia. Dara not choosing politics as a way to change Cambodia was understandable.
As Dara headed home to sit at his laptop persuading companies around the world that the circus was a great investment, he said: "Just remember when you write, Annie, no negative words in the title. This place is changing."

I had barely stepped two steps out of the hotel when I was swooped on by a teenage tuk tuk driver, introducing himself as Bruce Lee. Unsurprisingly, Bruce was eager for me to stop walking immediately and go on an excursion. He listed destinations. I thought it best to visit a place called The Killing Caves, before Sophea arrived.
Bruce listened to music from his phone while he drove. He also shouted greetings to half the city's population, waving at them, his motorbike meandering cheerily off-course. Then, when there wasn't much traffic, he focused on his driving. We made our way out to countryside that was far more lush and villages more prosperous-looking than the gaunt land and settlements around Siem Reap.
The Killing Caves were in sacred mountains; the Khmer Rouge had wanted to violate them, it was said, but the mountains were also well-placed viewpoints for a military installation.
The main mountain, Phnom Sampeau, had a complex of gold pinnacled temples, set in deep green forest, flashed with flame trees. At the foot of the

mountain, Bruce told me I could walk up to the caves but if I went by motorbike I would also have a guide.

"Better, yeah?" He said, hitching up his gangster-style drooping jeans, as he called an older man to come over from where he was lolling at a table by a row of small refreshment huts. "Driver, ok?"

Although the bike driver smelt strongly of alcohol and cigarettes, the winding ride was more exhilarating than terrifying. If our helmetless spin upward was the last moment I'd have, it wouldn't be a bad one: a view out across the rice fields to mountains beyond, flame trees and bougainvillea pouring down in the foreground...

At our first stop, the driver explained that although the building we were exploring was now a brightly painted shrine, it had once been a prison, where the Khmer Rouge had held intellectuals, then executed them. At one time it had been a mass of blood and skulls. In good English, the driver took a cigarette break as he explained Pol Pot to me:

"This is a horrible story but you need to hear it to understand what you see here."

When he concluded his history, about the length of a king-size cigarette, he told me he was thirty so he hadn't been born in those times but all his parents' generation had terrible scars.

The driver looked a lot over thirty; I wondered what scars he had to give him the ageing drinking and smoking habits. I was sure if I'd told him there were Cambodians his age, not a few miles away, full of enormous ambition, he'd have been amused. He seemed to have worked out that being well anesthetised was how to get by with what he had. Yet he was a smart man, a funny man. To go into the temples, I had to keep unlacing my mistaken footwear, trainers, then lacing them up again.

"Oh, you are so busy with these feet." He waved his foot in the air to show me what I should be wearing. "Flip-flop, not running shoe. Where are you running?"

At the steps outside the next temple we watched a war between loud snarling macaque monkeys. The driver said it might be a territorial dispute, or they would raid each other for food; sometimes they fought out of boredom. I asked if they killed each other in these monkey wars. He looked a little taken aback.

"No. They fight until one is scared, he runs away and he is out, out of the game."

Phnom Sampeau means 'boat mountain'. The story is that a beautiful woman was jealous of the king's love for a young girl, so she turned the land into water and sent her pet crocodile to eat the sailors on a boat full of gifts that the king was sending to the girl. Then the king turned the boat into a mountain and the crocodile into the facing mountain, Phnom Krapeu.

I asked what happened after that; the driver shrugged:

"That's it, that's the story. Even if you pay extra I don't have more."

Sophea had told me a few old legends like this, where narrative seemed to vanish into some meaning that eluded me. It was the sort of thing that stopped being a concern when modern Cambodian history came back into the conversation; then, bewildering princesses and magic spells were what you wanted to go on hearing about, indefinitely. A few moments after the crocodile story, the driver pointed to a small opening covered in chicken wire.

"That is a small cave where they killed children. Not yet open to see inside. Children bones still inside."

The main Killing Cave was vast, with a hole at the top. People thought they were being brought up here to do forestry work but they were cudgelled at the edge of the hole, dropping into the cave below. I told the driver it didn't seem a very efficient way to execute people. He looked, as I expected he would, shocked.

"They don't care about efficient. They care about cruel."

But if people didn't know why they were being brought up the mountain...

Then I realised that the cruelty was to frighten the men doing the cudgelling; so they would stay loyal and obedient, in case they were next.

A Buddha reclined along one side of the Killing Cave, with candles and fruit offerings beside it. At another wall there was a cage full of bones and skulls.

"No one knows who they are but people who don't know what happened to their lost ones, they come here to pray, in case theirs are here."

After the fall of the Khmer Rouge, funeral services were held over the piles of smashed up bodies in places like the Killing Caves. In our long conversation, Kiri had said younger people wanted to move on from all this, didn't want it to be what people came to the country to witness. If people stopped talking about it, Cambodia would heal. But although the cave had been cleaned, bones and skulls bleached and caged, it didn't seem that "least said, soonest mended" was a proverb that travelled usefully to this mountain.

A small group of young French tourists came in, shocked by the skulls, awkward and trying to find the best way to show to my driver and a monk who was lighting incense by the Buddha, that they were respectful. One of them opened his guidebook.

"Don't read it out." A girl in the group whispered. "Just pass it round so we're quiet."

We bowed to each other as I left; I have no idea why, except that it was to communicate something to the two Cambodians, not each other.

Descending the mountain was such a speedy roller-coaster that fear overcame the thrill element. I did try not to look scared to some Europeans toiling up the hill and set my face in what was probably a very unconvincing grin. I suspect I looked like a teeth-bared macaque monkey in battle; the one that's about to be out, out of the game.

The interesting driver disappeared with his fee and a good tip, while Bruce

Lee sent a minion to speak to me. I had to wait thirty minutes to see the next thing, I could get a drink and sit in his tuk tuk if I wanted. Where was Bruce? Bruce was at the back of the cafe tables, very busy with a card game.

"It doesn't start for thirty minutes, you are too quick." Bruce Lee's minion said. Perhaps the minion been sent over because he spoke better English but Bruce had just slapped down a card and let out a joyful yelp, so presumably it was more to do with me interrupting his winning streak.

I bought a soda and lounged in the tuk tuk until an unapologetic, scowling Bruce swung himself onto his motorbike.

"It's time."

I didn't like being quite so far from town, surrounded by lads who were clearly Bruce Lee's mates; but the minute I could run inside my hotel swearing at him and slamming the door behind me, Bruce was fired.

We drove five minutes down the road to a spot where some Europeans and a handful of Cambodians were gathered. The grass around us was littered with plastic bottles, food wrappers, carrier bags... I remembered Sophea, on passing a pile of litter somewhere, had pointed out that plastic was new to many Cambodians; they didn't understand that it wasn't like throwing down fruit peel.

It was getting toward dusk. Eaten alive by flies, we all waited, looking up at a fissure in the face of a mountain ahead of us. Then, a bat flew out, followed by a stream of bats, more and more, out into the evening sunlight.

"Millions!" Bruce Lee shouted in my ear. "Millions!"

Later internet searches told me that surveys had estimated one million. That was plenty really. More disappointingly, the bats had nothing to do with the city's name. Battambang means Legend of the Lost Long Stick, a story about four years long with no apparent logic. The moral seemed to be that if you had a magic stick, hold on to it. But you'd probably lose it and your kingdom anyway, so never mind. At least you had a go of the stick for a while... Oh, and there was a magic white horse too...The bats were far more deserving of a city named after them than frustrating legends. It was the sight of them. They kept coming, flapping in a curving line across the sky, hunting flies until dark, more bats, more...

The other bat watchers were jumping into their tuk tuks. We raced out to the main road and Bruce stopped in the plain, where the bats were moving across the sky like low smoky clouds. They changed formation.

"Sometime look like dragon!" Bruce shouted, ecstatic.

And some of the elongated black bat clumps did, or rearing horses, then they looked like coiling smoke again as they made their way across the plain to hunt around the trees of Crocodile Mountain.

The evening scene in Battambang was vibrant. Life seemed centred around the wide river, with little restaurant cafes and benches for watching the world go by. There were small parks where groups of quite old people jumped at their aerobics with alarming vigour in the evening heat.

On the broad, marble walkway, a small crowd had gathered to see what looked like a magic show. I asked Bruce Lee to pull over. He did, although his expression told me I was wasting my time. Probably I was, because I couldn't figure out what was going on. A man kept putting marshmallows in a child's mouth and making him spit them out. Cambodians around me were laughing or had a "seen it, not impressed" expression. The whole thing had an unsettling, Dickensian feel to it.

Climbing back into the tuk tuk, I asked Bruce what was going on. He pursed his lips, he shrugged. "Is show. You go hotel?"

Bruce Lee was cheap and I had liked his joy at the bat formations. So despite his patronising cockiness, I booked him for the morning. Also, there didn't seem to be that many tuk tuks around. Battambang did have a few tourists pottering here and there but we weren't the main business. Crossing into Thailand, if people made it, was believed to be more steadily lucrative.

My shiny floored hotel was one of the few modern buildings in the street. The creamy facades of old French colonial buildings, with small shops tumbling out of their ground floors and orange trees in the gardens of temples made the Battambang by-ways feel eccentrically restful. But the sign on the back of my hotel room door with a picture of a gun and a picture of handcuffs with lines through them made me wonder if I was getting the wrong impression.

I asked Dara about it when he called in the morning to check if I needed any other introductions around town.

"Ah, unfortunately that is because sometimes at weekends people stay there when they are drunk, from a wedding, for example, and trouble starts. It is to warn people who can't read they will be arrested if they bring a gun. Of course as many of the people who have guns and drink a lot are police... Don't worry. I checked and there are no weddings booked this week."

I'd heard from Sophea that Cambodian weddings, particularly in rural areas where nothing much happened in the way of entertainment, were raucous affairs. Girls would dress to the nines with make-up, as she put it, "thick like mud", and the men got fighting drunk. There were almost as many gangs in rural areas as there were in cities. They handled smuggling, drug trafficking, poaching and in a self-fulfilling prophecy, protected people from other gangs. So gang rivalries could break out at weddings, or there'd at least be a non-gang related fight over someone looking at someone else's sister too long. A punch-up could lead to men thrashing each other with sticks, to a possible shoot-out. As in an old-fashioned Irish wake, it was felt the occasion had been a bit of a let-down unless several people were unconscious and bleeding from the head at the end of the night.

I lay awake for a long time that first night in Battambang, listening. No gunfire, not even the animal chorus that surrounded Mr Kiri's guest house after dark. There was an occasional shout or car in the background. A couple of men who sounded drunk passed along the corridor. I waited. So much for being in a weddingless week. A gang would storm the corridor, get the wrong room.... But I seemed to be bullet-hole-free in the morning.

"Be careful." Bruce warned me as I began my climb of the steep but beautiful red laterite steps leading up to the Banan temple. "Three hundred and fifty-eight steps! Go slow, you not young."

To show him, I set off at a fast pace but, despite the shade trees, I couldn't keep it up. A little girl with a fan followed me, fanning with extra vigour when I stopped for breath. I hoped Bruce had gone to play cards somewhere and wasn't watching this evidence of my decrepitude. At first, I hoped ignoring the little girl and her anxious frown would make her go away but after a while I was grateful for her. We reached what I'd thought was the top but it was just a mid-level. I asked the girl her name and her frown vanished. She knew the routine – once she was acknowledged, she was in business.

Finally at the top were five towers reminiscent of Angkor Wat, pretty with trees and flowers growing around them. Built by an eleventh-century local prince, the temple now seemed to be a place for courting couples and picnicking families, gazing out over the views of the surrounding countryside. The little girl followed me all the way, fanning when I paused to look at a carving, or through a gap in the trees to the very flat land around us. Going down was easier, of course, and I felt a little less like the only reluctant memsahib in town when we passed a group of fairly young Koreans heading upward with a fanning child each.

My little girl seemed pleased with her tip and scampered over to a woman at a food and drink stall. The woman took the money and the child was given a juice drink. I wondered if this was the child's mother, or was she some sort of female Fagin. A lot of children with fans seemed to be resting in the shade with juice drinks or candy, peeling off to pursue a tourist when a new one appeared.

Bruce was resting across his tuk tuk seats.

"We go?"

But I had noticed a sign pointing to some caves and asked about them.

Bruce looked pleased and locked up his bike.

"I never go. I go also."

I was pleased to have his cheery company on the narrow, deserted path through the woods. He asked me the usual sort of questions about where I was from, what was London like, then he suddenly showed me the silver cross around his neck and asked if I was a Christian.

"Not really." I found myself saying this apologetically.

He said he was in a church in town and went every Wednesday evening. At

the church he sang to god, heard stories about god and learnt English. I wondered if this church of his, YWM, was American?
"I don't know. Some are Switzerland. Speak Khmer. I show you later." Apparently delighted at the mere thought of his church, Bruce skipped a little faster until we reached the caves.
An elegant-faced old man raised himself from a mattress, welcomed us and gave us head torches. He led the way, telling us to mind our heads in English that wasn't just fluent, he seemed to have learned it by imitating David Niven. His powerful flashlight pointed out stalactites, stalagmites and rock formations resembling elephant heads, the angel Gabriel...
"Oh and it seems to me this one resembles the face of an old man." The guide flicked the torch back to his own taut, old face. "You see?"
Then his torchlight flitted across more shapes in the walls of the cave, to a stalactite that dripped water into a bucket.
"They say if you drink this water you can see the future."
I wasn't sure I fancied roof-dripped water. "Have you drunk it?"
The old guide smiled; "I can foretell you won't drink it."
Meanwhile, Bruce excitedly took pictures with his phone, declaring he could see dinosaurs, trains...
The old man showed a shiny patch on the wall; "What would you call this?
"Like diamond." Bruce said, and was ignored.
"Quartz crystal," I chanced.
The old man smiled at me: "Yes, quartz crystal." As if he was remembering the word.
A little further in, he showed us a tunnel that had been cemented up:
"Now this is true, there's a tunnel here that leads to Thailand. During the war, the Khmer Rouge rebels used it so the government cemented it over. But eventually this tunnel leads into Thailand."
I couldn't find any evidence in later research that his tunnel story was true, or not true. I was in one of the areas where Khmer Rouge remnants had border-hopped to fight their last battles and they had probably hidden out in these difficult-to-access caves. Then again, a glance at the map told you they would have been very long tunnels.
While Bruce drank the water that promised powers of prediction and tested the echo sounds in the cave with various kung-fu-sounding noises, I asked the old man why his English was so impeccable. He nodded graciously; he'd heard this before.
"When I was young I was a clerk at the British embassy in Saigon. Of course, when Saigon fell, I fled – Oh do watch your head there."
As we came back into daylight he hustled some children to bring a mat for me to sit on. Bruce, he seemed to think, could fend for himself. Bruce was unconcerned, busy looking at his phone.
"Do you mind? I like to speak with English tourists," the old man said. "I

forget you see, there are words I forget."
We sat at the edge of the caves, greening rice fields below us. But the moment had a feel of black-and-white movie melancholy.
"The word for the paper to stop ink smearing?"
"Blotting?"
"Of course. And a word that means following but more formal, more for a legal document?"
I found pursuant.
"Pursuant." He savoured it. "And there is a word for if I crash your car but I don't have to pay, because there is a prior arrangement."
"Insurance." I tried.
"No. I know 'insurance'. A prior arrangement that I am generally not liable."
I suggested: "immunity".
"No, no…." Then he answered his own question. "I remembered! Indemnity!"
I asked him why he needed to know.
"No reason, I just sleep badly at night and try to remember things I wrote down as a clerk, conversations I had, and I realise a word has escaped me."
After fleeing his home in Saigon he had ended up in Thailand, found work translating for a charity and met his future wife in a refugee camp. Persecuted for having Vietnamese grandparents, she'd escaped the Khmer Rouge regime. When the volatile Cambodian border territory, last stronghold of the Khmer Rouge, finally settled down, his wife wanted to come home.
"Why not?" The old man said. "My Vietnam was lost to the communists. So here we are."
The fall of Saigon. It was a headline phrase, echoing through documentaries and fiction. This gaunt, sinewy man, searching for vocabulary at a cliff face far from Vietnam, he had been there.
His enemies, the Communist Vietnamese, invaded Cambodia in 1979 and defeated the Khmer Rouge. The Vietnamese troops left in 1989 but Cambodians didn't believe they'd really gone. The current government were muttered against as Vietnamese puppets. They had been corrupt, oppressive and their election wins had been dubious. The main opposition party whipped up the anti-Vietnamese feeling, although many Vietnamese had roots in the country, as traders and fishermen, that went back centuries. Some newspapers suggested this anti-Vietnamese feeling could result in pogroms, uprisings... Kiri insisted this was only opposition party propaganda, only something that preoccupied older people and uneducated people. But the uneducated majority had been exactly the recruiting ground for the Khmer Rouge.
In England there frequently was the same kind of talk: a radio phone-in, pub-talk culture, blaming immigrants and European connections for everything. The anti-Vietnamese talk might well be the kind of flailing scapegoating every

country erupts into during tough times.

I hoped the old Saigon clerk, flicking his torchlight across stalactites for tourists, wouldn't be harassed if something happened; age and constant displacement, surely he'd earned some kind of... what was the word? Indemnity. I'd also happily allow the endearing man indemnity if his tale of tunnels was untrue. Interestingly, there were the famous Cu Chi tunnels in Ho Chi Minh City, formerly Saigon. They were used by anti-French fighters, then as bomb shelters, then by anti-American fighters. Perhaps my old gentleman had taken the idea of the tunnels from his one-time home city to give a frisson to his cave tours.

When we'd walked some distance away, Bruce rolled his eyes and said: "Crazy, yeah?"

Hurt for my old gentleman, I said: "No, he's not." And decided it wouldn't be kind to point out that Bruce was calling people crazy but he had a tuk tuk with its back wall covered in pictures of the real Bruce Lee, and felt-tipped red hearts.

Bruce skipped along the path listening to his music. Judging the book of him by his clothes, I guessed it was rap. Suddenly, holding out an earpiece, he asked if I'd like to listen.

"Very nice. Chinese flute music."

Bruce was full of surprises.

His church, a big modern building at the edge of town, was not such a surprise. I suppose they did no more harm than any right-wing evangelical church, founded by an American twenty year old who had a vision at the seaside. This inter-denominational youth church, begun in the 1950s, had centres and mission ships all over the world. It was the sort of thing made Sophea spit feathers:

"I hate it, these Christians everywhere. Give you rice and go to school be a Christian. This is a Buddhist country but they want to destroy us, destroy us!"

I'm sure the pale, Germanic-sounding young man in glasses who barred my way as we came in didn't intend to destroy Cambodians, but he certainly didn't like the look of me. He had an air of dead-eyed superiority and asked me what I wanted?

I said that Bruce had told me about his church and would like to show it to me.

"Good." The pale young man said. "Come on in. Although I can't talk to you, I am busy. We're all busy."

He was very friendly to Bruce in Khmer but as he walked away, he gave me a look telling me he knew I was full of it.

We went around the large central building, where Bruce told me he had his singing lessons about God and the missionaries read bible stories in Khmer. We met more pale people in glasses, who were also wary but prepared to explain themselves. Yes, they talked about Jesus as they went out into the villages doing good works. They taught bible studies in the centre but also English and crafts. Bruce seemed delighted with the pale people, as if he'd got top marks for them after weaving them in craft class.

When we drove back along the river front I noticed some youths slumped under benches and a couple conducting a clear drug deal, according to my knowledge from American cop shows of what drug deals look like. Maybe Bruce's church had saved him from the dissolute activity Battambang seemed notorious for. I'd have preferred him to have been saved by the circus.

CHAPTER 7: WHO KILLED THE PANGOLIN?

Presumably coming from Siem Reap by ox cart, Sophea finally arrived in a flurry of pink clothes.

"Oh my friend, I have to explain so much to them in the restaurant, it took so long..."

She was eager to get going. After dumping her bag, we went down to the river front and the museum. I tried not to be childishly fidgety as Sophea admired carvings and Buddhas closely. She asked the museum guard endless questions. She'd pass on to me where things came from, what century they were made, what they represented... Since arriving in Cambodia I had tried to store the information about who was who, doing what, in the Hindu pantheon but there was a tumult to remember. Who churned the Sea of Milk? Who was an avatar of Vishnu, the wife of Vishnu or the turtle created to stop the world falling through the universe? By now I should recognise the be-necklaced cow, the elephant, the snake, and know the Lord of the Underworld when I looked him in the eye, but I was too sieve-headed to ever find alternative employment as a guide to antiquities. Sophea genuinely enjoyed discussing these pieces with the guard and he in turn was impressed by her expertise. Most wearying of all was pot fragments; once the gasping over how many hundreds of years old they were, back before Angkor was the largest city in the fourteenth-century world and held on to an empire longer than the Romans, what else was there to say about a broken piece of bowl?

I was much happier when we were out on the road again, in countryside so dense with greenery I'm sure I felt an oxygen rush.

As we passed flowering trees and brightly busy villages, Sophea smiled broadly: "Oh I don't believe it. I escape!"

The roads were better than the byways around Siem Reap and Sophea observed that Battambang had newer cars and motorbikes and the farmers used tractors instead of bullocks.

"This is all from working in Thailand. Thailand thinks this still belongs to them because their workers come from here. Cambodians are worms to them."

The district had been a province of Thailand: from 1794 to 1907 and again during World War II, when Thailand, a vague ally of the Japanese, moved in as far as Siem Reap. The Japanese, occupying Cambodia, allowed the Vichy French colonial power to administrate and allowed young King Sihanouk to keep his court in splendour.

We were headed for Wat Kor village, where many of the grander people of the Thai administration had lived. A couple of the hundred-year-old stilted houses, set in orchards and built from rosewood, were open to the public. After taking us to one that wasn't, Bruce Lee brought us to Khor Seng house, where an old man greeted us in French. He seemed completely beguiled by Sophea. Once he stopped giddily asking her where she was from, yes he could see she was Khmer but was she returning from abroad? – the old man began his sweetly formal, learned-by-rote, tour patter. He told us his grandfather had been the secretary to the province's last Thai governor and had built the house in 1902. He pointed to the wooden floors that had become shiny with decades of the family's bare feet walking across them; he showed us the low platform where people would sit to eat or converse.

"You will notice the windows on these old houses come practically all the way to the floor. This is because people used to sit talking, eating or working, on the floor. If you look at modern Cambodian houses, the windows are higher because people have adopted the European habit of sitting at tables on chairs."

He and Sophea agreed that this was a shame; getting up and down from the floor kept people more flexible.

As we moved through to another room, the old man explained that the house now did have tables and chairs, for home-stay visitors. The back part of the house had once been for servants but now the paying guests could have an authentic experience staying there.

He laughed with Sophea as he pointed out the mattress in the home-stay room was actually foam not the traditional kapok stuffing; this was far too lumpy for foreigners, or even young Cambodians. Talk of the drinking, discotequeing, heathen, physical puniness of Cambodians in their teens today bonded them through several rooms.

Between the servant section and the family section the doors had thick iron bands across them; his grandfather had been a wealthy man who worried that thieves might hack through mere wooden doors. Presumably grandfather wasn't too worried about thieves hacking his servants.

On our return to the main family room, our attention was directed to walls highlighted with sepia family photographs and a gilt-framed French mirror; the owner's parents had escaped with these treasures in the Seventies and

returned them safely. Sophea spotted a strange-looking thing hanging among the treasures – a dried pangolin skin.
"One time, there were very many pangolin in Cambodia but Chinese people think pangolin have magic in the scales and blood, they think it cures many diseases, so they kill them. Make a powder. There are still some in the Cardamom Mountains but enforcement against poaching is very weak, corruption of course, so now there are nearly none."
Politely she translated what she'd been saying for the old man, who then flurried to say: "This pangolin skin is very old, very old, from my father's time. Very old."
He and Sophea agreed that a poacher could get at least a hundred dollars for a pangolin – a poor, half-blind, scaly anteater that could curl into a ball.
On a table by the main door were framed photographs of the current family, including umpteen beaming children.
"This isn't everyone." The old man said. "I have two more grandchildren born last week. I'm waiting for pictures. Oh, you will ask me how many in total but I will have to sit here and write them down or I can't remember. Maybe that will waste a lot of your afternoon, waiting for me to remember!"
Then he modestly pointed to a donation box and suggested we contribute whatever we liked. Pleased with what we liked, he led us down the wide wooden steps to wave goodbye. As we looked back, we could see the real life of the house happened in the under-section, among the stilts. The family were cooking, swinging in hammocks, fixing motorbikes... A small boy was chasing chickens until an older boy told him to stop and wailing split the afternoon.
No more time to linger: Bruce Lee wanted us on the road. We called at the Battambang winery. A pretty, if unlikely, place. A very glamorous Cambodian woman ignored us when we arrived, busy doing her books, so we walked among the vines, Sophea sneering loudly about the quality of Cambodian wine.
"I used to like some wine, half a glass with dinner, but Cambodian wine? It is a joke."
Nevertheless, I thought I might buy a bottle to take home as a curiosity When the ignoring woman saw us browsing the shelves she asked us about ourselves in French. Where were we from? I answered because I could see Sophea was simmering.
"Ah, Anglaise." The woman said with some tone that may have been intended as charming but came off as a revenge sneer. Besides, the wine was fifteen dollars a bottle. Sophea said something in Khmer that was probably not friendly and we left the cold-eyed wine woman for an impatient Bruce Lee.
"Better go quick, bats come."
I just had a feeling that although they were close to the misery of the Killing

Cave, the bats would charm Sophea. They did. She also pointed out that it was a small, beautiful thing that made a little money for everyone – the tuk tuk drivers and the people with the refreshment huts up the road.

"Small money for everyone, not greedy. In Siem Reap the Apsara Authority will find a way to charge for the experience, or if there is no profit, kill the bats."

She watched the bats then glanced around the small crowd: "It is special, no? Each night, people from all over the world gather here to see a simple thing from nature together. Just very simple and free."

Out on the plain she thought the formation looked like a silk scarf, a silk scarf dancing in the breeze.

"It is so beautiful, so beautiful. You are right, I love it. It is amazing. But I don't understand. We know what time they will fly, about what time, but how do the bats decide? One bat must go first, no? Maybe they have a bat king, something like that."

Young Bruce, staring at the sky beside us nodded and let out an impressed whistle; "A king of bats. You think so?"

Sophea shrugged and smiled at me as we climbed back into the tuk tuk.

"I think I just make up a story, but I like it."

Clearly delighted with the thought that there might be a king of bats, Bruce sang along loudly to whatever unlikely music was coming through his earphones. But just as we came to the edge of town, his motorbike made an odd sound and juddered to a halt. He climbed off and looked at it. Making the sign of the cross he climbed back on and tried to restart the machine a couple of times. He crossed himself again and called up to the heavens – but still the bike wouldn't start.

Close to tears, he abandoned God for his phone: "I call my dad."

His father and a man with a tool box arrived in a tuk tuk. The father invited asked us to hop in, he would take us where we wanted to go. I felt he wasn't unused to Bruce needing rescue.

A guidebook had led me to believe the riverfront restaurants were lively at night. When we arrived we found there weren't that many of them and the atmosphere was peculiar. There were hostile looks, aimed at Sophea not at me. Was I imagining it?

"Maybe not. Maybe they think like the old man in the old house. They think because I am glamorous I am a Cambodian from France, or America. They don't like that."

Perhaps because she was talking loudly about being glamorous it made our fellow diners give her long looks.

As we went to the edge of the pavement after our meal, I realised there were no tuk tuks. I suggested we could walk, I knew the way, the hotel wasn't far...

"No, of course not, that is much too dangerous, of course we can't walk."

Then a tuk tuk carrying a huge woman and several bundles came by. She stopped her driver beside us.
The woman looked so tough you wouldn't be surprised to find all the bundles were wrapped-up heads.
"For one dollar she will drop us by the market near the hotel. It's better than walking."
I wasn't sure. The woman and the driver could be in cahoots, speed us to the border and sell us for parts... But Sophea was climbing aboard. It would be fine. No tuk tuks were so fast that you'd actually hurt yourself after a leap from one in motion.
It wasn't far. The woman dropped us and hurried away. She'd left us in the wrong place.
"Hang on, where's the market?"
The woman's gang would spring out now, haul us into a filthy warehouse full of trussed-up... I got my bearings. The covered market was all shuttered down for the night; we'd have to walk right round it, not shortcut through it. But now Sophea was in a high-pitched panic.
"We are lost?"
"It's ok, it's just round the other side."
I explained my disorientation with the market being shuttered.
"Ok, you're sure?"
"Sure."
She put her arm through mine and gripped tight as we went. Around the other side were people sitting on mats. Lit by candles in tin cans, or oil-wick lanterns, they were selling vegetables and fruits. Huddled in blankets, they were clearly not benefiting from the porous trade border with Thailand. Most of them were women. As we passed they looked up at us. Sophea clutched me tighter.
"Where is the hotel? We are lost, no?"
"No, it's just round the corner."
She was so nervous I began to doubt myself. But then we turned a corner, left the darkness and saw the neon glare of the hotel.
Laughing with relief when we got inside, Sophea said: "Oh I really think we get lost. Very bad at Battambang in the night. The way those market people look at us."
I'd assumed they were looking up in hopes we'd buy something. Perhaps the darkness had made everything feel a little edgy but I was really surprised to find myself the calm one.
"What scared you?"
She had gathered her dignity again. "I am very tired is all. Very tired. Better remember next time the market closes at night so there is no confusion."
She said a grand goodnight to the reception staff and left me, not for the first time, infuriated and laughing all in the same thought.

CHAPTER 8: TRAINS AND OTHER PLANES

It was definitely the first time in my life I finished breakfast and a man sidled up to me saying: "Bruce Lee sent me."

The man delivering what seemed like dialogue from a spoof spy film was a sad faced, middle-aged tuk tuk driver who introduced himself as Ted.

Both irritatingly and sweetly, Bruce had called me at midnight: "Sorry, sorry, no fix bike. I send friend, sorry."

More a friend of Bruce's dad, I suspected, sad faced Ted showed me an ancient teddy bear tied on to the backrest of his bike.

"Ted for Ted."

His smiling about this made him seem even more forlorn.

I explained to Ted that we might have to wait ten minutes for my friend. Long after ten minutes I went in search of my friend.

Sophea was dressed in grand style, with an embroidered Cambodian shawl over a white cotton tunic and trousers. On her feet she wore white plimsolls painted with tiny red roses.

"I decorated myself." she said, as she turned her feet for me to admire.

The television was blaring with a Bollywood musical. Hopefully there was no one with a gun nearby, trying to sleep off a hangover.

"I love this Indian dancing. But I am almost ready, I'll just put on my make-up."

As there seemed to be more dance-watching than making-up going on, I went downstairs, assured Ted it wouldn't be long and had an espresso.

I knew the strong coffee hadn't been wise when Sophea finally joined me.

"Did you have your breakfast? I don't have anything yet."

I'd had my breakfast over an hour ago. Sophea wanted to go to a stall in the market where she ordered several dishes, eating them with leisurely relish.

"I take rice soup. Many Cambodians don't like because it is the food in Khmer Rouge time but it is not like this. Then it is all water and some grass, no flavour." She looked at something being served to a woman on the next table. "Oh I don't realise they have this, I will order." She waved a hand to the serving girl.

I told her I'd take a look around the market. It was that or put cutlery in her eyes.

I breathed deeply while I looked at endless stalls of jewellery; then I was in the apricot net nightmare of the bridal gown section; then children's clothes; then replica branded sportswear, then luggage...

Having taken a round trip of all possible market merchandise, I came back to the table a calmer person. Sophea had eaten all the food and was talking on the phone anxiously.

When the call finished she shook her head: "Oh dear, two times last night the ladies in the restaurant ring me. Now they say the generator is broken. I tell them how to find the man who... You are ok? I am slow, I make you angry."

"No, not at all."

I felt like a very bad person. This was a short holiday from a hard life for her. Why shouldn't she revel in it a little?

In the luggage section I'd seen all manner of backpacks and Sophea had arrived with one that was raggedy in several places; I'd buy her a new one before we left town.

"We can go now. I just need to go where they change money. Riel is better than dollars for tips if we go to temples. I am not rich."

I took a breath and smiled at her. There would be something else before we got on the road but I wouldn't be impatient... To my great surprise she changed the money and headed straight for the tuk tuk where Ted was waiting, reading an English phrase-book.

"I learn." He grinned, put the book away and finally we were on route to the Bamboo Train that Sophea had repeatedly told me: "I am dying to see, I can't wait!"

Beside a collection of tumbledown buildings was the starting point for Battambang's famous Bamboo Train. This was a solution to a bad scheduled service that existed along several stretches of Cambodian track. Perhaps all commuters should consider this – if you're sick of the way the trains are run, make your own.

Originally, the bogie for these trains was made from the wheels of tanks abandoned after the civil war. Now they were made in local workshops, as were the flatbed trucks of the trains, the nori. The nori were three-metre by two-metre steel frames with bamboo platforms. On these passengers, livestock, rice and market goods were carried.

A driver settled us on a nori right away. No balefully watching the tracks for a delayed service here. So many drivers were hanging around it was more like picking up a rail taxi.

Telling us to hold tight, our driver started up the 6hp motor, like a boat's outboard, attached to the rear wheels by fan-belts. The single line had 1m gauge tracks that were warped and misaligned in places, so the nori's small handrail was reassuring. Clattering along at around 25mph, spinning through miles of remote scenery felt hypnotically peaceful, despite the engine noise.

Once in a while, a person beside the trackside bushes would be standing staring. Perhaps they were hoping for something, or someone, on the train. It seemed to be in the very second I noticed them that they'd vanish back into the greenery as fast as ghosts.

The meditative rhythm of the journey was interrupted by a nori with four European passengers, heading right for us. I wondered about brakes but there weren't any. Both drivers stopped their engines and drifted until they were almost edge to edge. Our driver asked us to get down; we had to allow the four-passenger nori to overtake. The other driver jumped down and helped us pick up the light-as-a-feather platform, the engine and the wheels, then take them to the side of the tracks. That driver returned to his vehicle, moved forward and jumped down again to help us reassemble our small train and we were back on our way.

Not for long. Two more nori were coming towards us. Again it was we who had to be dismantled and remove ourselves from the track. The number of nori, the number of passengers or size of cargo seemed to dictate who vacated the track.

We reached the end point, a small village with a few souvenir stands and cafes. "We take a drink?" Sophea indicated a cafe called A Taste of India. I braced myself for a three-course elevenses but they only served drinks. Sophea ordered fresh coconut juice. We were served by a wiry man with hair dyed that startling auburn shade that black henna tends to shock grey hair. More startling, the man was stripped to the waist and had massive, deep scars across his chest.

"He looks interesting for you, no?" Sophea asked him to join us and as an opener asked why his cafe was called A Taste of India when they just sold drinks?

"Ah, my friend has a restaurant with this name in Phnom Penh, and also he gives me these because I like the name." He indicated the menus for an extensive range of Indian dishes.

Mad as a hatter, I thought, then thought again; this was only part of his routine. The man had a range of peculiarities he knew would attract tourists. Not least, his fought-with-a-tiger-looking scars. Perhaps he had French, American, Japanese versions of his life story.

For me he had: "I studied in London, I am seventy-seven now, so that was more than fifty years ago. I live in a place called Clanricarde Gardens, near Hyde Park."

It was quite near Hyde Park. Though chic now, Clanricarde Gardens, Notting

Hill, would have been run-down, student bedsit land fifty years ago.
On his return to Cambodia he had been a soldier fighting with FUNIPEC against the Khmer Rouge in this area. FUNIPEC were a royalist force, who then formed a political coalition in the Nineties that included the Khmer Rouge. These days They were fairly marginal in politics.
Our scarred man had been a colonel; he pointed to photographs of himself in uniform on the cafe's back wall. FUNIPEC had been raiding the Khmer Rouge from the Thai side of the border when a shell blast cut open his chest. He was very lucky to be taken to Bangkok for treatment because Cambodian doctors...
Sophea nodded sympathetically: "No good, not good."
The scarred man was very cheerful, laughing at his grandchildren who kept chasing each other around the cafe tables and ignoring him when he tried to send them out.
"I am too old. They think I am a joke."
Seventy-seven was old in Cambodia but it was interesting how there wasn't anyone over sixty to get chatting to who was just a retired bank manager. Scars and strange stories everywhere.
A woman had been hanging around the edge of the cafe. When we finished our drinks, she politely asked Sophea if we would like to follow her.
She took us to strange round buildings that were explained as brick-baking kilns. A young man was shovelling from a mound of rice husks; these fired the kilns, where the bricks baked for several days. The young man was her youngest son; her husband and the two eldest were in Thailand working. She showed us the small, hand-operated machine for cutting the bricks. Behind this was a storeroom containing a few bricks and a lot of mud. There had been a disastrous flood the year before, destroying thousands of bricks, their family business. They had tried to catch up but the men lost heart. It was like that all around the area; people gave up and went to Thailand. Young wives went too; there was a local joke that a witch had put a spell on all the district's old women to get them pregnant, even at eighty. Things appeared that way because so many grandmothers looked after the babies, while the young women went away to work.
Not to be cynical, but it was after all this hard luck story that the woman waved a vague hand at her souvenir stall on the path back to the railway track. She sold hand-crafted scarves and shawls. They were cheap and seemed a fair enough fee for her time. I bought a few for myself and Sophea.
As we were walking away, Sophea turned back: "I decide."
The brick factory woman also sold carvings. Back at the stall, Sophea picked up a Buddha statue made from some scented wood. "Is expensive but..."
It was fourteen dollars. She was handing the woman money. I don't know if I was expected to jump in, offering to pay, but as I was paying for everything else, and scarves, meanness and irritation won the moment. Even if Sophea

hadn't expected me to pay, her altar at home was already crowded with Buddhas. Did it need another one so pricey?
I said nothing. I didn't know the statue was a gift for Chenda, who'd given her most precious Buddha to her daughter.
Our nori driver sweated up to us in an anxious frenzy. He'd dozed off, woken to realise how long we'd been and panicked he'd been abandoned without payment. Visitors usually took thirty minutes, we'd been over an hour... We apologised but he'd been stressed too much and wasn't speaking.
Back on the tracks, he kept a stern face and seemed to drive faster. Then we met one nori, with two tourist passengers – exactly the same as us. Who had the right of way now?
Our driver started shouting angrily. The other driver, much younger got down and asked his passengers to dismantle their train.
I asked our driver if we had right of way because the other driver was younger? His hot, cross face broke into a smile.
"No." He laughed with Sophea as he explained the rest in Khmer.
"He says he wins because he is in the most bad mood and shouting most. Sometimes it's like that, no rules, only which driver shouts most."

Ted was with a couple of other tuk tuk drivers in the shade, but most of the men sitting around were Nori drivers, along with the policeman who regulated the train driver rotations. Presumably he also arrested tourists who hiked several miles back through the rice fields to avoid paying their fare
Our next destination, as part of Sophea's quest for the history of her beliefs, was a site called Wat Ek, but I needed to know if we could get lunch out there – it had been hours now since Sophea had eaten.
"Ah Wat Ek," the policeman said. "Very interesting, madam. Eleventh century, there is also the giant Buddha..."
Sophea interrupted the policeman. I thought perhaps she was annoyed he'd only been talking to me, but she appeared to be making some kind of speech. All the men went very still, looking at her. When she finished they looked at each other, amused. Only our Ted kept a respectful poker face. I asked Sophea what she'd been saying.
"I tell him: 'Oh, there is no need to tell me it is eleventh century. I am a very old soul, I remember those times clearly from a previous life, so I will recognise the place and the date, he needn't worry about that.'"
"Oh," I said. "Of course."
I hoped I looked as non-committal as Ted.
Sophea stepped into the tuk tuk and didn't seem to notice that the men were smirking. And, I supposed, in a culture where the religion held the idea of reincarnation, her speech didn't seem that odd, perhaps just a little self-aggrandising.

We were stopped at a tollbooth outside Wat Ek and Ted was told he had to wait there. While I gazed at a Buddha the size of a tower block to the right of us, Sophea cross-examined the toll-collector about the restaurant inside. She looked very disappointed

"He says maybe she has some noodle, it's not a proper restaurant."

"Well I've paid now; we'll just have a good dinner later."

"Maybe we should have asked first. But never mind."

With an impatient sniff, Sophea led the way to the noodle stall. She had a discussion with the woman who was cooking; the woman sent a child somewhere in a big hurry. While we worked our way through very large servings of noodles, the child reappeared with a plate of fried chicken breasts and watermelon slices in a plastic bag. We might stagger through the afternoon.

The temple of Wat Ek was largely in ruins, so the clamber to the heart of it was hard work. I ended up as dirty as a toddler, while Sophea reached the top as if she had some stone-dust-repelling magic. I didn't ask about that, in case she told me she did.

At the heart of the temple was a Buddhist altar being tended by a very old man in a sarong. He didn't speak English but he could speak French for me. He said this but he didn't look at me at all, only at Sophea.

The man told Sophea he knew her soul was old from the minute he saw her; his was very old too.

Great. Now I had two of them making my head spin.

"This is a place where you may have been a priestess, before Buddha." He said. "That looks like a Buddhist altar but inside is a shrine to a female spirit, much older than the time of Buddha. Many women come here to pray when they need babies, many women."

Sophea nodded and told him she liked this place, it felt more holy to her than Angkor because the Apsara authority had destroyed Angkor with their greed. There was plenty of talk about the government and the Vietnamese puppet nature of them. The old man believed the government wouldn't last much longer because the spirit of the naga was about to rise in the country.

I knew the naga was the sacred, multi-headed snake carved all over Angkor and the temples of Battambang. The naga controlled the rains, prosperity and, in representing the rainbow, it was a bridge between heaven and earth. I knew that much, but it was not nearly enough:

"Oh yes," Sophea said. "My friend Chenda, who is my sister from another life, she prays very well and she says the naga will rise soon and drive out this government, drive out the Vietnamese."

I blundered in: "Is that metaphorical? Do you mean the Cambodians will rise up?"

The old man waited patiently, watching Sophea while she was polite but firm with me:

"No, it is the spirit, you won't see it, no one will see it but it will rise up in the Cambodians who pray to Buddha."

That was kind of what I... I just nodded. "Sorry."

Sophea went back to the old man: "I tell him you are nice but you are not here long enough to understand."

Still without looking at me, although speaking French for me, the man said: "The West do nothing because they don't understand what is happening here. And they are scared. Their governments are scared that if he is challenged, Hun Sen will start killing everyone. It already happens. He kills journalists, and politicians, and it isn't another genocide but slowly he kills many, many people with poverty and of despair. I wish the West were afraid of that."

Dara had told me that many of the older generation were fiercely loyal to Hun Sen because he had driven out the Khmer Rouge. But now they were noticing how much Hun Sen cultivated the military and was clearly grooming his son to take over. Older people dreaded political instability and where it might lead but even they were looking at the state of the country and getting restless. Feeling less obligated to Hun Sen, young people had the internet; they could read foreign papers and tell their parents how much money Hun Sen and his cohorts had stolen from them, and was still stealing. Perhaps the spirit of the naga was simply the truth dawning on everyone – that just because you'd had someone as bad as Pol Pot, you didn't have to put up with likes of Hun Sen.

Most Cambodia-resident Westerners I'd spoken to did think it was too late: corruption and greed were so locked in to the way things were done, demands for reform would lead to terrible repression. The 2014 election results had been dubious but protesters insisting Sam Rainsy's opposition were the winners had been forced to retreat when Hun Sen rolled out tanks. One Western tour operator told me he rented all his property, so that he and his staff could leave the country in a hurry;

"I tell my staff, enjoy Cambodia but be in the mindset that you might have to get on a plane tomorrow."

There were other tour operators who did buy land, designed and built eco-friendly hotels and invested in developing whole villages, with schools and health centres for their staff. They thought the old guard would just take their ill-gotten gains and go to live abroad.

Then, there were the educated young Cambodians like Dara; they fought hard to have things – education, a chance at travel and creativity – so many things Westerners their age took for granted. They enjoyed their own achievements, revelled in them and weren't losing them easily. There was definitely a change coming but whether it was with a fight, or an up-surging young generation, who simply enjoyed living well and had dropped all interest in old woes, shifting gradually into control as the old guard faded....? The only certainty was that the political future of any country was not predictable by the likes

of me.
In the ruins of Wat Ek, the old man suddenly started talking nervously to Sophea in Khmer. Still, and it had been nearly twenty minutes now, he hadn't looked at me.
"He wants to know who you are. He wants to know what your job is."
I produced my BBC identity card; sometimes the organisation was known in surprising places. The card seemed to be of more interest to Sophea than the nervous man.
"He doesn't want a card, he wants to know what you are writing about. He thinks you are from a guidebook. One guidebook asked him many questions, took his picture and he got no tip. I will explain to him that you write stories, stories as if for children, and you always tip."
She talked in Khmer and the caretaker smiled. He looked at me and nodded shyly.
"He understands, he is happy about that."

As we stood to go and I handed him the tip, he glanced at me again, then away, as if my blue eyes troubled him in some way. Perhaps in his belief system they meant something. I asked Sophea why he wouldn't look at me.
"He is shy and you don't introduce yourself properly, why should he look? Oh, how beautiful!"
There was a file of thin, standing, stone Buddhas along a water channel leading to the giant Buddha. Inside this giant were rich murals and golden Buddhas. The huge central one made Sophea look very vulnerable as she knelt to pray in front of it, slightly ragtag backpack on her narrow shoulders.
Outside, rain started pelting down. We ran to Ted who was hurrying to pull down the plastic sheeting that protected his customers, giving his tuk tuk the look of a small, mobile greenhouse. He wore a bright yellow waterproof, hood pulled tight around his face, that made him look even more teddy-bear-like.
"Where to?"
I'd been thinking I might make a second trip to Banan; Sophea would enjoy it. Or there were old colonial buildings to stroll around... Everything seemed to involve being outdoors.
"What about we find somewhere nice in town take coffee, cake, talk a little bit. Maybe the rain stops. In fact I am a little bit tired, the hotel is nice but the mattress is soft. It is difficult for me because my back is in an arch from dancing. I put a pillow under but then I am too high."
She laughed, pushing her belly forward. "Like a pregnant lady. Don't worry, I am always like this in hotels. I will have nice cake in a cafe and feel better."
Her lower back was unnaturally concave; perhaps the artificial elegance of her dance was something that should be let go, like corsets, foot-binding; perhaps the way forward was what they did in the circus, just suggesting the

traditional, but using modern, healthy bodies.

After cake and coffee, I bought Sophea a new backpack in the market. She managed to find one that was fake Chanel: it looked how their nylon backpacks might look, if they made them. Back at the hotel she swapped her belongings into it, folding the old one at the bottom.

"I can recycle. I have one for carrying dance instruments that is getting old."

I asked her why she didn't ask the hotel to give her a locker.

"The instruments for the dance can't stay there, they are holy. I must put them with my Buddhas and treat them with respect."

The rain had stopped. We ambled the fresh gardens of some of the town centre wats, bowing to passing young monks, looking at some of the really quite old gold-topped stupa – memorials.

"They are old, no? They say the commander in Battambong refused Pol Pot's orders to destroy the temples. But it is because Noun Chea, big Khmer Rouge leader, had family here. A mother who is very religious. All of them are hypocrites."

The contradictions of the Khmer Rouge. It seemed clear that most of the leaders were insane, so why we looked at the regime and expected sense...

We sat over an early dinner watching the streets close down. Battambang was so hassle-free compared to Siem Reap, with its central streets full of leafleteers and crowd-pullers, trying to sell you manicures, massages, day trips, bicycle tours, souvenirs, those pedicures where small fish ate your feet skin and every fish pedicure salesman had the same joke: "No piranha!" There were no dollar-beer nights and I'd only seen a couple of pizza places. Maybe the noisy, all-night street hustle of Siem Reap made it safer, but the relative indifference to tourists in Battambang's bedraggled elegance made a tourist like me feel, smugly, an un-nibbled toe-width off the beaten track.

Halfway through dinner, Sophea had to take a call about her restaurant.

"I have to tell them what to order. They know but they are scared to make decisions without me. Otherwise I would travel with you two weeks, three weeks..."

"Don't worry. Next time, next time. At first you didn't even know if you liked the look of me."

She laughed. "Oh I just wanted to make sure. But next time is better. We will travel to where the Khmer Rouge put me, we will see my brother and my old dance school, many places. I like to travel very much. If it is by my own idea."

She told me about her first plane trip, on tour with the dance troupe to Hanoi and Saigon.

She hadn't expected the plane to be so big and was delighted to have a window seat, while her friend beside her was terrified and far too sick to eat her airline meal.

"Another one behind is the same. I eat three meals, delicious!"

The food in Vietnam was very basic, as were the hotels. The best evening

was a reception at the Khmer embassy where they were given chocolates in a little palm box.
"I ate some, then thought my family will never have tasted chocolate. I left half and wrapped them in some paper, then back in the box. My friend ate all of hers and told me I was silly to keep it, it would melt. But I think, even if it is melted, my family get to taste it."
They were paid very well for the tour, so she brought her wages back to her parents as well as the Heidi-like gift of the chocolate.
"They are relieved when I come back, especially my mother who is nervous of everything. When I show them the chocolate they start to cry. My mother told me to keep the chocolate for myself as I am so good and bring them money. I tell them all about my journey in the plane, being above the sky. They are so excited because they have never been on a plane and they want every detail."
This is a précis, because Sophea told me every detail; she remembered the journey so vividly – everything was a marvel, from the look of the world from above, to the seatbelts. It became a little strange, as if she was right back there, describing it to her family.

In the morning we bought fruits and biscuits, along with a whole pallet of fruit juice boxes and loaded them into Ted's tuk tuk. We were going to the Wat to meet Sophea's dance and meditation wise monk.
The wat was outside town and seemed to stretch for miles. Temples, stupa, gardens and halls for the monks to meditate in. The only women I saw were sweeping or cooking outdoors. When we parked at the side of the main courtyard, Sophea called the monk. The phone went straight to voicemail. With a bow, Sophea asked a young monk passing to help her.
"He will get the monk, perhaps he is praying and forgot the time."
We waited, and waited. The young monk eventually came back, looking awkward. Sophea's face did that thing I've never quite believed when I see it on the page – it drained of colour.
"He says the monk is go away last night."
"Very sorry." The young monk said. To me.
"I called him when I left Siem Reap, to tell him we will be here now and he says he will meet us. But this monk says last night he goes away because his mother who lives in Thailand is sick. I am very sorry, I make the plan but it is broken."
Both Ted and the monk looked at the ground because Sophea seemed close to tears.
"You don't need to say sorry to me, he should have called you."
"Maybe, but his mother... But now you lose your time."
"I can come back next time."
"First my problem with Henri, now this... I think you will not come back. I

want to work with you, I am a serious person, please believe in me."

Now she bowed her head, as if waiting for me to rain curses down on her.

"It really doesn't matter. Next time."

Although it was a pain. And I didn't trust Henri not to sabotage attempts to change Sophea's life every time they occurred.

Sophea made a bow to me. "Thank you Annie, you are kind. We will see ancient sites where we can discover the history of this dance. The places where Angkor begins. The spirit lives."

"Why don't we give this stuff to Ted and get a drink in town."

Ted looked up.

"No, no, it is for the monks."

Ted looked down, as if spotting something wrong with a tyre. Sophea started hefting the pallet of juice from the tuk tuk. The monk went to help her, then a couple more monks materialised to take the gifts. I felt Ted could probably have used them more but this wasn't a fair time to argue with Sophea about how Buddhism worked.

In the mornings alone in Battambang, I'd found a good cafe by the market and watched a file of monks, every morning, at least a dozen of them, come along with begging bowls and bags. Every morning, the exhausted, hard-working market people rushed from their stalls, as excited as if rock stars had arrived. Eagerly, they gave money and food to the monks. Then they put their hands together, faces glowing with beatific smiles, as the monks chanted prayers with them. I didn't like it.

Not my business. In Cambodia monks and prayers were precious because their blood was only forty years dry.

Sophea's whole body was in a disappointed slump. I tried to cheer her up with an early lunch but not even food could do it:

"This morning makes my stomach bad, maybe just some coconut juice.

So we sat with our coconuts, watching the street. Sophea was unsettled by half-a-dozen young, tattooed Cambodian men at the next table who seemed to be out of their heads on something. They kept whispering and glancing at us.

"Keep hold your bag." Sophea whispered. "Let them go first."

We ordered more juice and sat there looking such a melancholy pair the men probably concluded we couldn't be that miserable and have anything worth stealing. They staggered away, carrying the beers they'd ordered.

Sophea and the proprietress exchanged a few disapproving words.

"She says if they understood how their grandparents had to live..."

The proprietress nodded at me; "This place before, bad, very bad."

She went away to serve a respectable-looking young couple.

Sophea sighed. "I hoped the monk would make me feel strong. He is good at this. Since the Khmer Rouge time I feel my life is not in my control. Only when I am dancing it is mine. I am twenty-five and I make a mistake in my marriage, then suddenly nearly thirty years have gone by and my chances are gone. No children because the Khmer Rouge and dancing hurt my body. And Henri will not pay to adopt a child. He says he only wants his own and as I do not love him, he will not bring a child in our house anyway.

"Suddenly I am fifty and I realise life is gone. I must tell you, Annie, I study Buddhism so I can get off my bed in the morning."

Some of this sounded familiar. The realisation of not being young anymore. The lying awake at four in the morning fretting that if I hadn't made that decision, said a wrong thing, chosen a wrong person, not known enough, soon enough... That casting back must be so much tougher for Sophea, whose choices had been so limited, or had been grabbed away.

All I could do was give her a floundering pep talk about how we'd live at least another thirty years, so many things could happen yet, we still had time. The situation with Henri was temporary and huge changes could happen, right up until she was eighty, ninety...

She held out her hand, palm upward. "Every time I think something happy will happen to change my life, it escapes."

And she made a motion, clutching after something.

CHAPTER 9: GOOD CROCODILES, BAD CROCODILES AND THE END OF THE WORLD

"One dollar, one dollar!"

The very small girl, who looked as though she'd cut her own hair with a sharp stone, kept following me, pushing a plastic bracelet at me. She had three more in a shoebox, all a bit chipped and all ugly. I'd already bought a guidebook, some badly printed postcards and a bead necklace, so I wasn't giving in this time.

Apparently, to stop the local children begging, some official had come up with a scheme for them to sell the books and postcards but the children often improvised with whatever merchandise they could scrabble together. Getting them to go to school, or to be allowed to stop helping their parents out financially, was unlikely to happen in the near future, because officialdom didn't trouble themselves with looking at solutions to widespread poverty.

"One dollar one dollar!" The little girl was still dancing backwards in front of me.

"Sorry."

In deep disappointment, eyes filling with tears she walked away. Then she was back, shaking her head. She was going to make allowances for me, give me a last chance:

"Ok, ok, for you... One dollar."

Her addled notion of bargaining made me laugh so much I bought her ugly bracelet. Maybe not so addled. She skipped to the next group of Europeans chanting: "One dollar, one dollar." And probably knew that for some unfathomable reason, Europeans, when she persisted, found her hilarious.

We were at Banteay Srei, City of Women, said to have been built for a princess. But it was also said the very fine dance carvings must have been made by women.

Sophea shrugged when I asked her what she thought:

"It is made by someone who sees in a different way to the Angkor builders. That is someone who likes battle. This is gentle place but it could be a man who likes women, wants to make a gentle place for them to be happy."

Banteay Srei was a Hindu temple in pink stone, with very delicately carved women, flowers and mythical guardians, built hundreds of years before Angkor. Perhaps its prettiness was the reason it was one of the first restored, as far back as 1930.

Soft-toned Banteay Srei was hushed compared to Angkor, in look and atmosphere. Against the sharp green sea of rice paddies surrounding the temple, two boys poled along on a flat-bottomed boat and water buffalo were wading with their odd combination of majestic and comical gait.

Sophea looked a little sad.

"Yes it is pretty but I don't like it now. The Royal Ballet started a school near here but when I asked to teach they say it is a lie about my grandmother, they have no record. Maybe not, papers are destroyed in the Khmer Rouge time. But they say it is my mother who lies, not me. That makes me so angry. My mother is not a liar."

So, significant as it was, we spent a little less time at Banteay Srei than I would have liked. We were looking for inspiration particular to Sophea's dream of a dance school and performance group. Without the royals how could she manage? "How can you write the history of my dancers if I can't show where my dream belongs… Oh who needs them? I must think for myself, no?

Outside Bantea Srei, Mr Ponleak and a handful of drivers were listening with alarm to one of their colleagues. Sophea was instantly cheered up by the story:

"He is driving and a snake flies down, nearly lands in his face, he is nearly crashing. The others say it came from the trees, fell down from the trees, but he says no, it is a long way from the trees...."

Ponleak said: "No trees, no trees."

The driver shook his head, actually quite troubled.

Sophea said: "Maybe it is from god."

I said: "Maybe you were dreaming."

The driver laughed, shook himself to indicate how unsettled he was; "Not dreaming. My customer don't see but I see. A snake fly down."

Everyone muttered and tutted. As Sophea and I walked away with Ponleak the answer occurred to me:

"Some kid threw the snake as a joke. Maybe with a catapult."

Immediately Sophea shook her head. "No, no, he says it is from the sky, it is a sign."

She translated because my sentence was too much for Ponleak to understand. He looked apologetic, more dependent on me than Sophea he seldom disagreed with me, but nonetheless: "No madam. Probably sign."

"Sign of what?"

They both shrugged. I gave up.

As we drove away I could tell by his gestures that the snake-struck driver was telling his tale to a newly arrived driver.

Sophea suddenly slapped her hands on her thighs: "A snake, of course, the naga."

"So that's a good sign, yes?"

She shrugged. "It depends. Maybe you are right and it's child making joke."

I'd have to go back to London soon, before I was driven crazy.

On the way out of Banteay Srei, I also saw my 'one dollar' friend in discussion with the boy, about twelve years old, who'd sold me the postcards. Perhaps they were family. The number of sales-children out at this temple was nothing compared to the numbers around the Angkor complex. Although education was free in Cambodia, the children hustled, worked in the fields, helped around the house – they did all manner of things, except go to school. Part of the reason was that school wasn't exactly free. Cambodia's corruption poisoned everything, right down to the best intentioned primary school teacher.

To keep their jobs, teachers had to pay a percentage to the headmaster, who was having to pay bribes to a local school inspector, who was paying some higher official and on up the chain... Meanwhile back at the lower end, to feed their own families, teachers were having to declare all manner of things 'extra', requiring a fee. This could be English lessons, exercise books... And there was more to it than that.

A volunteer programme I spent a day with was funded by the profits from a top-end tour company; the owner, Andy, was a wealthy Englishman who had no need for his profits. He wanted a small, circular scheme so there was never 'ownerless money' resting anywhere to pique the interest of corrupt officials; there was no rattle of a collection tin to exacerbate the compassion fatigue that could set in for tourists in Cambodia. Particularly as half the charitable projects were so ill thought out.

Ponleak's village, under threat from the developers, was also blighted by dozens and dozens of grey cement rectangles – as if aliens were starting to invade and had begun with constructing ugly sentry boxes. These incongruous frights were a gift from a Japanese charity, who had decided the village needed public toilets. But then they'd run out of money or lost heart – no one in the village knew. And no one had been asked if they wanted dozens of toilets scattered through the landscape – except, presumably, the local government official who'd been given a fee for his consent. Perhaps he'd gone back for more money and the Japanese were put off. The only certainty was that Ponleak's village had fifty empty cement boxes. Some people used them to store animal feed but mostly, like Ponleak, the villagers just shrugged it off as the sort of thing that happened.

Every second restaurant in Siem Reap advertised itself as supporting some charity. There were establishments that put notes in the menu asking customers to be patient because they paid staff to train with them – but didn't that just mean they had cheap waiting staff? Then there were the fake orphanages. Children were borrowed from their parents for an establishment that allowed tourists to visit and asked for a donation. After a week or so, the children might be returned to their parents and a new batch brought in. There had recently been a newspaper story about toughs from the orphanages driving off vulnerable parents, such as single mothers, when they came back for their children. A mother might only have loaned her child so it could be well fed and sheltered while she improved her circumstances. But she'd be forced to leave the child for good, earning money for the 'orphanage' owners. There were cases of poor families finding their very attractive child had gone – perhaps sold into the sex trade, or adopted out of the country.

Posters around Siem Reap and Phnom Penh warned ORPHANAGES ARE NOT TOURIST ATTRACTIONS. But a clean-up of the charity industry in Cambodia had barely begun.

The About Asia Schools, a small tour-company-funded organisation I'd spent time with, was impressive in this tangled world. And they constantly checked themselves, to be sure they were actually were helping. Sarah, their energetic manager, was a teacher. She had arrived as a volunteer and pointed out to owner Andy that the volunteers weren't properly trained. He hired her to solve the problem and now their volunteers all had a crash course in cultural awareness and interactive teaching. This Teach First programme was something Sarah wanted to pass on to local Cambodian teachers, who used very old-fashioned, standing-at-the-blackboard methods. This particularly didn't work with undernourished children, tired from chores at home and working on the land. These children needed to be drawing pictures, shouting out, playing clapping games, running to write things on the board.... The class had to be constantly rebooted with energy.

The children's enthusiasm wasn't helped by the schools being so dilapidated, with broken classroom equipment and insufficient desks. The buildings were stifling because broken fans were never repaired. More often than not, purchase and maintenance budgets were lost in someone's pockets. Andy avoided involvement in funding for equipment or repairs, because this ran too much risk of providing 'ownerless money', or of challenging Cambodian authority. The volunteers were a more targeted way to help.

Even negotiating with schools to take the volunteers in a straightforward way could be tricky. Yes, their teachers had free training in modern methods but where was the backhander? Eventually though, the organisation had placed volunteers in a hundred schools.

As much as possible, local staff were employed both in the tour company and to train volunteers. The goal was to one day hand the whole thing over to the Cambodian employees.

"What I realised I really don't want to be part of," Andy explained, "Is creating a mentality in the children here that how the world works is that white people come in and help the brown people, because the white people always know best. A lot of places in the world have been messed up with this."

A couple of local staff were working with Sarah on a research project: they went out into the villages to find out why children might only come to school half a day, once a week, or why they never made it at all.

There was a feeling, as life was tough and unpredictable, of people living very much for the day, so the benefits of long-term education were hard to communicate. Pointing out that an ability to speak basic English could lead to a good job in the city didn't always help; many very traditional rural people worried their children would be corrupted by Western ways. Or perhaps look down on their parents and not come home.

Nhean was a supervisor of the volunteers and engaged in the research with Sarah. He told me: "Family is so important here, the memory of losing family is still close. My father lost seven siblings in the Khmer Rouge, seven. So people think the Western habit of leaving home is bad and will influence here."

In this wet season the children were often tired at their desks because their parents took them out at night to hunt for a type of frog that was eaten or sold. Girls were more likely to be in school than boys because boys were needed to work on the land; girl's tasks, sewing and cooking, could be done in the mornings or evenings. Often the children couldn't concentrate because they were hungry, so the volunteers provided cooked rice, vegetables and clean water at the back of the classroom.

"Of course the word got round and parents stopped giving their children breakfast because we'd give it to them." Sarah said. "All the time I have to remember what Nhean told me about the good crocodile and the princess." She grinned at Nhean.

"Sometimes I come in with something I think is a brainwave and he just looks at me and says 'C P'. Shall I tell her? Ok, so... The princess wanted to cross a field full of bad crocodiles. The good crocodile had the idea that the princess could climb inside him and hide in his stomach. She got in and the good crocodile swam through the bad crocodiles. But when he got to the other side he found the princess had suffocated inside him and died. He tried to explain to people but they didn't believe him. They beat him and told him he was the worst crocodile of all."

I must have looked bewildered. Nhean made sure I got the message.

"It means watch out for big ideas, they might not be that great. Think once, think twice."

At a school far in the countryside, Nhean took me to a classroom where children, wild with excitement, were learning a song. The walls were decorated with paperchains and their desks littered with debris from making these chains.
"They're having a party for the king's birthday tomorrow. The song's about the king." The volunteer smiled at the local teacher she was assisting.
The teacher said: "They're very happy now, but we had to explain because these children don't know what a birthday party is. Villagers don't have this kind of event in their lives."
When I met Sarah, the NGO manager, for a drink later, I told her about the party arrangements.
"I know, there's always something. We've just started trying some nutritional education, teaching kids to grow vegetables, giving vegetable plots to the villages because nutrition is really poor. Rice, rice, rice. Everyone is obsessed with rice as a cash crop and meanwhile the kids are malnourished because it's all they eat. We've also noticed that whatever way we teach, the children don't retain things very well. And what's really worrying is I've just been reading research from a big international charity that says if children are malnourished under the age of five it can damage their brains. So yes, the party thing can make them enthusiastic about school but if they aren't retaining anything... All the time we have to keep adjusting." She shrugged. "Or worst crocodiles of all."

A few kilometres on from Banteay Srei was a charitable project that seemed to be run by fairly good crocodiles. It was a landmine museum and a small school. Sophea had seen it before but came in with me.
"Good man," she said, pointing to the Cambodian founder on a wall poster. This was Aki Ra, who had started the museum and school. After being forced to fight for the Khmer Rouge from the age of ten, he then, as they started to lose, was conscripted into the Vietnamese army. When the Vietnamese left Cambodia he was conscripted into the new Cambodian army. Finally he had a job he wanted: land mine clearing with the UN. He decided to make clearing landmines, some of which he had helped plant in his youth, his life's mission. As he worked, he collected odd bits and pieces – old guns, gas masks, uniforms..... He had the idea to make the museum to teach people about the worst of war. And to educate visitors about land mines. In the Siem Reap province alone there were 27,000 victims. Aki Ra wanted to clear every land mine from Cambodia.
The reason Aki Ra had posters and booklets about his life all around the premises was that he didn't want to do any more interviews; he wanted to be

out clearing mines. With the help of volunteers and donations he had also established a small residential school for child landmine victims, although, thanks to the clearing operations, the school was now used for orphaned children of parents who had died from AIDS.

One of the most significant donors to the landmine museum was Tom Shadyac, an American producer of films such as Ace Ventura Pet Detective; Evan Almighty... I'd have to remember, next time I passed over them in the DVD library because I fancied myself too foreign-film-sophisticated for that sort of thing, that they were worth more than my pretensions.

Sophea pulled my sleeve and indicated we should stalk an American couple being shown around by another big American with an ex-military air about him. It seemed he ran the place, voluntarily, and I wondered if Aki Ra wasn't the only person connected to the establishment doing some sort of penance.

As the American explained Cambodia's modern history to his visitors, he pointed out that American bombing had killed three times as many Cambodians as Pol Pot. The visitors, a group of people in their fifties, possibly older, didn't seem shocked.

"We've been very surprised by the people here, we half expected there'd be anger at Americans." One woman asked. "Why is there no anger?"

The museum American answered with assurance: "It's because they've moved on. And they're Buddhist, they let things go."

"Not true," Sophea hissed in my ear.

We carried on stalking the group. The museum American pointed out that many of the people who had lived through the Khmer Rouge times were dead now, simply from what counted as old age in Cambodia.

"I'm sixty-five, they don't believe it. A sixty-five year old is like a ninety-five year old here." Although even for a Westerner, the museum American was a robust sixty-five, with well cycled legs.

I thought he'd noticed us and our stalking, so I pointed Sophea toward the giftshop. I bought a book about landmines and decided against a T-shirt with a silhouette of a person with amputated limbs, leaning on crutches. The T-shirt bore the logo The Perfect Soldier. I was self-righteous enough without wearing a T-shirt advertising the fact.

As we went outside, the American was ahead of us, concluding his tour beside a cluster bomb. After he'd explained this brutal piece of weaponry, the woman asked about King Sihanouk; she couldn't figure out his place in Cambodian history.

"Well, he knew the Khmer Rouge were going to win so he switched sides, then he knew they were going to lose, so he switched again. Incredible. What can I tell you but the man is one of the consummate politicians of our age."

"True," Sophea whispered.

When the Americans were gone, we looked at the large cluster bomb, a thing that would hit the ground, explode and deliver small bomblets that didn't

always explode because they hadn't landed right – these were the things children tended to find, drop....
"Actually when I am a child," Sophea said, "I quite liked the bombs in Phnom Penh. I didn't understand. I see the light, the colours, I think the noise is exciting. I only think this at first. Then I see. And it's not true we forgive Americans. I mean the ones in the past who bombed us. They must go in to hell. The ones now are OK."
"I thought the guide seemed like someone who used to be a soldier, bomber pilot, something like that. Just a feeling I had."
Sophea didn't think my feelings were worthy of attention. She glanced back at the museum entrance; "The man who started this is brave. And he makes his karma good, just by his own courage. I wish I could do something like this with my life."
Really, didn't we all? Then again, I could have done without the whole being a frequently starving orphan, conscripted to three different armies and risking my limbs in minefields route to Paradise, or sense of a life usefully lived.

Prasat Kravan was off the main temple circuit. It was a Hindu temple with bas reliefs of Vishnu and his consort Lakshmi. Ponleak had heard talk from other drivers of a ceremony and he'd a feeling we'd want to see it.
Most of the participants were women, although there was a young man in white who danced in snake-like movements, possessed by the spirit of the naga. Children clambered at the windows but were moved aside by their mothers for us to have a good view of the ceremony.
There were musicians playing traditional instruments, particularly drums. There were piles of offerings – fruit, flowers, bowls full of cigarettes, and bottles of alcohol. I could smell alcohol sweating out of participants.
"They drink something, they chew betel, they go into a trance." Sophea said, as two old ladies got to their feet and danced in an arm churning motion.
"Ah, that is the dance of the horsemen." Sophea eyed them critically. "We use it in the ballet too but with more control. They summon strength."
The ladies didn't have the strength to summon much strength and soon sat down again. The snake dancing boy writhed up, then stumbled, almost falling back into his seat, where he trembled, eyes closed and chanting.
One of many women at the ceremony wearing military uniform, got to her feet dancing and brandishing a perfume spray. She was an army captain, and the ceremony was for her protection from black magic; she'd just been promoted and might be spiritually thrashed by the envious. The music, the dancing, some strange singing – it was mesmerising, but it didn't feel Buddhist.
"No, no." Sophea seemed to find the ceremony quite usual. "It is a mixture. Old from India, older than even Hindu. But it's also Khmer. The women are possessed by spirits of warriors from the carvings of Angkor. Always dance

is how spirits are summoned. They will feel strong in the army, protected. They do this before a full moon, when the spirits are strongest. You see the gifts? They must give five of everything – five lotus, five candle, five cigarette..."

"What about the boy?"

"He is a monk, maybe a relative."

"Do you believe in this?"

"From this we have Buddha, it is the earth Buddha grew from. We are lucky in Cambodia, we have many traditions. That's why I have to study and pray because the next incarnation of Buddha is the last one, then after five thousand years there is no more time. The end of time. If we are not good, we will never see God. It is also the last incarnation of Vishnu, the end of Hindu time. Everything is together and all time is finished."

Despite not believing a word of it, I was a bit freaked. It was in the words. If time began, it ended. Imagine being around when scientists had the date, give or take a few months, when we would all vanish. It was the sort of thing that, if I thought about it too long, made me want to chew betel and dance like a snake until I fell over.

Sophea's phone was ringing. Henri. Yes, yes, she was on her way back. Good Karma to look after him, what with the very end of all time being so close... If Sophea turned out to be right, would she put in a word for me?

We turned to go as she ended her call, tight-lipped.

"Sometimes it is very hard to be Buddhist, very hard."

I stepped out to cross the road and she pulled me back. A speeding Range Rover had appeared out of nowhere.

"There, nearly the end for you."

The road cleared and she led me forward; "Cross together. One they will kill but not two."

Ponleak, parked on the other side of the road for shade, had been playing with a stray dog. He'd paused, horrified, in his activity when I was nearly killed.

He said something to Sophea.

"He says is government cars, drive how they like. Like babies who stole a car."

They both seemed to find this hilarious – hey, my time had nearly ended and my karma was undoubtedly appalling – no laughing matter.

As we'd watched the temple ceremony, Sophea had talked about the spirit of her dance bringing prosperity back to Cambodia.

"These dances today are like... folk dances. They protect people but they are much lower down. The ballet brings the strongest spirits. If ordinary people can learn it, if it is performed not just in the grand places, it is like we have part of our language back."

I wondered about her classical dance for the people idea. Not just from my disbeliever point of view, not only because it was unnatural – if dancers learned very young it was no more outlandish for the body than European ballet – but because my previous day with the school's volunteers had made me see that a child with a few plastic bracelets to sell might be a lucky one. Official reports had Cambodian poverty levels improving but there were still 6.9 million people, twenty percent of the population, who were what the World Bank called "type-one poor", meaning regularly going without food. Then there were those on the edge; the 8.1 million who, in World Bank classification, were, "near poor": living on around two dollars thirty a day. That Mr Ponleak and his wife were managing to keep their children alive, let alone in school, on a tuk tuk driver's money, made them remarkable people. So their need for the decorative flourish of an archaic form of ballet dancing...? They had enough to do.

In the morning, before dawn, Mr Ponleak's wife was leaving to work in Thailand. Her wages in the housekeeping department of a hotel would be a very helpful one hundred dollars a month. She'd only be able to come home in her three-day break in the middle of the month, so Ponleak had donated me to Mr Kiri for the evening, in order for his family to have a farewell meal. The rain was pouring but Kiri came into the building flapping his arms, looking like some crazy beetle in head-to-foot black waterproofs.
"Tuk tuk ready. We go?"
I was headed for the elegant old temple of Wat Bo, as a guest of Sophea's hotel manager. The trees around the temple were strung with fairy lights – fairy lights in trees would be one of the abiding images of Cambodia for me. The pathway was lit by elegant lanterns and liveried hotel staff were bowing to grand-looking guests.
"You go here?" Kiri clearly didn't think I was from a high enough drawer for the occasion. I promised him I'd been invited. It was a display by the Royal Ballet Company.
Wearing lavish costumes, accompanied by a full orchestra, the young dancers enacted scenes from the Hindu epic, Ramayana. Behind them was a finely painted, antique mural of the Cambodian, more Buddhist version of the story, called the Reamker. The audience were guests from the expensive hotel, or local dignitaries, or wealthy foreign residents – actually Kiri was right, I was very lucky to be here.
The dance was gorgeous, of course, but Sophea managed to be spellbinding with so much less. The performance went on for well over an hour. I thought of speaking to the princess who'd been introducing the segments but what did I care about this rarefied world? The country was full of hungry children, children who couldn't read – Sophea and I had to find some more practical way to get good karma than bringing ballet to the people.

Outside the rain had stopped and Mr Kiri had moved his tuk tuk closer to the building. I thought this was so I wouldn't have to weary my grand, ballet-attending legs.
"You moved." I said, so he'd know I'd noticed the consideration.
"Closer to hear the music." He said. "Very beautiful."
Kiri looked at the fancy guests leaving, some getting into the whimsically retro tuk tuks of classy hotels, some getting into cars with tinted windows.
"How is dancing?"
"Very beautiful."
Then, burly Mr Kiri said, with a breath that was all wistfulness: "One day I hope I see."

Claiming that it was in the interests of getting everyone fed, the Khmer Rouge had made Cambodia plain, colourless and cruel. Taking away detail had made the country insane. Everyone was more than a type on the poverty scale. Losing details – colour, music, dancing – were losing part of a language expressing who we are beyond types. Decorative flourishes kept us human.

AN INTERRUPTION

AT THIS point in the story, Annie was back home in London, working through her notebooks, research and experiences gathered in Cambodia.

For months she had been plagued by a near constant pain in a small area of her upper back. The GP put it down to long days crouched over the laptop and sent her to a chiropractor, which only made things more painful.

Finally, Annie was sent for a biopsy.

Dr Tom, the oncologist, was friendly, immediately trusted and brutally honest. He lit up an x-ray on the lightbox on his desk. It was lung cancer; it was advanced, and it was inoperable.

Other hospitals might talk about palliative care, he continued, but not here at the Chelsea & Westminster.

He would check with the clinic about starting chemotherapy the next day. Then set up an appointment for Annie to talk to his radiotherapy counterpart at the Royal Marsden.

Annie snapped out of the numbness that followed diagnosis.

She couldn't possibly start chemo tomorrow, she had deadlines, meetings, writing to finish.

Dr Tom leaned in and met her gaze. He talked quietly.

"What do you want to do Annie? I don't mean tomorrow. I mean what is the thing that is most important for you, in your life, at this moment?"

Annie paused, taking in the weight of the question.

"My book. I want to finish my book about Cambodia."

"Okay then. I will do all I possibly can to help you finish your book about Cambodia."

"That's what I want."

Two weeks into treatment and Annie almost died. The plan had been to run the chemotherapy concurrent with radiotherapy. Annie started chemo and, on this day, we struggled into the radiotherapy unit in the basement of the Marsden to begin that portion of the business.

Annie collapsed. All treatment was suspended. She spent a week in a sealed hospital room where her family had to wear aprons, masks and hairnets to visit.

If Annie's body couldn't take the chemo there would be nothing for it.

Dr Tom re-drew the battleplan. He reduced the dose of chemotherapy and suspended radiotherapy until after chemo was completed.

Annie tentatively started down this new course. It was unspoken but both of us fearing a replay of the extreme reaction. If that happened, we knew that would likely be the end of treatment, the end of hope.

It did not come.

The weeks passed, and gradually we allowed ourselves to believe the worst was not coming.

We fell into our new routines quickly, constructing our days and weeks and months around the diary of Annie's hospital trips and regime of drugs, moving through chemotherapy and then to radiotherapy.

The treatment was intrusive. It made Annie ill. Her hair fell out. She was often exhausted, frustrated by her body failing her; and angry and terrified. There were days when she struggled to walk more than a few steps.

And all the while Annie continued to work, shifting the office space from her desk to our bed.

Those that knew she was ill were kept to a tight circle, as small as Annie could manage.

Scheduled work appointments were postponed; social events put on hold, Annie always citing writing commitments.

And she was writing, completing the early chapters, working as long as her strength on any given day would allow.

I had been nursing a suggestion about her book and looking for an opportune moment to bring it up.

"Have you thought about incorporating this thing, this illness, into your book?"

"I was going to mention it," she said, "in passing."

But my idea was that it should be a larger part of the story, part of her journey.

My Cambodian Twin had grown out of a half joking idea that Annie, so defiantly secular, would go on a spiritual journey – about life's meaning – alongside the physical Cambodian journey. But progress of that book had been hijacked by this life threatening… spectre; one that had forced Annie on some other journey, a trip that could not help being spiritual because it involved facing up to her own mortality.

"I will think about it," she said, firmly.

Which I knew was Annie code for 'keep your nose out of my business McNamara'.

Annie had already decided to treat the cancer in the book with the same lack of attendance that she treated it in her life. She was determined not to let it define her. or allow it to make her someone who could wallow in self-pity, or navel gazing.

I would open the door of our tiny flat with shopping and hear her on the phone to friends, talking animatedly, catching up on gossip and laughing, always laughing. There would be no mention that she was lying in bed, too ill to walk to the bathroom unaided, wearing a scarf to cover her baldness.

Or that she had this disease that was life threatening and these casual promises to catch up in a month or two might not happen because she might possibly be dead by then.

Cancer was to be treated with disdain, ignored wherever possible, both in life and on the page.

The long gruelling months of chemo and radiotherapy were followed by more anxious months, waiting for the scarring around her tumour to heal, so that the medical team could properly assess the state of the cancer.

Another X-ray on the lightbox in Dr Tom's office.

"It is good news Annie."

The tumour had shrunk; just a tiny degree but it was significant.

It almost seemed like an anti-climax. After all the drama and all the fear and sleepless nights; just to be told that to go home and get on with our lives.

Annie had one question.

"I want to go back to Cambodia. What do you think doctor?"

"What I think Annie, is what is the point of going through all you have gone through these long months if you cannot do the things that you want to do." - MM

CHAPTER 10: THE LONG JOURNEY BACK

"They live in the boats all the time?"
"Of course."
"I don't think I'd like that. I'd be scared I'd roll over in the night and fall in the water."
"Or wake up and find a crocodile in your face," Sophea laughed. Then she put on a gruff voice and made a comical wide-mouthed grimace. "Hello, what's for breakfast? Is it you?"
I'd forgotten how she could suddenly be very funny. We were looking at the tiny, precarious-looking fishing boats on the other side of the wide, dark Mekong water, in the threatening lee of a high, glassy hotel. The boats belonged to a Muslim population, descendants of people called the Cham. The Cham had arrived from the Borneo region in the ninth century. Once they'd been traders, pirates, conquerors but time had pushed them into the background. In recent Cambodian history they'd faced many threats; at the moment it was land-grabbing modernisation. Their homes along the Mekong and Tonle Sap rivers were in the way; developers wanted river frontage for hotels and fancy apartments. The Muslim fishermen stood little chance of being allowed to continue cluttering up potential docking facilities for yachts and luxury cruise boats.
The Cambodian Muslims were treated viciously by the Khmer Rouge, their mosques destroyed. Their roles as fishermen and running slaughterhouses had kept some of them alive – the skills were necessary. Although the Khmer Rouge killed Buddhist monks, the religion's squeamishness about the taking of animal life remained with Cambodians, so they let some Muslims live. These days, the Cambodian Muslims moved around the rivers and in their stilt house villages very quietly. It didn't seem their situation would improve.
A few nights before our river trip, there had been bombings and shootings in Paris. By what seemed to be coincidence, a Cambodian restaurant had been at the heart of one of the target areas. Sophea had checked – her sister and

family were safe. But now in Phnom Penh, as we watched the rickety fishing boats, the green light on a recently built mosque just visible on the land behind, the Cambodian Muslims faced a new threat.

"I am sorry for them." Sophea said." These are quiet people, hardworking. They are here long time, since before Angkor. Maybe some Cambodians will use this as an excuse to hurt them, break their boats. It is nothing to do with them. But if people don't like them or want their place..."

Our little steamer went on out to the point where three rivers met – the Mekong, the Tonle Sap and the Tonle Bassac. To one side were cranes, skyscrapers and docked cruise ships; ahead, water and a sky clouding in spectacular formations; and behind us, young monks out with girls were taking selfies, laughing and letting balloons float away. It was Sunday night; fun night in Phnom Penh. I was so happy, and so lucky, to be here.

I'd loved Phnom Penh immediately. The roads were brain-shatteringly noisy, there was no apparent pollution control and where old French colonial buildings weren't slumping down with dilapidation, constructions were high, shiny and space-alien new. There also seemed to be a digging things up festival going on, with men surrounding big dusty holes in the street looking at men working below who were brandishing crazily dangerous bundles of wires and cables – a prize for the man putting his life most at risk in the deepest, most unnecessary hole. Everywhere were displays of a national certainty that life was cheap, as tuk tuks, four-wheel drives, battered sedans and teenagers three on a moped wove intricate patterns through it all, usually in the opposite direction to women with bundles and three babies on their mopeds... Occasionally, at the edges of this, wiry men pedalled embarrassed looking tourists in the pushchair-like cyclos: the bicycle transport that seemed out of date but came into its own in the flood season.

Across the main river-front road, on the lawns outside the Royal Palace, Cambodian families picnicked as tight-packed as a Benidorm beach in the Seventies. Lights, tunes and cries came from the nearby food stalls and balloon sellers.

"In the week this is not people, only birds." Sophea had told me and I wondered if there was a translation confusion but it was true: the weekday lawns were thick with doves and pigeons, the stalls sold food for them and passers-by threw seed for them. Sophea thought the birds were supposed to be lucky but wondered about the luck/dirt ratio.

At night, the riverfront felt more cheery than it did in the daytime frenzy, with lantern-lit stalls and those fairy lights in trees. There were spot-lit pagodas; full-blazing headlight beams and luridly lit bars, pizza and burger joints. Tourists sat at pavement cafes looking slightly shell-shocked.

As we stepped into the night frenzy from the fun of our boat trip, Sophea was laughing.

"I enjoy so much. Because you are here I have hope again. Light at the end of the tunnel is what you say, no?"

It was. For both of us.

Despite all that was happening, Sophea still looked far too young for her age and had the elphin chic of a girl in a Godard movie. Both Sophea and Chenda, who'd arrived with Sophea's brother and niece to meet me at the airport, had declared I looked younger, because I'd put on weight, I'd been too thin before, far too thin...

I had been thin when I went away. Then I had a backache that nothing eased and a shortness of breath. It seemed that I had a tumour in my lung. But it was a small one, that the NHS had fixed so well I could get back on the road, even if it was many months after I'd intended. Still, as Sophea had cheerily put it:

"It's so good you live in London. If you were in Cambodia you would be dead."

Although I'd come back as fast as my body would let me, there was another setback. Sophea's father was very ill, probably dying and she didn't want to travel far from him for long stretches of time. She had hoped he could share some memories with me but his mind had flickered away. A few times a day, he knew who was in the room. A few times a day, he managed to speak.

She'd warned me about this before I left London: "I can show you our history in Phnom Penh, where we were taken. And you can talk to my brother. I need to go to Siem Reap for work, in one or two days we can go from there to Battambang, to many places. But I may have to come home suddenly.... Oh, I waste your time, the book will never finish."

The book would never finish if I didn't get on a plane and try.

The book was about Sophea's remarkable past, surviving the Khmer Rouge, it was also to be about her current attempt to start a traditional ballet school, where a ballet school had no place to be – in an impoverished Cambodian village.

Sophea believed if the traditional ballet spread out from the palaces to muddy and busy byways the ballet had a spiritual element. If the dance was widely practiced, ordinary people would discover a harmony in their daily lives. It might not heal but it might soothe.

My illness hadn't given me any great philosophical insight except to just shrug and enjoy things more. Travel and not plan too obsessively where I wanted to arrive. Wasn't a Buddhist country a very good place to be thinking that way? A mission to soothe seemed appropriate.

Not far from the river, Sophea's family had a little store-front restaurant, selling small, mysterious snacks to locals. Most trade was take-away but some customers ate at plastic tables in a long, cement-floored room behind the counter. Above the room of plastic tables was an open space, like a wide window without glass. Clearly visible up there was a mattress and the top of an old man's head. Sophea saw me looking up for too long.

"I know, strange for Europeans. You put someone dying where you can't see. But for us he is still in our family. And he likes it, his business, the family, everyone talking, the music on the radio..."

I was invited to sit with him. Up winding stone steps, past the paint peeling walls, to a room cluttered with heavy wooden furniture, mats, cushions and family photographs – all post 1979. There were several Buddha statues in a corner, surrounded with artificial flowers, incense and candles. A very old lady in white prayed at this home altar. Through the glassless window I could see the restaurant and the edge of the street below.

Sophea's father was gaunt and breathing with difficulty but his expression was calm. But he must have been in pain, despite pain-killers the doctors had administered; his feet and lower legs were black, some toes were eaten away.

"The doctor says I remembered a friend's mother had diabetic leg ulcers. But the missing toes, wasn't that gangrene?"

Sophea didn't trust the doctor and seemed to think, perhaps because I'd spent so much of the last few months in hospitals, that I could give her a medical opinion.

"If you don't trust the doctor, you can't find another one?"

"This is the second one. Both the same. My father is very old, leave him alone. I know that. I know. Also my father prefers traditional medicine and wants no more doctors. But his poor feet..."

There was nothing I could think of except to find an internet cafe and look at the NHS website. She made a note of the web address:

"That's incredible. I can look things up, just for free?"

"We're still sort of guessing."

"It's incredible. There, gangrene..."

For both gangrene and the ulcers there was not much to do except give antibiotics or penicillin, keep the legs lifted, apply a plain ointment and elastic bandages. I felt terrified that my guesswork was completely wrong.

The Phnom Penh shops kept the French custom of closing for a long lunch. Metal shutters were descending just as we reached the pharmacy. Sophea bent down and begged the pharmacist to let us in. She not only let us crawl in, she spent a good twenty minutes checking her own online resources, choosing an ointment and bandages for us and being very sorry that she wasn't a doctor and couldn't help with the antibiotics.

It would cost Sophea ten dollars for a prescription, then the drugs themselves could be five dollars, as well as the painkillers they were paying for...

Sophea, her brother, or her sister-in-law took it in turns to sleep on a mat beside her father. If he needed water, or was anxious in the night he wasn't alone.

"In the night, the past comes, you know. Or sometimes he is crying and talking to my mother, telling her to keep strong."

Keeping her father fed was also something they took turns with, as everything had to be pulped to smoothie consistency. Today it was her brother's turn and he'd returned from the market with mounds of fruit to mash up a healthy lunch. Sweetly, he came up to his father's room and presented me with a coconut and a straw.

"These are good. Very fresh," Sophea said. Sann flustered back downstairs. Sophea had said he was nervous but he really was. As twitchy as a mistreated puppy, moving his head this way and that, alert for the worst. Then he'd be fine – the man could drive in Phnom Penh, for goodness sake. Perhaps it was a stranger in the house....

When everyone had left us alone with her father, I asked Sophea about it.

"No, it is not you. It is my father, it makes Sann scared when he sees him. He is so scared my father will die, but he will, very soon."

I realised Sophea's father was looking right at me. He started whispering. Sophea beamed, and leant towards him to hear.

"He is inside his mind today. He says he knows who you are, you are my friend from England. I told him about you, so he is very pleased to see you."

Then he closed his eyes.

"He will have to sleep now." Sophea squeezed his hand. "He prayed when you were sick. We all did."

As we went back to the ground floor of the house, Sophea said:

"Come and see my room."

As if we were ten years old.

Her room did have a bed but was mainly a storage room for everything from clothes to restaurant supplies. On the wall was a picture of her in dance costume, actually she looked ten in the picture, but it had been taken in Paris, when she was twenty-seven.

Speaking of Paris, Sophea had cut all ties with Henri since my last visit. As his eyes recovered, he'd had a few more drinks than usual and tried to make love to her. That was that, she had told him to go back to France and die. As for the restaurant, she didn't care; maybe she was entitled to money if it was sold but she'd rather die...

As we went out in to the hall, a teenage boy came past us.

"Is that one of your nephews?" I knew there were nephews.

"My nephews are at school. These are lodgers on the top floor, students. My family used to rent the whole house but since my father got sick, Sann can't afford it."

Paying for their father's hospitalisation earlier in the year, his medicines and doctor's visits, had cost the family a fortune. Sophea had sold part of the land around her Siem Reap house to help out. No one was happy with the Paris sister who had announced that as her husband had bought some of the land for Sophea, it was their contribution.

"Maybe you should use a third party to speak to Henri if he's selling; don't be proud, you helped build that place."

"No. It isn't some fortune, it's only a lease and the building, the land is Apsara Authority. And don't worry, he will stay here to die so I have to do his ceremony. I promised, so he will make sure. What is the expression? Have my blood? Come on, I will take you to see nice things. Here ..." She rifled in one of many boxes around us and found a basic mobile phone and charger. "You can buy some minutes for this outside in the shop and I will put my number so you aren't lost." She looked at the small phone with disdain. "It was my first but it's ok for you."

She also wanted to find a reliable tuk tuk driver for me. From the drivers resting on a grassy traffic island nearby, she selected plump, middle-aged Jack. "Young is not good. Not respectful."

Jack – drivers did seem to have a policy of adopting names Westerners could say – was English-speaking and delighted to be given Sophea's barrage of stern instructions in Khmer before he was allowed to type his number into my medieval phone.

At the entrance to the Royal Palace I declined, I thought politely, the services of a couple of official guides. Then a young uniformed guard said something to Sophea about her scarf, which she wore thrown over one shoulder. She moved the scarf to hang down on either side.

"What was that?"

"He says I mustn't have the scarf like that, it must hang down either side."

"What?"

"I know. They say anything to be important."

She took it in her stride. I looked back; the guides were smirking and nodding at the guard.

In all the smiling, kindly prettiness and jokiness of Cambodia, a thought kept occurring: if this is you, in uniforms, of any kind, was where the bad blood seemed to flow. When Kiri gave us the number for his policeman relative in Battambang, Sophea had explained to me why it was a good idea to have a contact number for a specific policeman.

"They are corrupt. They will want money even to give you a number for the insurance form. It's better to have a recommendation."

Sarah, the manager of the of the small NGO whom I'd met on my last visit, had moved apartments after the one she'd had in a cheap but rough area of Siem Reap had been broken into four times.

"Our local guide said I could hire an off-duty cop as a security guard but he might rape me, so better to just move, get back closer to other Westerners. If you join the police here it's because you're looking for a career as a bully."

Sophea, however, had nearly screamed the Bayon temple down when the guards there had stopped our filming. It surprised me that she let the bizarre scarf-bullying go so easily. But I hadn't understood how exhausted she was, how close to breaking point.

A hundred yards or so from the raucous bedlam of the riverfront road, the Royal Palace was a vast, peaceful complex behind high walls. The various buildings were separated by lawns hopped with birds, the tiniest birds can be before they're insects. The open-sided pavilion where child Sophea had sometimes danced had gilded standing Buddhas along the back wall. The dance pagoda faced the pubic lawns for picnickers or pigeons, invisible now behind the high walls, but once there had been railings. Sophea showed me where she used to stand, able to look in very easily. Having seen the photo of her in her father's room, a face full of sparkle and character as well as beauty, I understood why a dance teacher would have seen her at the railings and jumped easily to the conclusion that this girl should be invited in.

It was very hard to reconcile the Aladdin's-cave bling of the silver pagoda with the religion it was supposed to represent. Wouldn't Buddha, who preached of abandoning worldly goods, have had to say: "What part of abandoning worldly goods are you people not getting?"

Probably the donkey-riding, carpenter's assistant Jesus would say the same thing about the opulence in the Vatican. The modest-living thing that most religions began with didn't seem to pass on very well. But the display in the Cambodian Royal Palace would make a Kardashian stagger, and made the British crown jewels look like a car boot sale. The floor really was silver. Five thousand silver tiles. A carpet covered most of it, coyly pulled back in one place for us to see that talk of this floor wasn't just a fairy-tale.

As we padded around on our shoeless feet, we saw display case after display case containing jade Buddhas, gold offering plates, crystal Buddhas, cigarette boxes encrusted with jewels, ivory Buddhas, silver Buddhas, marble Buddhas, little gold Buddhas and a Buddha said to be made of emerald – but recent analysis had showed it to be mere Baccarat crystal. The mistake was a nuisance because the pagoda was often referred to by an alternative name – Wat Preah Keo, Temple of the Emerald Buddha. But there were emeralds elsewhere in the temple, and rubies and sapphires...

In the middle of the gaudy display was a life-size golden Buddha, decorated with diamonds. I started to read about this in my guidebook: it had been made in the palace workshops around 1907 and...

Sophea dropped to her knees, bowed her head to the Buddha and started chanting.

A cynical part of me wondered about this child-like emotional display. Praying so ostentatiously, in front of all these tourists? But it was also possible that Sophea was overcome by emotion and religious fervour.

An elderly guard rushed at her and for a moment I thought he was going to haul her away, but he had a handful of incense sticks. He lit them and gave them to her with a respectful bow. He walked away; it wasn't the hustle for a donation this kind of thing usually was. He looked back at her, clearly moved. When Sophea finished praying, everyone in the place was watching. She gestured to me that we were going.

On the marble steps outside, I asked if the man who gave her the incense knew her?

"Oh yes, many of them know me here. They know I am poor now but I am from the royal family."

Presumably the scarf monitor hadn't been given that memo.

Sophea maintained her haughty demeanour and led me to a building displaying royal wedding garments and richly decorated dance costumes. She wanted her picture taken beside these with her own phone.

"I would look nice in these, no?"

I was starting to feel very tired. I was going to have weeks of her, but I was already mentally rolling my eyes and wanting to resign my role as her Boswell, her mere note-taking sidekick.

We looked at royal wedding portraits. She asked me how many palaces the British queen had and did they ever find out who killed Princess Diana? Diana wore beautiful dresses, were they in a museum?

I told her there were about five palaces and I didn't know about Princess Diana, it wasn't something that interested me.

She looked irritated and disappointed, so was I. But of course Princess Diana would fascinate Sophea.

We pressed on. I reminded myself of her father, just up the road in the dilapidated house, his blackened eaten-away feet. I pretended I'd suddenly remembered seeing Princess Diana open a primary school – how she looked, the pretty lemon-yellow hat and dress she wore...

We came to a pagoda containing massive gold representations of footprints. I asked Sophea what they were; she shrugged.

"I don't remember."

Even I knew the footprints represented those of Buddha, on the path for us to follow; I thought Sophea might have a deeper explanation. And I was just interested to hear her version of the story. But she was too tired, or too plain miserable to keep explaining things. Perhaps she knew I'd made up the Diana story and was punishing me.

I stuck with my guide book as we passed a high mausoleum to the king's sister who had died of leukaemia; then to an odd, artificial wooded grove with music playing; a place, my book told me, to pray to the gods. There was a hall displaying royal sedan chairs and another with a life-sized carved white elephant to display the royal howdah. Then there was an exhibition of photographs of people in traditional Cambodian costume and a traditional wooden house to explore, alongside an exhibition explaining the different styles of architecture to be seen in the country.

Sophea suggested we find the rest room, drink some water. She came out with her face and the front of her hair wet.

"You're tired, you want to go home."

"No, no."

Doggedly she led me on to a building where she had rehearsed with the dance troupe but it was closed for repairs. Then we back-tracked to an outdoor cloister with a mural of the Ramayana, some patches of it peeling or marred by damp. The mural, painted around 1900, was delicate and subtle. Modern murals could be very broad-stroked and brashly coloured, as if there'd been a hurry to restore any kind of religious art to the country.

A sign on the wall informed us that the mural was being restored by a Polish company.

"Can't beat those Polish builders." I joked, to myself really.

"Yes, always someone getting rich not Cambodians." Sophea muttered and crossly led me off to the next thing.

I wished I'd annoyed her with a wittier remark.

As is the way in a long tour, especially when there was a great deal of looking at things and little conversation, it was all becoming a blur to me, until we came to a long room displaying photographs of Sihanouk's life.

King Sihanouk was very handsome when young, compared to the squat old fellow he'd become. The main thing the photos showed was a man of extraordinary vanity. Not the endearing vanity Sophea had: this was the dressed-up different ways, posing and laughing at the world type of vanity, familiar from every portrait of a dictator humanity has ever endured. Here was Sihanouk hunting, here in army fatigues, in a sports car, on a yacht – and look, there he was wearing stylish modern suits with De Gaulle, Haile Selassie.... Sihanouk even managed to have an in-love-with-himself eye on the camera in photographs where he was comforting the poor and victims of landmine explosions. This shameless man had always manoeuvred himself into the limelight, as well as onto the winning side.

Sometimes, in the case of Western leaders like Thatcher and Reagan, Sihanouk had convinced them of what the winning side was; that there were reasonable members of the Khmer Rouge who could be worked with. Sihanouk then manoeuvred into the coalition of so-called democratic government that included former Khmer Rouge leaders. But Sihanouk was subsequentially out-manoeuvred by the even craftier Hun Sen who made himself look very clean to the West by taking Western funding to end the Khmer Rouge rebel enclaves and capture the remaining leaders for trial. Sihanouk's parry was to persuade Hun Sen that he really needed him to cover the 'Vietnamese puppet' accusations. Together, they enjoyed a large percentage of the billions the UN poured in to provide food, build hospitals, roads....

Until recently, ordinary people believed that the royals were the keepers of Cambodia's spirit, passed down from the days of Angkor. But patience was wearing thin. People, particularly the educated younger generation, spoke angrily about the royal family's greed and betrayals.

In later pictures, Sihanouk's face was that of a wily man. His main characteristic had carved itself into his features. As if he'd begun to re-incarnate into something reflecting his behaviour before he was even dead.

Out in the sunlight, we realised the palace had closed and we were locked in. Clearly the guards were too busy organising peoples' accessories to actually do anything they should be doing, like clearing the building.

Sophea had her fists clenched, was close to screaming.

"We have to get out. I need to go home."

I saw a metal gate open a fraction of an inch.

We pulled and pulled to try sliding the gate open further. Sophea was sweating, muttering what had to be Khmer swearwords. Then a woman came through a tiny door in the one we'd been hauling at. She gave us a puzzled look and hurried on her way. Mercifully, this had made Sophea laugh. Just like that, she was at her best, joking with Jack when we found him in a terrible panic because he'd seen the museum close half an hour ago, we had his number but he didn't have ours, had his phone stopped working...?

"Poor Jack, he didn't get paid. He thinks we ran away."

"Oh no," Jack grinned. "I know your house. She can run away, not you."

"Now you give her the idea, she is very bad, she will do these kind of tricks."

Sophea kept on laughing with Jack. I felt like flinging myself down somewhere to pray for an emotionally stable day. Hour.

CHAPTER 11: THESE THINGS HAPPEN

"I think you are Jesus."

Jack wasn't having some moment of revelation that I was the Christian messiah. He was just surprised that I had given some money to two monks who'd stopped outside Sophea's house with their begging bags. I'd seen monks go in and out of the house to pray with her father, so I'd done it for him, and for Sophea. Presumably the monks had stopped at this specific house because they knew prayers were needed; as I was the only person out front at that moment, I didn't want to let the household down.

I thought it was probably beyond the scope of our mutual vocabulary to explain to Jack that I was agnostic. And in a silly way, I liked the way he'd looked so impressed with me.

"The monk and me, don't see tourist give. Never see."

I was surprised; I was sure earnest Westerners would often give donations to the monks, probably with a lot less of my secret so this is a job is it? resentment of them.

Chenda, who seemed to be wherever in Cambodia Sophea went, beckoned me in to the house. Sophea was at the foot of the stairs in a thin, cotton tracksuit that I'd have worn as clothes but Sophea wore as pyjamas.

"Sorry, Annie, my father is bad in the night, I must help my sister. You can get soda in my room, wait ten minutes please."

She went back to hand-washing something in a bucket.

"My father makes a mess in bed, is not his fault." Then she laughed as she went to refill the bucket at a wall sink. "This is the washing machine here."

She pointed to a shower stall behind a plastic curtain: "Our bathroom."

A shower in the corridor where the lodgers passed, next to the toilet also used by the restaurant customers...I'd given up being awed by the Sophea that emerged fifteen minutes later from that life behind her glamour.

Tourists are reminded by signs outside Tuol Sleng, Security Prison 21, to be respectful. We were respectful and very, very uncomfortable. Signs also reminded us to be "spiritually concentrated" and not to laugh on the premises. Of course we didn't laugh. And sitting on benches all around the grounds I saw young Westerners with expressions that read: "I am trying to spiritually concentrate on this, trying to find an emotion appropriate to where I am, or even a thought that isn't part of a cold numbness."

Should S21, Pol Pot's prison and torture centre, even be a tourist attraction? That thought too was part of our discomfort; should we be here, then go on a boat trip? I came to think that we should. To know what our governments were a party to in the Seventies and beyond, for a start. To understand that although some younger Cambodians wanted to move on, this – this – had gone pretty much unpunished, and the damage was passing down the generations.

Then again, it was quite hard to elicit the big feelings S21 merited with the drinks stalls, souvenir stands and tuk tuk drivers hustling outside shouting: "Killing Fields next madam?"

Perhaps the visitors on the benches were having better-quality thoughts and it was just me, pompously floundering to express the inexpressible.

The prison had once been a large school, built around a courtyard. If it hadn't been for the rolls of barbed wire below the windows, to stop prisoner suicides, the building would have had all the banality of evil required.

"The Vietnamese opened this place for people to see in 1982. I came with my friends and it was not cleaned like now. You see, there...." Sophea was pointing to dark stains on the floor of one of the rooms. "They can't clean out stains of blood but when we came it was..." She was struggling, she switched to French. "It was all sticky , every floor sticky with black blood. And it stank."

Some rooms had metal beds, manacles for hands and feet still in place. There were photographs on the walls of blood-glistening bodies, crumpled on the beds as if they had been flayed to death. Information notices told of women having their nipples cut off with pliers; men being forced to eat a bucket of faeces; boys hung up by the feet and plunged repeatedly into water... There were paintings on the walls too, of babies being swung against trees by the feet, or of children being chopped in the neck with a machete. The notices told that these things happened in the courtyard while the parents watched, so they would confess to being CIA, or KGB, or both – there was no sense to it.

In a prayer room incense sticks were burning, surrounded by pictures of the Killing Fields and skull after skull on wooden shelves. In another room were glass cases holding piles of clothing taken from the dead.

We came to a bewildering photo exhibit about the Kampuchea-Swedish Friendly Society, taken in 1978. There were photographs of happy young people welcoming the Khmer Rouge into Phnom Penh. A central picture showed a group of Swedes with Pol Pot, looking at smiling, plump children in luxuriant fields.

"These fat children are from the leaders." Sophea said. "We are not fat. We are skinny like crickets."

At this stage, Pol Pot was working hard to persuade the West that he was a victim of Communist Vietnamese propaganda. The Swedes from this group of visitors released a statement that they believed Pol Pot had tortured and killed some of his enemies, yes, but that reports of genocide were lies.

Sophea shook her head: "How can they say it? I never understand it."

When I later told her what I'd found on the internet, that the Swedes were a young Maoist group, publicly regretting their naiveté within six months of the 1978 visit, Sophea wasn't letting them off the hook: "They get a free holiday and say sorry afterwards. Pol Pot invited them to stay in the Royal Palace. They don't think this is strange communism?"

As we were moving on from the Swedish room, Sophea said: "I will go outside now, I don't like to see this part with the faces. I will meet you in the garden."

I went into a long, long room – photographs of the dead, filling walls and the several high screens dividing the room. The Khmer Rouge liked to record everything, including taking pictures of the prisoners as they arrived at S21. There were men, women and children; most had the plain, cropped hairstyle and black clothing of the Khmer Rouge era but some of the men wore colourful shirts and had long hair. These might be the lost Cambodian pop stars filmmaker Rithy Panh remembered in his film The Missing People. Some of the women wore thick make-up; one or two had long, curly hair. Most of the people had a neutral, passport-photo expression, although more than was comprehensible had a slight smile. They'd probably been bullied into making a pleasant expression; they must have known what was going to happen to them.

It just welled up, face after face, an occasional one standing out – the shaved head of a Buddhist monk; a woman with intricately styled hair; a couple of Western men; a very dark-skinned, wavy-haired woman with a child. This woman looked terrified and as if she was weeping....

Sitting in the shade outside, Sophea was staring at her phone, playing a computer game.

"I don't disrespect." She said. "I just can't think about this. Although this is not so bad for me, the fields are worse because I was working in the fields. Fields like that. I saw people being taken away who had been working just a few metres of earth from me and my mother."

"You don't have to come with me."

"It's ok."

We walked out past a rather hard-faced woman drumming up trade for an old man sitting behind a trestle table of books. He was Boumeng, a handyman

and an artist, who was deemed useful and not killed in the prison. To stay alive he had painted portraits of chief torturer, Duch, and of Pol Pot. Today, he was sitting under an awning signing copies of his autobiography.
"Speak to a survivor!" the woman shouted at Westerners.
Presumably we could speak to him if we bought his book, or a t-shirt that read: Say No To Genocide. The poor old man sat smiling. Obviously he wanted to tell his story and make a living, but the shouting woman tipped this into being something unsettling.
At the gate, a young English-looking man was hurrying out, wiping tears off his face. I realised I already knew a lot about this place. To see it, without book after book after film to prepare you, S21 was a cold shock.
"It made you cry?" Sophea asked as we got back into the tuk tuk.
No, for some odd reason it was the crying man who upset me.

"Take one, maybe I can't speak very well for you." Sophea urged me to pick up one of the audio guides as we went in to the Killing Fields site.
This wasn't the only Killing Field. There were probably hundreds, all over Cambodia, but this was the largest and the one where prisoners from S21 were taken.
"People who came here from S21 would be relieved," the commentator speculated. "They would know, after all the torture they were about to be set free, about to die."
How could he know that? Who was there to ask? Sophea and I agreed we'd be angry, not relieved. We'd want some more life.
"But we think this now." Sophea said. "Even without torture it was too much for some, like for my mother."
As we walked in to what appeared to be a large park, Sophea said:
"I am a child and I know I am hungry and my skin is burning in the sun, even through my clothes but I don't understand what's happening. To not understand is better."
This would have been fields and an orchard in the middle of nowhere; now there was a road was lined with high-quality housing.
"Who'd want to live here?" I asked. "Is it people who want to be near their dead?"
"Or the family of people who make them dead and don't care." Sophea shrugged. "Or more likely foreigners, Koreans, Vietnamese... they don't care."
It seemed impossible that human beings could live close to this and not be disturbed, but then the place itself existed, so my mind was clearly soft and naive about what people could and couldn't do.
It would have been night, blazed with arc light, when the prisoners arrived.

The audio guide gave a description and then played a sample of the soul-scraping noises prisoners would have heard as they pushed forward – the roar and grind of a diesel generator, shrill partisan music...

The dead, at least nine thousand, were exhumed in 1980. Despite tidy walkways and signposts, there is still a rising horror on a visit here. The audio guide plays descriptions, often in the faltering English of local voices, of how people were killed.

Prisoners were often bludgeoned to death to save on bullets. The crude weaponry, usually sharpened agricultural equipment, didn't kill effectively so the piled, injured bodies in the pits had DDT and lime poured on them to finish them off.

Signs beside grassed-over burial pits warned that rains often washed cloth, teeth and bone fragments on to the path. Within moments we saw a strip of faded cloth and a sliver of bone. Sophea's picked them up and put them on one of the flat stones marking the paths.

"These could be neighbours or my cousins. Dancers I watched dancing."

Notices explained what had been found in some of the hollows – headless corpses in one, mothers and children in another – there was a tree where babies had their heads dashed. Twisted-thread prayer bracelets were fastened to wooden guard rails.

I didn't know if it was suggestion but I was sure I could smell something bad around the burial pits.

"It's true." Sophea pointed to the red mud sliding from the edges of the grass into the walkways. "Like the small bones we find. The rains make the earth turn over and there is always something to come up from below, something that smells bad, like flesh."

In the night there had been heavy rain. It occurred to me that each breath could have microscopic fragments of all the bodies.

We went around what looked like a lake at the centre of restful woodland. Not a lake; the largest of the burial pits, believed to be full of bodies under the water. It had been decided to leave them to rest in peace. A pagoda had been built out over the water for the souls of whoever was there.

Looking for her words, I asked Sophea the crass question about how this place made her feel. As she began to answer she put her arm out to stop me in my tracks. A clump of Australian teenagers behind tumbled into me all making "What the...?" noises.

A thin snake was on the path in front of us.

"Green mamba." Sophea said.

An Australian gasped. "Deadliest snake in the world isn't it?"

The snake had disappeared into the undergrowth.

Sophea put her arm through mine and walked on. Australians were thanking her for saving their lives but she ignored them.

"Answering your question, I feel a mixture of emotions going around, sad and angry and sometimes afraid because all this happened in my childhood. If it comes once it can come again. Many Cambodians feel this. This is why we are quiet about Hun Sen."

We stopped for a while to look at the lake pagoda. I switched off the audio guide – although informative, there were moments when it became intrusive. Visitors could pick up flowers or incense to place around the high central stupa, containing seventeen layers of skulls, classified according to age, sex and type of injury. They had been cleaned and treated to preserve them. We walked around and around this high tower of bone. Sophea had seen it several times.

I don't like it. Why should these be here for show? They should be like the ones in the lake – left in peace, not for show."

We crossed the grounds to a small museum with Khmer Rouge uniforms, Ho Chi Minh sandals (made from tyres) and pictures of Phnom Penh after it was emptied of human beings. There were photographs of the leaders, maps and explanations of how the Khmer Rouge had happened. Although there was a great deal about Pol Pot, there seemed to be more about Duch, his chief torturer.

This sadistic, manipulative man designed all the horror to assuage Pol Pot's paranoid psychosis, making himself appear indispensable. When it was all over, Duch thought he could outsmart the world and make them pity him. After his capture he had been brought to the Killing Fields and started weeping, begging forgiveness.

"Look at his face." Sophea stared at photographs. "Even in the pictures of him old, his face is strong."

In a small theatre a film was showing. Sophea said she didn't mind going in. I still chose seats near the door.

"We can leave if you want."

She shook her head: "It's ok, I saw it before."

The film began with as soundtrack of howling wolves. Then, some grainy footage, in black and white, of the Khmer Rouge marching, of people digging something, more marching....What happened in the Seventies was outlined. There was footage of Duch, now a Christian convert, weeping and begging forgiveness. The preparation of the skulls in the stupa was explained. A very young, very English-sounding voice wished all the souls in the Killing Fields a place in paradise. This sentiment caused a few of the white people in the audience to make scoffing noises. Sophea sat in her very upright way, expressionless. Outside I asked her what she thought of Duch's conversion and weeping.

"I don't accept this sorry. If you are sorry you kill yourself."

Sophea showed me where her old house had been, now a street of flashy modern shops, then we drove past a primary school. Children in blue and white uniforms were coming out for the end of the day.

"I had the same uniform. I loved it so much."

Jack dropped Sophea outside her house and took me round the corner to my hotel. She'd spend time caring for her father, putting in the hours so her family didn't think it was unfair when she went travelling with me. And helped her to feel less guilt about it herself.

The doctor had been and said there was nothing to be done but keep her father comfortable. He could go in minutes, or hang on many weeks. Apparently it was her sister in law who had been grumbling about Sophea not pulling her weight.

"I do much more than her, much more. And they know I must go to Siem Reap to dance. And my brother wants you to tell our story. So we should go."

In my hotel I watched the aftermath of the Paris shootings. Piles of flowers, interviews – French passers-by defiant. Isis spreading, gathering recruits to kill the privileged Westerners. I took a shower to wash off the tiny dust of Cambodian dead that might be on my skin.

CHAPTER 12: PONCY WRITING

Two men with guns were summoning a third to take a look at me. I wasn't close, half-way across a park, but perhaps it wasn't the most sensible time to be taking pictures of the French Embassy. I wanted pictures because it figured so much in foreigners' stories of the Khmer Rouge. It's where they had gathered, allowing Cambodian friends and staff into the grounds. What had always puzzled me was the number of people in accounts of the siege, a thousand people at least. How big was this embassy? Looking at it, I was satisfied that the embassy and its grounds, now behind high white walls, covered quite an acreage.

The French embassy in Phnom Penh was a place to stand and worry at yourself, asking: "What would I have done?"

The Khmer Rouge, negotiating through French scholar, Francois Bizot, had insisted that all the Cambodians on the premises be handed over, or the foreigners on the premises would no longer be protected by diplomatic privilege. There was a flurry of fake passport making and pretend marriages between Cambodians and Westerners. It was the beginning of Pol Pot's regime but already it was clear that prison would be the least of the fates for Cambodians who had associated with Westerners.

The various ruses weren't enough to save all the Cambodians hiding out at the embassy. The last helicopter escapes had been made and now trucks came to take the remaining foreigners – a French, American, German, English assortment – to Thailand. Most of the Cambodians left behind were never seen again. The rare escapee like Dith Pran, subject of the film, The Killing Fields, had been left by colleagues to face certain death. The guilty search for Dith Prahn after the regime fell was very typical of how the West treated Cambodians: betrayal then guilt.

Meanwhile Cambodians endured and most of them quite liked the Westerners who'd returned to have fun, or a fulfilling lifestyle.

"The more of us there are here, the more they feel, well there's money to be made and help being dished out, why not? But a few Cambodians have told me the more of us there are the safer it is. If the country's full of Westerners, how can their government do something terrible? Not that Hun Sen doesn't make threats. Not that he'd let a few old white blokes and teenage backpackers get in his way. But it's a thought."

While Sophea rested, Will, a friend of a friend, was taking me on his designed for the eccentric tour of Phnom Penh. Will was in his early sixties, working part-time in tourism, married to a thirty-five-year-old Cambodian woman and blissfully happy. He'd obliged me by stopping near the French Embassy but, judging by the guards' reaction, we were too near.

I told Will that the French Embassy was making me wonder what I'd have done: save myself, or desert a friend? Big, amiable Will was more worried about the situation we were in at that moment.

"I really think we should be getting in the tuk tuk and moving on: those guards are still not liking the look of you."

When we were further away, Will, tones of north London rich in his voice, said he had been thinking about my question.

"The obvious answer is we don't know till we're in the situation, but you got to think, if you do some saving-your-skin thing, and you're basically an all right person, then it's going to be there the rest of your life. Especially if you're like the Killing Fields bloke and everybody knows. All you'll do is try to live it down. Better to be brave to save embarrassment later. Anyway, I wouldn't leave my wife behind. Wouldn't bloody dare!"

I said I hoped Cambodia was a tamer place these days and I wouldn't be spending any time in extreme situations having my courage tested.

"Not that tame." Will said. "I still think its edgy here, so I've made sure all the paperwork is rock solid for my wife and her daughter. I think I've adopted the girl a dozen times now, just to be sure."

Although we had hurried away from the Embassy, the remnants of French colonial times featured centrally in Will's tour for eccentrics. His system of travel was quite eccentric too. But ingenious. He had taken photographs of everywhere he wanted to go and would just hand these to tuk tuk drivers.

"They only know main sights, a lot of them can't read, or speak much English..."

He'd been here years. "You don't speak Khmer?"

"I'm trying, but I'm too old a dog really so learning it isn't going so well. All kinds of extra letters that we can't pronounce... I told the wife, you're younger, better you polish up your English. Obviously she ignores me, she's the stroppiest woman on earth. That's why I like her, I suppose. Always liked the stroppy female. A lot of Europeans come unstuck in the East. They think they've found some beautiful china doll and turns out they've got Wendy Deng... Not that I'm saying at all that my wife – look!"

Will pulled himself out of difficulty pointing to a woman at the roadside who had a push-cart glistening with fried beetles for sale. Planted in the middle of them was a sign that read: Photo One Dollar.

"Smart isn't it, I'll bet the sign gets her even more photos. Really, just the street life of Phnom Penh's enough entertainment in itself. Sometimes I have to drive in it, then it's no fun. Normally, though, I'll just take a tuk tuk and I never get bored with looking round at it all. I'm not one of these British ex-pats who says they'll never go home but I do love a place where people are living their lives outdoors."

The first stop on Will's eccentric tour was the Van Family Restaurant, with the yellowy-creamy, square build of French colonial architecture. Now behind decorative metal gates and high walls, the building had been constructed in the early twentieth century for the Indo China bank. In 1960 the wealthy Van family, Cambodians, had bought it for a family residence. Sensing that life might not continue to go well for rich people, the Vans had fled Cambodia in 1970 and didn't return until 2003. They bought their dilapidated former home back from the government and lovingly restored the colonnaded balconies, the patterned tiles, the carved wooden panelling... They still lived there but had turned most of the building into a high-end restaurant: all velvet-draped chairs and linen napkins folded into bird shapes. Small real birds hopped around the gardens and the traditional spirit house outside.

Spirit houses did look like little decorative bird houses. This one would be a Tevada, a home for the protective sprits of an individual family. Neak Ta were spirit houses that protected communities. On the platform of the housesfruit, flowers and incense were offered to the guardian spirits. The houses were from an animist belief system, predating and, in Cambodia and Laos, often intermingled with Buddhism. There were also spirit houses made for tourists to ship home for their gardens.

Another elegant French colonial building was the old post office, built in 1910 and refurbished in 2020. It retained many features from its last busy time, the 1960s, the best being the heavy rosewood desks to sit at and feel very grand at while writing a card.

We crossed the street and Will began a cheery exchange with an old lady as he bought bottles of water from her. She kept pointing and nodding at the elastic bandage around his wrist.

"When I was doing my photography round here, I slipped and fell over, got all dizzy like an old fool. She put ice on my wrist, got me a tuk tuk home...It helps, you know, because now they understand I'm harmless, not some developer. They hate developers around here."

There were over-thin men and a couple of women with babies sitting on the stone steps to the building that Will ushered me into. This was the dilapidated Hotel Margolis, now home to thirty nervous squatter families. They'd lived for decades in what had once been a very grand French hotel. Architectural rescue might mean they'd lose their homes along the paint-peeling corridors, where they cooked their meals and boiled big kettles for washing the clothes strung along the tiled balconies.

"A lot of the people who came back to Phnom Penh after the Khmer Rouge squatted buildings in this area because it's near the bridge out of town. It took people a long time to feel safe. And the people in here might be on the move again soon. Doubtful anyone will care what happens to them. Look at it, it's taking up a whole city block in an area developers think can get very trendy."

A famous former resident had been Andre Malraux, locked up in 1923 for stealing treasures from Banteay Srei. Malraux had argued that the French government were also appropriating statues and treasure for museums but Malraux and his band of adventurers clearly intended to sell what they'd taken. The main persecutor of Malraux had been Georges Groslier, French colonial functionary, archaeologist and writer. Groslier admired Khmer culture and wanted to leave it in its place. With the Cambodian royal family's co-operation, he helped set up the National Museum. He also wrote extensively about the ballet dancers at King Norodom's court, finding them, in the end, very sad figures. In his 1912 book Cambodian Dancers he thought the art form was going to decline. A sensitive and honourable man, Groslier was killed under Japanese interrogation in Siem Reap, 1945.

After his five-star imprisonment in the Hotel Margolis, Malraux was expelled from Cambodia. He went on to become a celebrated novelist and French Minister of Culture in De Gaulle's government. It seemed the French couldn't help being charmed by roguish Malraux. And he would probably have fitted right in to modern Cambodia.

We passed the former police headquarters, again once an elegant piece of French architecture, now looking very seedy. It was at the centre of a dispute between conservationists and the owner, who, Will suspected, was simply letting the dispute run on until his price rocketed.

The police headquarters had earned the owner some income, as it had been the setting for Gerard Depardieu's bar in the 2002 Matt Dillon film, City Of Ghosts. Although the film's plot was a little disappointing, it captured something about Cambodia today. The local corruption and the resident Europeans finding a place where they could live a cheap, hedonistic life, some of it harmless and doped-up silly. Some of it darker.

Although it was mid-morning, a street we drove along had a couple of local girls in short skirts hanging around shop-fronts. The Khmer term for prostitutes was srei khouch – broken girls.

"A lot of the ones you see on the streets are Vietnamese. Their culture got corrupted earlier. Cambodians are more conservative, they'd rather die."

I wondered if this was Will's wife's opinion, defensive about her people but other foreigners had made the same observation. It was a conservatism that meant a raped woman was the one disgraced in the community, not the rapist. He would usually get off with a fine; the police preferred this, so they could take a cut.

Will went on: "But girls get tricked into it, kidnapped into it. What you see on the streets isn't the problem. It's what happens indoors. Phnom Penh's terrible for paedophiles but they prefer the coastal resorts, like Sihanoukville. Much more lawless down there. They say it started going bad down there with the Russian soldiers on R and R, you know, who came in with the Communist Vietnamese, but the real child abuse here, for money or just in families, that's all behind closed doors." He smiled apologetically. "I know my wife's twenty years younger than me but we've only been married a year; she's a grown-up. More grown up than I am."

Will took me on foot through what he pronounced: "a really dodgy part of town, probably all right in the daylight, probably."

I wasn't sure how much of this was Will's showmanship and how much was true but the tuk tuk driver did look very relieved when told to meet us at the other end of the block. And as we passed, people stopped what they were doing to stare. Or they were junkies doing nothing, so staring at us made their morning busy?

When I mentioned the staring, Will laughed.

"Probably surprised to see a middle-aged white bloke with a white woman."

By coincidence, we were walking past what was known as The White Building, in rather grandly named, for the current state of it, Sotirous Boulevard.

In the 1960s, one of playboy King Sihanouk's interests was architecture. He wanted Phnom Penh to incorporate modernist use of shape and form and commissioned Cambodian architect, Vann Molyvann, to build a sports stadium, a national theatre... A long list of structures, many now in danger of collapse.

Van Molyvann's White Building was intended as prestigious housing, mirrored in the Grey Building opposite. Today, under all the dilapidation, boarded balconies, washing lines and carrier-bag-covered windows, the Corbusier-influenced, criss-crossing, light use of concrete, is still visible enough to show this was a great building.

"Are you going to find it hard to write about architecture without sounding poncy?"

Will was right. I am. But Vann Molyvann's creations around Cambodia are refreshing after all those gilt, curly roofs, and high, characterless glass towers. The wary residents we walked past were washing babies; selling food or cheap clothing; playing chess in teahouses or drowsing beside crates of roosters for the evening's cockfighting. Although the area had a rough reputation, it was actually very mixed. There were prostitutes, junkies and gangs but there were also artists, musicians and working families. In 2015 the government served an eviction order on all of them: whether the White Building was restored or demolished, the current tenants were to be pushed out.

Built to house 1400 people, the White Building currently had at least 2300 residents. There were some collapsed stairways, and creepers clawed through walls. The ramshackle changes, such as cementing in balconies, had spoilt some of the look of the building and officials claimed they had added weight, making the structure unsafe.

The open concrete staircases of the buildings, going up four storeys, where children dangled their feet, watching the foreigners pass; or where a few protest flags drooped and teenagers played radios, were full of an outdoor life that gave the district a feel of something from a J.G. Ballard story crossed with French Quarter New Orleans. I didn't go at night – Sophea rolled her eyes and tutted when I told her I'd been there at all, but I felt I'd missed out by being such a coward.

Next, Will and I meandered the narrow alleys of old Chinatown, where shirtless men squatted in doorways playing cards, and trails of flip-flops led into every house. Perhaps the shirtless men were waiting for one of the many services offered at the long laundry building, each service deserving its own explanatory sign – 24 hour, 3 hour, Special Plan, Fast Plan, Super Plan, Extra Plan...

Staggering toward us, a very thin shirtless man, low on teeth, offered to show us: "French church, Catholic!"

Will sighed to me that he did know where it was but he didn't like to hurt the man's feelings. Besides, the man was oozing alcohol fumes from every pore. Who knew how his mood could turn if he was refused?

People had built homes inside the 1910 French church, little plasterboard huts under the high, vaulted roof. There had been five Catholic churches in Phnom Penh in 1975 but only this one survived.

The drunk man had an explanation: "This morgue for Pol Pot people." He made a throat-cutting gesture. "Put dead people."

He made the gesture again, grinning.

A thick-walled extensive building with small windows; turning it into a morgue made sense.

Out in the sunshine, drunk man lead us to the old presbytery, now rented to several Chinese families. Then he pointed back, his piece de resistance: an old stone cross on the church roof.

"See, logo of Catholic Church! Logo of Jesus!"

Will's tour rounded off with lunch on the terrace of the Foreign Correspondents' Club, overlooking the river. There was old-world elegance and a sense of history from photographs of cosmopolitan 1960s Phnom Penh around the walls. These days, the club was largely a genteel tourist attraction.

Will was going to the coast in a few weeks.

"It's supposed to be a family holiday in Kep, that's the nice resort, but happy to show you and Sophea the dodgy parts of Sihanoukville if you want to catch a ride."
I hoped we could take him up on his offer but I had no idea what was going on with Sophea today, let alone how she would be in a few weeks' time.

Later on, Sophea came to my hotel with Jack. She looked well, if a little tired; elegant in white and pink, her sunglasses on her head. All fine, except at the open neck of her blouse I could clearly see two long red scratches below each collarbone.
"You hurt yourself?"
"No no. My stomach is very bad. This is a traditional Cambodian cure. I cut and put in herbs. It's a good cure."
I didn't think it was good at all. Wasn't this more like self-harming? And why hadn't she worn something to cover the slashes in her skin?
Several times I'd told her to rest, told her she didn't have to travel with me if she was worried about her father. Of course I wanted her to come with me but there was an increasing listlessness about her that made me feel she was being polite, saving face. And now these cuts? Like a cry for help.
Jack trundled us out to look at her old dance and art school, the Royal University of Fine Arts. It was nicknamed the red school, after its crimson painted walls. Sophea spoke to a gatekeeper.
"He says the woman I am looking for is on tour with a group. He says if we want to look inside we must make an appointment."
"Can't we do that?"
"I will telephone them tomorrow. Sorry, I thought my friend would be here. Sorry, I waste your time."
I assured her it didn't matter; we'd go another day. I really didn't want to be the cause of more skin-slashing.
We ended the day at the National Museum. Briefly, Sophea rallied, greeting many of the guides and guards.
"My friends. Same school. I lived around here such a long time. They ask after my father. There are many wall writings in English Annie, sorry , I can't explain too much, I am tired. You want an audio guide?"
I took one so she wouldn't feel obliged to speak to me. It was a little bit old-fashioned school history class: dates and names melting into dull chaos. The museum was a beautiful place around an open courtyard, dotted about with statues and carvings of gods and dancers. There were jasmine scents, bowls of white chrysanthemum, lotus ponds and Buddhas – elegance I hardly dared appreciate once I registered the mood Sophea had snapped into.
A group of French people came past, laughing.
Sophea glared at them: "Oh fine to be laughing, meanwhile in Paris..."

They looked at her but seemed at a loss what to say to this small, angry woman. They walked away, clutching each other.
At least they couldn't hear her when she added: "They should keep quiet when they are bombed. But no, I see them on television, 'We are great, we are French, bomb us, we don't care.' Really they are silly."
She said this making a chest-puffed, wide-armed gesture that I suspected was more an imitation of Henri than the French in general.
I kept quiet, in case she started on the British.
"I think I will go home now, I am feeling too sick. You can stay. Look at more things, take some coffee, I really can't help you."

She was a gush of desperate apologies when she rang later. She didn't want to waste my time, we would travel, I could interview her brother, the dance teacher...
I felt exhausted with her and her temperament. Perhaps I would leave her in peace, cut my losses, just have a holiday and go home soon.
I went out with Will to watch the sunset from an outdoor cocktail bar, nineteen floors up: lychee martinis a speciality. Looking across the whole city, I felt a rush of happy disbelief. Six months ago it looked as though I'd not be travelling again, ever. Getting back to Cambodia and finishing this book for Sophea had been powerful among driving thoughts during treatment. Sophea was down there somewhere, washing her father's sheets in a bucket.

CHAPTER 13: DON'T FIGHT THE MONKEYS

The dollar I gave to the bony woman imploring at the top of the steps seemed to set off a wail of complaint.

Sophea spoke sharply to the woman, then beamed a smile at me.

"She says it is not enough. She says she is dying, I tell her we are all dying, especially you."

Finding this something to laugh heartily about, Sophea moved on up the temple steps.

I didn't mind. If finding my illness hilarious made Sophea feel better, so be it.

I felt better than I'd felt in months. I'd climbed up a very long flight of steps, admittedly by what was called the Lady Steps, the more staggered, easy route through the Udong temple complex, and I felt fine. On the other hand, Sophea, so convinced my demise was imminent she might as well chivvy me along with jokes about it, had found the climb a struggle.

After sitting on a low wall to catch her breath, she explained that the piled timber and stones outside the temple we'd reached were from an older temple that had been bombed by the Americans. She touched one of the wooden remnants.

"Look, this has gold-leaf paint on it but it is being eaten by termites."

As an old monk appeared at the door to the new temple, she seemed to tell him off. He both nodded and shook his head at once as he answered her.

"He says they want to put the old temple pieces in a glass box to display, but it's too expensive. I tell him hurry up or there will be nothing left."

Inside, the monk pointed out a frieze of bright-coloured paintings depicting the life of Buddha. He talked a while to Sophea in Khmer, then pointed to a bowl in the centre of the room.

"For finishing the temple." Sophea said, as she dropping in some riel as a donation. "He wanted to know if I would mind him asking you, which is respectful, no? I think a dollar at least."

As we walked out to attempt the next section of the climb, Sophea said: "He says the old temple was destroyed by the Khmer Rouge. They did kill a lot of people and monks here. But many people, Phnom Penh people, say the temple was already destroyed by American bombs. I think it is both. Americans first then, the Khmer Rouge want to spoil it more."

Udong was the site of an old capital; the name means Victorious, although it was where the kings retreated to in the years of constant attack and defeat by Siam in the seventeenth century. The blown-up temple, Vihear Preah Ath Roes, had been constructed in 1911 by King Sisowath. In every guide and history book, I could only find reports that it was destroyed by the Khmer Rouge in 1977. But modern history in Cambodia was muddy. Verbal accounts was all there had been for years: no newspapers, no recordings of what happened at Udong... It was certain that monks and local residents were murdered by the Khmer Rouge when they came here; a memorial on the other side of the mountain told of a hundred mass graves, containing a dozen corpses each, and buried instruments of torture. Near these, there was a pavilion of paintings, mainly by an artist called Vann Nath, who made it his life's work to depict the horrors he'd seen the Khmer Rouge commit.

We climbed, passing grand shrines and small thatched-roof shrines, up through trees with glimpses of fields flung flat and far to the horizon. We came to a sweet-faced woman who pointed us to sticks of incense planted around a hole in the rock. A magic place. Around the magic hole were plates and bowls with local notes in them, held in place with stones. This was an old, old system of benevolence. If you were in need you would 'borrow a plate', to buy food to put on it. You would pray as you took it, making a promise to return the plate and money by a certain date. A sort of mystical credit union. If you didn't keep your promise, you could never come back – spiritual credit rating spoilt.

I made a donation that would be split between the guardian woman and the plates to be borrowed.

"You can pray for something now." Sophea said. "Tell the hole in the rock. Doesn't have to be out loud. Just in your mind."

I asked for good health. The air was thick with incense and the smoke of scented wood in a brazier by the plates. I felt a real sense of well-being.

This place was part of something ancient, far older than Buddhism.... Perhaps the sense of well-being came from something in the smoke other than scent. It was hot, it was high. I might be too. Time to get away from the fire and take a brisk breath of fresh air..

At the highest point, the views stretched far across an uncannily level plain. Over to the right was the gold-roofed compound of a monastery and meditation centre. Near this were squares of water, for growing Lotus flowers.

Behind us was the gigantic white memorial to King Movivong (1927-41). A few flights further down was a modern temple believed to contain a sacred relic: an eyebrow hair of the Buddha.

"They say it is there. I think was lost in the war." Sophea said forlornly.

She was tired now and even if I went into some sort of slapstick routine about my imminent demise, her mood wasn't going to improve until she was down on the ground among food stalls.

First we had to negotiate a part of the steps down that were prowled with macaque monkeys. I don't know if the people we'd just passed going up had provoked them but they were definitely in a mood as they surrounded our feet. Then one put up its little hands and snatched Sophea's water bottle.

"Go!" she shrieked.

We cantered down the steps, hissing monkeys coming after us. I wasn't going to take this. I stopped, turned, stamped my feet, shooing at them. They hissed and circled me.

I stamped harder and, ridiculously, shouted: "Want a fight, do you?"

This did give them pause.

From much further down the steps, Sophea pleaded:

"Stop it, Annie, don't fight the monkeys!"

This did seem to be wisest. I was in Planet of the Small Grey Apes. They were all looking at me and moving closer, except the one struggling to open the water bottle. I ran to join Sophea and the monkeys came after me. Then they stopped. As if one had said: "Leave it, she's not worth it."

Perhaps the one who hit me in the back of the legs when he threw the water bottle after me.

"Don't pick it up," Sophea said. "It has monkey spit."

As I'd hoped, Sophea was happy when we sat down on a bamboo platform in one of many shelters by the market at the foot of the mountain. We could order food here.

It was quiet today, Monday, but during the weekend people from Phnom Penh came out here to picnic, evidenced by the litter we'd seen dumped along the approach roads. The only tuk tuk parked by the empty shelters was Jack's.

"I can invite him to join us, yes? He must be hungry."

I felt ashamed I hadn't thought of it. Then again, if I was ever in some flush situation in London and asked a cab to wait for me outside a restaurant, would I also invite them in for the meal? I tried to imagine what Jack's fare would be if his tuk tuk had a meter. Forty-one kilometres, both ways, with three hours' waiting time....? A London cab meter would probably explode. Luckily, Jack would be delighted with twenty dollars.

A woman brought us roast chicken, rice, soups, sauces and various vegetables that made a feast far too much even for Sophea. Jack asked me if he could take the left-overs home for his children; he had nine. We found him a carrier bag while a son belonging to the stall was loading the tuk tuk with a pumpkin, a water melon... Then, as if it was some sort of comedy sketch about how much would fit in a tuk tuk, another boy brought a bananaplant, two plantain stems, a sack of banana leaves, two fat marrows.... This was all to make traditional healing foods and poultices for Sophea's father. I asked her how she knew these things.

"When I went to study in the pagoda I learnt meditation and I learnt these things. Also, everyone in Cambodia used to know, because we had no doctors."

Jack nodded. "Soon, go..." He lost his English.

Sophea translated: "He says young people who are poor don't learn this, they want only Western medicine they can't afford. So they get nothing and die."

Cramming ourselves into what now looked more like a mobile market garden than a tuk tuk, I was very glad Sophea had brought a pack of face masks; the dust and pollution were bad enough for anyone, let alone someone a bit lung ropey.

Jack had told me he was hoping to hear from a friend who was opening a restaurant. He could work there and maybe only tuk tuk drive once in a while. I willed this to happen for him because he not only had to endure the pollution, the bone-rattling noise and the stress of just holding the machine on the potholed roads – there were his fellow road-users, driving like babies, thundering blindly between lanes, backing out of nowhere, plunging right in from side roads.... Meanwhile Jack stoically puttered on, not missing an opportunity to overtake and never failing to swerve us out of a near-death moment.

I had only been a passenger in the long tuk tuk drive but back at the hotel, before six, I fell asleep in my clothes. I woke up again in the very small hours when a text from Sophea beeped: "My father is going. Come at nine."

At nine, Sophea was taking breakfast at the back of the restaurant with a group of very old, shaven-headed ladies.

"These are friends of my family, from the pagoda."

The ladies bowed and smiled at me. One stood up and began fiddling with the radio to find music Sophea's father would like. Up above I could see the top of his head, very still.

"He will not eat or drink now. I gave all we buy yesterday to the pagoda because my father will go soon. I am sorry, Annie, but I must do everything for him because I did not do it for my mother."

Chenda arrived with Sophea's four-year-old niece, Chantou. They sat with me. Sann brought me rice and soup.

"Later, Annie, you can help if you like, but eat now, everyone else has eaten."

The rice was plain, the soup thin and bland, just the way I liked it; nothing to be afraid of. I found Cambodian food like very harsh Thai food. There was

a big difference between the food Cambodians ate at home and the milder, tidier versions of it served in restaurants where Europeans ate.
With all eyes on me, I knew it would be a dreadful thing not to clear my plates. I was managing. Sophea told me to come upstairs when I'd done.
She wanted to perform a ceremony for her father, but we would still go to Siem Reap the next day. She needed to dance; she needed the money.
As I walked up to the father's room, Chantou yelled something after me. To my surprise, everyone at the deathbed was smiling when I walked in.
"Oh Annie, you will laugh." Sophea giggled. "My niece shouts to her mother: 'This one didn't pay! Give this one the bill!'"
They were all laughing but I felt a bit embarrassed. "Well she's right, I never pay."
"Family." Sann, said, pointing to me.
Sophea smiled at me. "Of course, it is just funny. My niece is too clever."
Meanwhile Sophea's thin, elegant father lay breathing shallowly, his eyes closed. But there was the slightest of smiles; he was following the joke.
The mood changed to something far more sombre and focused as a half dozen monks came in. Sophea and Sann greeted them, then went downstairs, leaving me as a puzzle in the corner for the monks. The monks didn't pray; they just sat whispering to each other, watched in awe by the old ladies. Then the old ladies sprang into action. They put metal bowls, like wide chalices, in front of each monk. Sann reappeared with an envelope for each bowl. Money, I supposed. Sophea and Chenda brought in soft drinks; brand new orange umbrellas and yellow cellophane-wrapped baskets containing candles and incense sticks. Sophea put more envelopes in bowls. The monks did nothing, sat smugly taking the piling of gifts around them as their due. In my initial opinion.
I was wrong to think that. Sophea's father was a devout man, who had not been allowed to pray for at least five years of his life. These new monks, replacing the murdered ones, were a blessing to him and he would want them honoured.
The monks started chanting, one flicking scented water with a flower stem. All heads bowed. Chantou jumped into the room, shouting. I wondered what she thought I'd done this time. Chenda got to her feet.
Sophea whispered to me: "Annie, can you help, so that my sister in law is not distracted?"
Outside, Chenda summoned Jack who was dozing under the trees across the road. Our destination was a vast modern shopping mall, where we filled a trolley with soft drinks and biscuits. As Chantou was getting bored with the expedition, I bought her a plastic toy. I told her she could play with it as we walked along but she scowled at me and put it in the trolley. She was definitely headed for a career in law enforcement and had me pegged as the wrong sort.

When we delivered the groceries and Chantou back to the house, Sophea told me the prayers were said, we could go for a walk by the river if I liked. She'd planned to show me a place where Buddhas where made but just wasn't in the mood.

A walk was fine. I had an appointment for dinner with Will and his family. Will had included Sophea in the invitation. The dinner was on a river barge, something I knew Sophea wanted to experience but she'd wistfully declined.

"I am not in the mood for people I don't know."

It was understandable, so we strolled beside the water, feeling the light breeze through the city fug.

"I walk by the river by myself in the evening many times, to get out the poison in my head."

Sophea paused, I could tell she had more to say.

"Maybe I will only stay two days in Siem Reap, so you will have to go to the other places without me. I will arrange everything with Ponleak, you won't be lost. I am so sorry."

It was disappointing but of course she had to come back to her father as soon as she could.

She went home to rest. As I was halfway up the stairs to my hotel room, I had a text. Sophea's father was dead.

In the morning, I arrived to offer my condolences, to see what I could do to help. No one met my eye. Sophea, I knew, had seen me but left me standing there as she helped her sister-in-law lay mats on the cafe floor. I felt like some tourist who'd stumbled in.

"I'm so sorry, if there is anything I can do...."

No one acknowledged me. I'd obviously made a huge mistake. No one wanted or needed me there.

Sophea turned, snapping: "Annie, I am too busy."

"Of course."

I left feeling, inappropriately, a little hurt.

I headed for the internet cafe with Jack. As well as arranging some meetings in Siem Reap, I emailed home and played around on Facebook, a culture where I knew what to do.

In the evening, Sophea called, apologising.

"I have arranged everything for you with Ponleak and if you come in the morning I will give you the bus ticket. Jack knows where to take you. Everyone will help you."

At the front of the house was a big marquee festooned with black and white streamers. Inside, the tables had white cloths, and there were monks everywhere. A garlanded portrait of Sophea's handsome father in middle age was the focus of the room. The scruffy fast-food cafe of yesterday was transformed for the funeral. I had an envelope with a hundred dollar gift for Sophea and was about to ask the shaven-headed woman approaching me where she to find her, when I realised it was Sophea. Her head was completely shaved, eyebrows gone. She wore a chin-high white blouse and long black skirt. Everyone was dressed in white and the women from the family had their heads shaved.

Upstairs where his father had lain, Sann was on his knees, rocking to and fro. His hands were up to his face, as shocked as if he'd just discovered the corpse. Sophea seemed serene; perhaps now all the caring and watching her father suffer was over, there was some relief.

She had a nephew fetch my bus ticket and she hugged me a great deal, getting a little tearful, telling me she would pray for my health.

A Land Cruiser packed with monks had arrived. I could see Sophea wanted to welcome them.

"I'll see you in a week, or when you're ready." I said.

More people were arriving dressed in white – friends, neighbours – this had been a quietly significant man. He'd done no harm and he'd endured.

CHAPTER 14: FLOAT LIKE A BUTTERFLY

"If I no here, they no washing."

Ponleak combed out Maly's wet hair. He called after his son, Vibol, who was giggling and disappearing up the stairs wearing only underpants.

That the house had a second floor, and that the purpose of Ponleak's chasing them around to wash and change from village school civvies to town school blue and white uniforms, showed how hard he'd worked.

"Next year, town school all day."

He'd also learnt more English. Apparently, when they were involved in refurbishment work on the little guesthouse, Kiri had practised with him.

Ponleak fastened Maly's hair into elastics and leapt after Vibol to get him into the crisp school clothes that, for a family like Ponleak's, cost a fortune. His wife was still away in Thailand. On a couch in the corner of this main room Ponleak's mother was watching television. She did basic housekeeping and babysitting but she wasn't up to the speed of movement required for Ponleak's gleefully energetic children when they needed to be organised. It was good to see that the children were healthy; while I'd been away, Maly had scarlet fever, though. Recovered. Everyone's held breath exhaled. Although he was as dusty and scruffy as ever, Ponleak's slog for his family was paying off.

Out on a porch, cluttered with a pink scooter, two bicycles, tubs of flowers and pieces of building material, I noticed some concrete blocks holding a bar bell. A metal rod through two round stones – Flintstones-style gym equipment.

Ponleak saw me looking at it.

"For exercise, "he said.

He pointed to wooden cages with colourful tweeting birds festooning the porch: "For singing."

Then he laughed, pointing to the tuk tuk parked in the road: "For going."
Enough of affably humouring my nosiness, it was time to herd the children into the tuk tuk – there were only two of them but it did seem like herding. Maly went to sit with her grandmother, Vibol skittered back upstairs.
Ponleak took off his hat and rubbed his head. "Each day."
He said something sharp in Khmer. Maly smiled sweetly at him and didn't move. I heard Vibol laughing.
In the end, my camera lured them and we set out, with them making poses and faces.

Then Vibol started jumping around, getting up on the seat and trying some terrifying gymnastics. I stuck my leg out to make a barrier but it probably wouldn't have been effective enough to save Ponleak's precious cargo if he'd hit a pothole at that moment. I'd barely settled Vibol back to sitting in some mildly less death-defying fashion when we pulled up at the school. I was relieved to wave them off and not to have to tell Ponleak I'd let his son bounce head-first into the traffic. Especially as Ponleak had taken such care shepherding me back in to Siem Reap.
First he had called to check I was on the ten o'clock bus. Good, he'd be at the other end to meet me in five hours. About half-way, the bus stopped. I did what Sophea had warned me to do – get out and run into the service station to get to the toilets first. This meant I had time to get outside and stroll around a while in the fairly fresh air and at this moment, by what I thought was astonishing coincidence, Ponleak rang. But I suppose he knew roughly what time the bus hit the half-way point. I told him I would call when we were coming in to Siem Reap.
"Ok. Bong Sophea say looking outside after now."
I knew what he meant. The countryside around this stopping place of Kampong Thom was where she'd been marched to as a child.
It didn't appear different to the countryside I'd just been passing: flat, rice-producing land, with rare hillocks of woodland, suggesting a landscape that had been changed for the fanatical rice growing of the late seventies; or by the lucrative present-day logging of valuable hardwoods. A great deal of rural Cambodia looked repetitive and bleak. Perhaps knowledge of the repeated brutality that had occurred out here tainted the picture.
Our young driver took the minibus at an astonishing pace along a road that was, at least for half of it, only red dirt. Skilled as he was, the driver was tense and muttering the whole way. I wondered what the human burn-out rate was on the Phnom Penh to Siem Reap journey?
People at the roadsides were thrashing and bashing, fishing and hauling, mending, pulling, digging – and in the blistering midday heat they were filling in holes in the tarmac manually. Then I saw some European on an equipment-laden mountain bike, cycling Indochina for fun, for a challenge

and thought I'd like to shove him. I immediately saw my hypocrisy. And how did I know the cyclist wasn't a charity doctor taking medical supplies to a remote village or some such? What help was I?

I hadn't stayed in Phnom Penh for the funeral because it hadn't felt right to be there. For the umpteenth time I wondered if I'd misread the situation. I should be there for Sophea. But I wasn't even a friend. I was someone who'd be there noting her grief, thinking of ways to describe the funeral guests and the rituals.

On the day of her father's death, this extraordinarily courteous woman hadn't been able to even speak to me for ten minutes. And her brother's silent rocking anguish was pulling the air apart, like screaming. No. I shouldn't be there to witness any more.

At the Siem Reap bus-stop there was a het-up clamour of motos and tuk tuks for hire. I was very relieved to see Ponleak skidding in to the parking bay. At first he made the polite formal bow but I thought, to hell with it, and hugged him. He wasn't shocked, hugged me back and kept looking over his shoulder to grin at me on the drive to the guesthouse.

The guesthouse had changed.

"For Japanese." Kiri explained, showing me where the clean lines of Japanese-style wooden seating and low tables had replaced half the trees full of Kiri-bothering night creatures. The other half of the yard still had high tables and hammocks swinging from trees, along with streamers of fairy lights. The guests at the tables did all seem to be Japanese, perversely ignoring the seating area constructed for their culture – the only person I ever saw use it was Kiri, when he took a rare nap.

The laid-back Japanese hippy owner had spotted a good thing in Kiri and made him general manager, as well as maintenance man, driver... In return Kiri seemed to have become fairly fluent in Japanese. In any other life, Kiri would be on at least a hundred thousand a year, not seventy dollars a month – his pay rise under the new regime. Last year it had been sixty.

I could tell by the worried expression passing Kiri's face that Ponleak was explaining why I'd been away so long. I lifted my own bags from reception to my room along the corridor to show them I wasn't going to be a medical emergency.

"No, No." Ponleak said, taking command of the bags.

"All decorated."

Kiri waved at the whitewashed walls and new floor tiles.

"And has window."

I'd have preferred one of the wood-panelled rooms upstairs but perhaps the bland look of this was supposed to be more to a Westerner's taste.

Kiri then had to sprint back to the entrance; a small uproar was starting in the lane. It must have been a terrible choice for Kiri: he still hadn't extracted all my gossip – where was Bong Sophea, my husband etc... But in the lane, a Frenchman from the guesthouse opposite was screaming about a late pick-up by the Battambang bus, he wanted his money back, he demanded his six dollars immediately, refusing to understand Kiri's explanation that if the bus had a lot of people to collect before setting off.... The Frenchman was still screaming when the bus arrived.

As Kiri came back, grinning broadly, it was clear he felt he'd made the better choice of unusual incident. A screaming Frenchman? Hilarious. But he was gone now. I could be around for weeks yet; plenty of time to make a fool of myself.

Last time I was here, an American had been swearing and shouting about a broken shower. Holding silent through the man's continued yelling about how long the room maid had taken to summon competent help, Kiri had fixed the shower quickly, courteously – but then rushed to the lane to regale his mates with the tale, mimicking arm waving and stamping.

Not having the force of personality to get things done without raising your voice was a shaming thing in a man. It was also a way to be unpopular in a country where shouting was usually done by men in uniform, with guns. Also in a country where a poor person like Kiri had an everyday struggle, yelling about a bus being twenty minutes late, or not having a shower at the exact moment you wanted it, well it was just laughable.

The down side about sharing a guest house with young Japanese was that they all smoked like 1950s film stars; the up side was they were as quiet as slippered mice. I hadn't heard most of them go off for the sunrise tour in tuk tuks with drivers, including Ponleak. When they returned at eleven they took to their beds but Ponleak took a soda, chatted with me about my plans and then we headed for his village.

I'd been thinking I needed to go somewhere contemplative. The next few days were full of meetings and expeditions with people, so just a little thinking space seemed useful. I'd texted Sophea to tell her I was fine, she needn't get in touch until she felt like it.

"Quiet place." I'd said to Ponleak and after dealing with his wash-resistant children, he took me on the long drive out to Kompong Pluk, a village built on stilts soaring as high as cathedrals, most around seven metres above the water. When Tonle Sap river flooded, the waters could come much closer to these houses and walkways of bamboo and planks. Sometimes the water reached them. The dwellings went up level after level, so that there was always somewhere to escape.

I watched a toddler negotiating a very long, very thin wooden ladder, far, far above me, as if he was just on a playground climbing frame. I couldn't stop watching but I didn't see the end of his journey as he had so far to go. Presumably he was fine; nobody rushed to stop his precarious-looking descent because it was nothing, it was where he lived.

I was moving quickly, on a motorboat meant for a dozen tourists but as it was the quiet season there was only me, and a man the driver introduced, a little apologetically, as: "my uncle". Uncle reeked of stale urine, sweat and alcohol and had just a triptych of teeth. I wondered how someone lost all their back teeth and kept the front three in such perfect order but felt involving myself in conversation with uncle might go very wrong. After a grin and a bow, uncle sat up front and didn't bother me with so much as a glance. With a gut thump of shame I registered that uncle was about sixty years old. How something so odd had happened to his teeth could be a horrible story. One that meant the whole family understood why he drank all day.

The boat trips were touristy but the majority of water activity was people living their lives: fishing; keeping pigs in floating sties; mending nets; ferrying logs, tractor parts and old ladies with bundles, or young women with babies; people were building new stilt houses or repairing old ones – the water was dense with goings on and different kinds of craft.

We passed a stilt pagoda where people in white were gathered. I knew this now: a funeral. Somewhere near the pagoda, we dropped off uncle, then the boat puttered out into the main Tonle Sap lake, as blowy and wide open as heading out to sea. I told myself the boat driver went out here several times a day but I wasn't unhappy when we turned back for calmer, more crowded waters.

We pulled in to a stilted tourist restaurant and transit point for transfer to a dugout canoe; the best mode of transport for exploring a submerged forest.

I knew I looked Michelin Man foolish once I was strapped into a fat lifejacket and then my backpack was bundled on top of this. As I stepped in, the teenage girl with the canoe told me:

"I live here all my eighteen years and never get attack by crocodile."

Oh. The boat was the size of a dressing table drawer and there were crocodiles? I was already assuming I'd meet an unseemly end by tipping over backwards into the murky flood water but now I'd be eaten as well...

The girl paddled further into the trees and the peace of it stilled down any alarmed thoughts. Occasionally, other women paddled up, trying to sell me snacks and cold drinks but when they went away there was a very quiet, magical strangeness to meandering a drowned forest. The paddle, this side, that side, barely making a sound in the water.

A brown and orange butterfly, the size of a sparrow, landed on my arm and sat there a gentle, bewildered moment. I tried to keep very still but it realised my blue shirt wasn't what it had been hoping for and flipped away.

It didn't mean anything. But I felt it should.

"My friend! My friend!" Ponleak slowed down.
He was pointing ahead to a line of young men in sports gear jogging along the roadside. They stopped and greeted Ponleak very respectfully .
"Champion," one told me.
"Champion?"
Ponleak put up his fists and made a pummelling gesture. "Boxing." He dropped his fists. "Finish now."
He drove on, waving and shouting encouragement to his friends. Back at the guesthouse I could ask more.
"Is true." Kiri said when Ponleak asked him to explain his boxing career. "Champion for all this region of Cambodia."
Then Kiri told me Ponleak's On the Waterfront saga of how boxing sometimes functioned in South East Asia.
A lot of it was controlled by gangsters from the Philippines and, as Ponleak rose up the ranks, he was flown to Manila for a championship match. All paid for, all very exciting. But he was told to take a dive. Ponleak wouldn't. The gangsters gave him only fifty dollars of the five hundred dollar prize money and told him never to fight again or he'd find himself at the bottom of the Tonle Sap. Ponleak used the money as a deposit on the tuk tuk, found a nice wife and didn't regret a minute of it.
"Respect for him." Kiri patted a bashful Ponleak on the back. "I box also but not good like Ponleak."
I thought about the Flintstones barbells outside his house.
"You still train?" I mimed weightlifting. To Kiri's amusement.
Ponleak pointed to his forehead. "If I get angry."
Then he demonstrated lifting barbells very quickly. "One, two, twenty and finish."
He slumped, demonstrating a calmed mind.
"There is boxing Siem Reap Wednesday, Ponleak can take you."
"Really?"
Ponleak shrugged. "Looking, no problem."
Kiri nodded, satisfied, then charged toward the lane, hissing and stamping his feet.
He came back shaking his head. "Is cat."
"But you cut the trees."
"Same cat monkey lizard coming, make me crazy."
"Maybe you should shoot them?"
Kiri liked this and went out again to tell the drivers in the lane what a good line he'd heard.

There were crowds, flashing signs and eight different kinds of music playing from the bars and restaurants; all of these had someone outside punting for trade. The boxing show was pushing hard, with two microscopically dressed girls handing out leaflets. If Ponleak and Kiri hadn't already warned me the show was going to be aimed at tourists, the blare of the lights, music and glossy promotion girls made me suspect this wasn't a seedy, exciting world of illicit gambling and gangsters threatening to drown people. This was boxing that Ponleak thought suitable for a lady. And risk-free for himself.

As Ponleak and a ridiculously young policeman attempted to make space for the tuk tuk among the ill-parked vehicles in front of the building, I saw that Sophea was ringing me. There wasn't any quiet place to retreat to, so I had to shout questions, finger in one ear, about how she was coping with her bereavement.

"We do the cremation, many monks, many people. It made me pleased."

There were prayers and meditations she still needed to do, and she was very worried about her brother but she was also worried she'd let me down...

"Nonsense." I said, because I knew this word always made her laugh. She said it sounded too English. "I have lots to do, background research."

"Today was the burning, that was very, very hard. "

"Of course it was, but nothing in your life can ever be that bad again."

I was trying to shout something useful, while gesturing at a persistent leafleter to leave me alone. The leaflet, of course, was for an Apsara dance show, with dinner. Sophea had been quiet for a long time.

"Sophea...?"

"You're right, Annie. I like what you say."

And I will come back Sunday for the dancing but I don't know what to do about my hair, I have no hair..."

I knew this situation.

"It'll grow back. You could wear a scarf."

"I can't dance in a scarf, it won't look right. Maybe a wig. What do you think?"

I thought it was a very good sign that she was worrying about her appearance.

"A wig could look very good." I said. "A whole new style."

"Yes, I think so... Maybe I will find a wig to make me look very nice – where are you? You are outside in the night?"

It was only around 7pm. I explained I was at a very tame boxing event.

"Boxing? Let me speak to Mr Ponleak."

I handed him the phone. He was nodding and saying, "Yes Bong" a great deal.

He handed the phone back. Possibly he muttered something to himself in Khmer.

Sophea said: "I tell him to be careful. I will speak with you soon."

I looked at Ponleak and he laughed. "Like we child."

The bossiness was good though; another sign she was getting through it.

The boxing ring, square like all boxing rings, was in the middle of a vast room of tables. This was Las Vegas style, dinner-show boxing, accompanied by music that varied from local pop to the wrong-headedness of Oasis with a disco beat. There was no admission fee; we just had to buy a drink. Presumably the promoters were hoping for the likes of the dozen Korean businessmen to the left of us, chain-smoking and ordering whisky after whisky. The promoters would not be delighted with Ponleak and I, one Coca-Cola each. The waiters also pushed dinner menus but I didn't see any takers. If the food was as overpriced as the drinks...

Ponleak assured me the boxers were the real thing.

"Fight many, many times."

Looking at their run-over faces would have told me this.

A few of them seemed to know Ponleak, greeting him with surprise and delight. Ponleak was enjoying himself, at first.

Very thin, woefully uncomfortable-looking Khmer girls in mini-skirts, long hair ironed flat and pokily high heels, teetered around with the boards indicating what round it was. They smiled wide, trying to summon the brassiness the job required, but they all looked as though they'd like to burst into tears and run home to their mums.

The bouts were pacey, exhilarating and short, with very long intervals for shoulder-kneading and flapping with towels.

"Only five rounds?" I asked Ponleak.

I hadn't intended any slight but he answered scornfully.

"You ten, twelve, only hands."

There was more body part usage, yet this boxing had less sense of the object of the game being to give each other brain damage. The fighters fell to the floor often and must break a lot of bones, particularly ribs and toe bones, but it seemed more about skilful entertainment than brutality.

Ponleak always knew which of a pair would win. Over-excited, I asked if he knew how the fight was fixed?

He gave me a scathing look: "No. I know who good.

He also knew the fighters would be lucky to get the fifty dollars they were supposed to be paid for the evening, perhaps a little more for the winners, but...

He looked around the quarter-filled room: "No tourist. Maybe twenty dollar."

There was a cheer and applause, as two alarming looking men came into the ring. They had black headbands over long hair; binding and coloured strings wound up their arms. Over their shorts they wore the nappy-like garment of sumo wrestlers. Neither were young; one had quite a sag to his stomach.

They began a very long, very formal preparation ritual, breathing and centring themselves but then they started moving sinuously around each other, striking out so suddenly a movement was over almost before I registered it was happening. These unfit seeming men were transformed in whirling, swooping, jabbing bursts of action. From apparently dawdling around the ring, the saggiest man jumped to plant both feet on the side of his opponent's head, then went back to dawdling.

"Bokkatao," "Ponleak told me. "Very old Khmer."

This lethal martial art was believed to predate Angkor. There were carvings on the entrance pillars to the Bayon temple showing warriors twisting their bodies in the stances of Bokkatao fighting. Bokkatao use every part of the body and has thousands of moves. Like Khmer ballet it has a spiritual element and Bokkatao was even closer to extinction than the ballet. The Khmer Rouge had killed most of the practitioners of a skill associated with the past, with royalty. These days, fighters and audiences preferred the faster thrills of kick-boxing. Or the arts they'd seen in the movies, such as Akido or Kung Fu.

Like Kung Fu, Bokkatao based many of its forms on animal movements – snake, eagle, tiger...

But when I said to Ponleak: "Oh, it's like Kung Fu," he looked sternly affronted.

"No. Kung Fu Chinese." With such Sophea-like disdain in Chinese, I felt as though I'd said something obscene.

After what was clearly a short display fight, the Bokkatao practitioners came off to hearty applause but they looked fed up. As he shook Ponleak's hand, one rolled his eyes resignedly as if to say: "What's it come to?"

When the men were out of earshot, Ponleak shook his head: "Bokkatoa go away. Too much difficult."

Kickboxing went worldwide, big events could be arranged for fighters who needed a much shorter training time than Bokkatao fighters. Bets could be laid.

And as the next kickboxing bout started, Ponleak's life as a thing to be bet on came back to him. He was suddenly very uneasy. He kept glancing sideways at a young South East Asian man dressed in expensive, preppy style, who'd taken a seat a few tables away. The man was laughing and ordering drinks for two girls who looked Italian, maybe Middle Eastern but certainly with the grooming and classy casual clothes of wealthy international lives. At no time did any of them pay any attention to Ponleak, but I could sense some sort of rage rising in mild-mannered Ponleak. This might be a night to go home and heave the barbells. Whatever it was, it might be better to ask in the morning, with Kiri to help out.

In the morning, Ponleak was nearly half an hour late. I worried it was some problem with the children, but it was Henri, Sophea's ex-husband. He'd called Ponleak at five in the morning to take him to hospital. When he got there, Henri had gone. Apparently one of his few remaining French friends had also rushed into the forest on a pre-dawn rescue mission and Henri had chosen to travel to the hospital in the friend's car.

"Sorry him sick but I finish Bong Henri."

Kiri started to translate Ponleak's exasperation but I got it. I didn't know if I should tell Sophea when she called. She didn't need this. Henri wasn't desperate, he had a friend. I'd say nothing to Sophea.

Kiri explained to Ponleak that I thought he had every right to be furious. And maybe Henri wasn't that ill. Just drunk.

Kiri laughed, repeating in English: "Only drunk!"

I imagined he was noting this line for his retelling of the story out in the lane. I knew I'd probably upset Ponleak further but while I had Kiri to hand, I had to know why the preppy boy had annoyed him last night.

"Ponleak know him from boxing. He is nothing. He is son of boxing business man, always at party and sport. Does he work, no. And look at us."

Kiri threw his hands in the air.

Ponleak laughed; "Kiri also not working. Only talking."

And we left Kiri behind, talking alternately on the phone and to some Japanese guests, switching from English to Japanese, while fixing a broken pot handle the cook had brought to him. Bone idle.

CHAPTER 15: THE END OF THE WORLD, AGAIN

We sheltered under a stone overhang in the Bayon temple but the rain was pouring through cracks and crevices, changing direction to hit us in the face. The guide, Yeng, couldn't get a phone signal to beg the van driver to rescue us with umbrellas. No luck with my phone either.

Never mind the umbrellas. Within minutes, despite the apparent shelter, we were soaked through. I suggested we might as well just make a dash for it. Yeng looked horrified. Like so many Cambodians, he reacted to rain as if it were a meteor shower, a hail of frogs, a crash to earth of plaguely locusts – not something that happened every year through regular rainy seasons, and sometimes in the middle of the dry.

I had a feeling Yeng didn't like me much. My indifference to rain seemed to confirm his suspicion that I was mentally deficient. He was a top-class guide, lent to me for a few hours by Andy's luxury tour company. Yeng's archaeological knowledge was vast and detailed, based on his own researches as well as study. He was also an expert in ornithology, history, local flora and fauna. And wasted on me.

As he talked archaeology, my attention may have meandered. And I knew I looked as blank as a henhouse wall when he showed me nests and tracks, or told me about symbiotic bird and animal relationships in the forests. When he asked if I had questions, I had none. Because I hadn't been paying full attention.

I had thought, when offered the guide, that another wander through the temples would refresh a sense of wonder at them, add new information – all this was happening, but a real dancer was more intriguing than a carved one; real fighters, real people at their work and prayers were what I wanted to know about, not the stone reliefs of them stretching around Angkor. Very much as it was for Kiri, for me the best of life was all about chatter, laughter and beauty in this moment now. This might seem zen-like, but it's also, in my case, to do with having the concentration span of a gnat.

Finally, the rain cleared to a drizzle. Yeng, shuddering as if he had several types of pneumonia, hurried me to the tour company's leather upholstered minivan.

Tourists were beginning to creep out from under trees and cafe awnings. We passed the elephant with red and gold decorations that took children for rides. It sheltered forlornly under some very wide spreading ranches. There's no sadder sight than an elephant all dressed up and too damp to go anywhere. Perhaps there was: I noticed as we drove past that Chez Sophea was shuttered. I felt a short pang of sympathy for Henri but, whatever happened to him, I hoped it wasn't going to lead to more sick-bed minding for Sophea.

The van driver suggested we have coffee and croissant, let the ground dry a little before touring further. He presented a perfect little hamper containing flasks of coffee, milk, chocolate and plain croissant.... Yeng joined me but the driver had a great deal of polishing to do outside. This wasn't the sort of company that had muddy vehicles.

To warm the mood of our so far silent breakfast, I told Yeng about how much baking and baguetting I'd found when travelling through French West Africa.

"The people there say: 'All the French left us was bread.'"

Yeng made a grim sort of smirk. "Here we say all the French left us was nothing."

I liked him for that. Such a shame he'd noticed me not listening several times. It was probably far too late into a bad relationship to worry if my next question was stupid or not.

"So would you say the French were the worst thing to happen to Cambodia?"

Yeng stirred three sugars into his coffee.

"I'm torn between them and the Americans." After thought, he stirred in a fourth sugar. "Perhaps the French gave pieces of our land to Thailand, made the Vietnamese the more educated administrators of their Indochinese empire to weaken us, made puppets of our kings, stole our art and our monuments. But they weren't our only enemies. So many things happened to the Khmer people they wanted to shout – here we are! Americans pushed us over the edge and Pol Pot took advantage. Nearly broke us. But there is still this voice trying to speak, saying 'we are Khmer'. We've been a people as long as the English, the French, certainly for hundreds of years longer than the Americans. That is why I like to talk about our history and traditions. Because we are still here, fighting to breathe sometimes. Perhaps it's difficult for you to understand."

"Not really."

Yeng clearly didn't accept this. He asked me how long I'd been in Cambodia? The answer made him look sceptical, not so long really, to write a book. Ah, so someone in the company had told him this. I'd seemed dim and fidgety in his lessons and now it turned out I'd barely spent a few months here. I could see why I seemed unfeasible to him.

"It's not the whole country, my book, it's a focused thing."

I explained a little about Sophea, even confessed I was worried about her, telling him about the skin-cutting.

"Well, there was no medicine here for a very long time. There still isn't for the poor, so if the person knew the right plants and the cut didn't get infected, it would simply be like an injection."

Now that he had my explanation for my journey, and he was drying out, Yeng seemed to find me less irritating. He told me things that were less formal and museum-catalogue-phrased. Less like a stern teacher marching his class on a nature trail.

Yeng, in his late twenties, was from the countryside, so although he lived a more modern life, older members of his family could heal all manner of ailments and believed a thousand magical things. For instance, until he was seven he'd been called Lizard, because in the naming of a child it was very important to keep envious evil spirits from harming them or stealing them. So, the child was made to sound unappealing. If it was a hairy child, it might be called Buffalo; if it was stocky it could be Frog. The child's real name was a secret until they were past six or seven, especially if they were boys. In traditional beliefs there was also a thing called "motherism". The spirit of a deceased mother in a family was sacred. If, for instance, the daughter was dating someone unsuitable in secret, the mother spirit would make another child in the family fall ill. Ceremonies would have to be performed to calm the mother, but also the family would start looking into who was misbehaving.

I told him how Sophea hadn't stopped crying until her mother came to her in a dream. Did people obey dreams?

"Dreams are very important. Quite often, traditional families will sit down to breakfast and they will tell their dreams. Sometimes, the father will interpret them. The family discuss them. But your friend, don't you think she simply stopped crying when she'd grieved long enough?"

A down to earth man. But he believed wholeheartedly in Buddhism, in reincarnation and in the next incarnation of Buddha being the last. That the end of time wasn't far. That in the Hindu faith, the last incarnation of Vishnu would be at the same time as Buddha's. The end of everything.

Not this again, I hated this.

The thought of earthly time ending didn't worry Yeng. He would do his best to live good lives and reach Paradise. He was talking about the relationship between Buddha and Vishnu, suddenly he asked: "Did you see the film Avatar? "

Now where were we? Yes I'd seen it.

"The last incarnation of Vishnu is half human, half horse. In Avatar the people are half horse in Paradise. I think they got the idea from Hindu stories."

I told him about the Four Horsemen of the Apocalypse.

"There, you see, horses at the end for everyone. I must read up on that, perhaps there's other imagery the same."

I wondered if it came from times when people first saw warriors riding at them on horseback It must have been a mind-blowing sight. No horse romped paradise. Why depress Yeng with my feeling the end of the universe would be just that. Gone. Nothing. We have to make the best of this.

Then Yeng told me babies were born who remembered past lives and could be very disturbed as children if they were not given magical cures.

Like Sophea, he made my head spin with his shifting between worlds.

I told him that Sophea remembered her previous lives. I wasn't sure if his long silence was summoning a polite reply, or deciding whether to share special information with me.

"There are people, particularly artistic people, who can remember and cope with it. That is where their ideas come from, what they describe as imagination, or inspiration. Do you know where your ideas come from?"

"Not always."

"No. You would say inspiration, imagination.... Speaking of imagination," Yeng did look as though inspiration had struck him, "I have to show you something."

We went to Ta Prohm, the creeper-climbed temple featured in Tomb Raider. Leading me to a wall of carvings, Yeng asked me if I noticed something unusual.

There it was: a dinosaur. I think it was of the type that any child of seven would know to call a stegosaurus. Yeng beamed delightedly.

"You know, you have to ask, where did they get that idea? Did somebody see it? Remember it from a past life?"

I pointed out that the carvings just below were of a lion dancing like a monkey, or a monkey with a lion's mane, so perhaps this was a carver with a wild imagination, who let it rip in this one small perfectly preserved panel.

"Or," Yeng smiled. "Is it a much later hoax?"

"Is it?

"I don't know, that's my main theory."

He was probably right but I did prefer the notion of an imaginative stone-cutter, hundreds of years ago, who'd never know his vindication – being a fascination for people in the twenty-first century.

Yeng pointed to another row of carvings.

"Do you know how to spot a true Khmer?"

The men in the wall friezes had shaved heads and what I thought were those long, inside the lobe, flesh-stretching earrings. The sort worn by Masai warriors or comic-book store staff in Shoreditch.

"It's the earlobes." Yeng explained. "The true Khmer has long ear lobes and dark skin, like someone from South India."

It was true. I looked at Yeng and the other local guides around the temple – long, narrow earlobes.

"My skin is too light because I had a Chinese grandfather but pure Khmer is dark."

Sophea definitely had the ears and covered up her skin with creams and long sleeves: "Or I will be black, black like night."

In the wall carvings the lobes were very long, though.

"I think the carvers were proud, wanted to show how we look different, special."

As we walked the smaller temples that Yeng preferred to the brash busyness of Angkor Wat itself, we came to one covered in bamboo scaffolding.

"We hope this time the restoration will be done properly. The authorities will sometimes accept a cheap bid, or there might be bribes involved. But now the bad restoration that used harsh chemicals and acids, eating into the stone, that all has to be repaired, so it will cost double. There's also the problem of foot traffic wearing away the stone. You saw earlier, we were climbing all over the Bayon temple, but with more tourists every year... The Apsara authority have made the tickets as expensive as they dare but they won't restrict the number of visitors. I don't know how we solve that."

We, he said – the temples belonged to the people. Something Sophea had shouted a great deal the day we were chased out for filming. And Yeng had no more respect for the Apsara authority than Sophea had. As we drove out of the park, he pointed to an elaborate memorial.

"This looks nice, it is for those dead in the Khmer Rouge times but actually there were individual war graves all along this stretch of roadside that the authority dug up, so they could sell the land to developers. I don't know what will happen but there's increasing discontent."

"What would be the best thing to happen?"

"Oh, I think our boss is right, more widespread education. I was lucky, my parents didn't have much but they believed in education. Rural people often don't see the need. They also remember too clearly when educated people were hunted down for execution. They think it's safest out in their own villages, working the land. But we're trying to persuade them."

Part of the persuasion was a project the local teachers and Sarah and Nhean in the charity branch of the tour company came up with. If the villagers suspected, or just couldn't manage school for their children, then how could they be met halfway?

A few days after my tour with Yeng, I went with Sarah to a small wooden building at the edge of a country village. Outside, some children were playing with a skipping rope; inside a local woman called "the librarian" was teaching half a dozen girls, and one boy, to make flowers from coloured tissue.

"This is a traditional art, for decorating at weddings, parties," Nhean explained.

Nhean was the schools' supervisor and now managed these village projects. Sarah hoped she'd soon be able to hand everything over to Nhean.

The room was already heavily decorated with paper flowers. There were also children's paintings and drawings. Shelves were filled with bright-coloured books. There was a reading corner with cushions, floormats and two comfortable chairs for adults. A basket was filled with skipping ropes, rubber balls, beanbags and building blocks.

Late every morning, an English class for different levels was held in the village centre and in the afternoon there were different levels of literacy classes in Khmer. They had just taken on a woman to teach mathematics and geography.

"We try to have the classes when people are least likely to be working." Sarah told me. "And we'll change times with the seasons because there's planting time, harvest time, that sort of thing. Our teachers have to be flexible but in each village centre there's a librarian as the constant person. The teachers are part-time, but their pay is as good as a full-time state teacher's. We keep these village projects small and quiet. So much easier than dealing with the school system. That will go on but this is the next phase."

The books in the library were picture books and storybooks the children could take home. There were comics as well as learning-to-read books. In a separate section were adult books on vegetable planting, pig-rearing, constructing simple buildings, sanitation projects, catfish-rearing...

"The adults were very wary at first. Old men coming in like they expected a trap, but now they're easy with it. They come and ask if we can get a book on such and such in Khmer. And the kids really own this place, they keep it clean, nothing ever gets broken or goes missing."

I noticed that it was mostly little girls in the classroom. Was this the case, even when it wasn't a flower-making day?

Nhean said: "No, it is because most boys are scared to make flowers, they don't want to look like a gay or a lady boy." He looked embarrassed. "Acceptance of these things is in our future."

Action for gay rights in Cambodia was in its infancy. It was not unheard of, but culturally it was a long way down most people's list of political concerns. Still, one boy was in there making paper flowers.

Meanwhile, more and more people were arriving for the English class due to start; mostly older children and a few adult women.

Now the teacher was ten minutes late.

Sarah asked Nhean to phone the missing teacher. Nhean claimed he didn't have the teacher's number with him. She said nothing but stopped smiling. It did seem odd that the supervisor for the project wouldn't have contacts for his teachers in his phone. Sarah called the office and got the number – no answer. Nhean looked very distressed as she asked him how often this teacher let them down. With a sigh, Nhean admitted that it happened, sometimes. It was bewildering because this was a great teacher who loved his job, was better paid and treated by this company than he was in the state system but still he would go on drinking benders and not show up.

Sarah pondered a moment; decided. She would be docking the teacher's pay. She thought part of the problem was that in the state system teachers were paid their small salary regardless and no one cared. Did the teacher think things were the same in this organisation?

"No, maybe. No, he understands." Nhean said carefully, distressed. "He does like his job, very much. His problem is, he doesn't like himself."

"So, you have been covering for him a bit?" Sarah asked gently.

Nhean watched the skipping children for a moment.

"But he is such a good teacher." He said. "I will talk to him."

Sarah smiled very intensely, to lift him out of the plunge of shame he was taking.

"It happens, doesn't it? People start so well with us, then they let themselves down. But you didn't, Nhean. What do you have that we can bottle?"

Nhean regained his cheerfulness: "Yes, we need to think about it. The motivation situation. There is always this... We feel still a little bit "why bother", especially the poor people. Good luck such as a nice job cannot quite be trusted. Something will happen, we'll be let down, tricked. Children here are discouraged from ambition not out of cruelty, or jealousy, but because their parents fear disappointment for them."

I didn't contradict Nhean but it suddenly occurred to me that perhaps people just wanted to be left alone. Whether or not they had to live a tough life, it was theirs. How weird it must be, to live in a place where strangers appeared, offering to help your community, because obviously, left to your own devices, you weren't doing things right.

I hoped I didn't sound critical when I asked: "Don't some people feel offended to be offered help?"

Of course I sounded critical. Both Sarah and Nhean bristled at me. Nhean stepped in first: "I don't think the problem is with offering help. It is as I say, making people trust a good thing when it happens."

"Like with this building." Sarah said. "One of the guiding staff told us about this building in his village, a nice, new wooden building, just sitting empty. It had been a clinic set up by an NGO but they left after a year. The village elder told us we could have the building and he'd encourage people to cooperate with our project – as long as we don't go away. He said it would be bad for the villagers to be disappointed again, so we had to promise."

"I understand. Sorry, I wasn't criticising." I said.

But I still thought it must sometimes be a difficult thing, to be on the receiving end of help. To know you're perceived as not living well enough.

Sarah nodded and broke the tension I'd caused with a smile.

"I hear you, Annie, but don't worry about us, we're always navel-gazing about wanting to get it right."

Another part of the navel-gazing was concern over how not to become part of the corruption problem.

"We have to be a bit sharp. If you're a well-meaning soul and call a village elder to ask what they need, they might say: "a clean water pump". If you go there, you'll see they have a pump, or several. What they actually want is money, or a second pump for the elder's private use. A few times schools have called us and asked for things like a desk, or a filing cabinet, or even a laptop for the principal's office."

Nhean was laughing again: "Really, it's disgraceful. Oh, here's another thing..."

He showed me a pile of textbooks that they used for teaching English. A teacher Nhean knew in Phnom Penh had worked, voluntarily, with the government education department for eight years to get this textbook right. Suddenly they said they wouldn't use it; they had found better textbooks in Singapore. Nhean and Sarah had looked over the Singapore book; it wasn't as good as the one the teacher had created but clearly, somehow, this Singapore book meant more money for the government.

The other great shame about this was publishing in Cambodia really needed all the support it could get. After the years of book burning and execution of intellectuals, new Khmer writing was rare.

Small organisations held writers' workshops and festivals, trying to rebuild a new body of Cambodian literature and find modern voices. In Phnom Penh I'd met with a couple of writers from the donation-funded Nou Hach Literary Association. Named after a Cambodian novelist and cultural attaché, murdered in the first week of the Khmer Rouge regime, Nou Hach held poetry and short story competitions, leading to publication for the winners. Poetry readings and slams happened in the buzzy Java Cafe. Everything was very young, very new. As for the chances of anyone making a living from publishing books, let alone writing them...

Even in the cities, few children grew up with books in their homes. Dara had told me most of his childhood reading in English was from photocopied books because the real thing would have been too expensive. News-stands still ran their book trade by buying one copy of a popular novel and making a few hundred photocopies.

This was why the villagers were so careful with their library; to damage, neglect or steal something as precious as original books would have been shaming behaviour.

The library part of the village education scheme worked but getting the teachers to like themselves enough to hold down a job they wanted...? That wouldn't be so easy.

The villagers who'd arrived for the English class began to meander home. This might mean they wouldn't bother coming next week. No one complained; Cambodians expected to be let down.

"It looks like acceptance." Nhean said. "But it is resignation."

Sophea rang in the evening to tell me she had bought a wig. It didn't look so bad, she could dance in it. She ranted a little while about her sister who hadn't been there to help with her father and hadn't sent enough money from Paris for the funeral. By the way, had Ponleak told me that Henri was sick? She hoped he would be ok. She was a little angry with Ponleak now because he was refusing to go out to help Henri. Sophea had to arrange another tuk tuk driver to deliver groceries. I explained how Henri had pushed poor Ponleak to the limit.

"Oh, ok, he didn't tell me that part. He just told me he can't go. But Henri is really very sick."

Despite everything she felt, she might have to look after him.

"It makes me feel tired but if he cries on the phone I feel too bad. People who drink like this, they kill themselves. I feel too bad about him."

She'd looked after her father, now it would be back to Henri. Resigned to it.

CHAPTER 16: NO SOPHEA, I'M NOT THAT BRAVE

It was hard to know if the atmosphere felt edgy because I knew this had been the last stronghold of the Khmer Rouge, or if the majority of the people stared, not friendly, because quite a few of them were former Khmer Rouge. Or they were their defensive descendants and the likes of me were bound to have the wrong idea about their side of history.

There seemed to be two ways Pol Pot was rationalised. He was the well-intentioned father of his oppressed people but his evil underlings, such as Duch and Ta Mok, had ruined everything. Or there was the belief, widely spread by surviving Khmer Rouge leaders, that Pol Pot had been the psychopath who ruined their people's revolution, and they'd only followed his horrific orders because they were afraid. There was also the theory that a heart attack hadn't killed Pol Pot while he hid out on the borders with Thailand. When the leaders around him knew the battle was lost, they poisoned him, so they could adapt theory number one to suit the Americans, and Britain. They could be the people with a seat at the UN. The people Margaret Thatcher had called "the reasonable members of the Khmer Rouge."

Somewhere near here, Sophea's brother had been a child slave. Sophea thought I might take photographs to show him.

"If he is a little bit strong maybe we can see if pictures can help his memory without hurting him too much at this time. Imagine Annie the woman who took Sann might still be around, perhaps she is being taken care of by people who thought they were orphans. Maybe if I go there I can see her face.... But even for me it is not possible. It is for you, Annie, to discover what people up there know about this woman."

So, my first discovery was the lack of smiling in Anlong Veng. Then just some gut feeling that the people watching me were as poor and war-damaged as they'd been at the time when Pol Pot led them down to punish the privileged and westernised in Phnom Penh. Led them to kill monks and dancers.

The most affable person in Anlong Veng was an old woman charging a dollar to see Pol Pot's cremation site. She wore black and had the short-cropped bob of Khmer Rouge times. With her in her bamboo kiosk she had two very cute little girls, grandchildren perhaps, eating lollipops while helping granny take admission fees. A crudely made sign: Pol Pot Cremeted Here, had led us to granny and her post at the end of a dusty, litter-strewn lane.

I was with Art – another driver with a pseudonym created for foreigners. Art and his elderly Toyota had been approved by Kiri and Ponleak as a trustworthy man to take me this distance.

When we walked into the overgrown cremation site, in a field surrounded by trees and small farmhouses, Art stood at the back fence, arms folded, looking up at the spangly, multi-storied luxury hotel and casino on the other side of the main road. Something that seemed purpose-built to spite Pol Pot.

Pol Pot's own memorial had no gilding or painting. it was a crude wooden frame covered with rusting corrugated iron. Someone had left a Pyrex bowl of fruit; some incense sticks were burning. I stood there a while, trying to think what to think. There was a loud thump behind me as Art lifted an old door lying in the long grass and dropped it again.

"Good door," he said. "We go?"

Granny and the girls grinned and waved as we walked back to the car. Art was about forty years old. I had been assuming he had the sort of back-story he spat out as soon as the car doors were shut.

"I hate Pol Pot so much. I am poor because of Pol Pot."

Art's father had a prosperous small business and Pol Pot's people had killed him. Art's mother died young of an illness and there had been no medicine to treat her. For most of his childhood, Art went hungry. I had noticed, in outlining the itinerary for our journey, his main emphasis had been on where we would eat.

Pol Pot rested in quite obscure conditions but Ta Mok, known as Brother Number Five, had a gigantic memorial, constructed by his grandson. A rock the size of a house was in the middle of the highway, with carvings of soldiers at the base, gilded spirit houses and marble flooring. Bowls of flowers, fruit and incense were abundant. It was said a tribute to Ta Mok could make you dream the winning lottery numbers.

Ta Mok had also made himself appreciated in the area by building schools and orphanages. But the house Ta Mok had built for himself was notorious and something Sophea wanted photographed.

"Always I hear it is beautiful. If I can't go, I can see the photograph. A palace they tell me, palace."

It certainly was a lavish spread for one of the leaders of a communist regime. Built by a lake which Ta Mok had created to enhance his view, the house had murals over two storeys, and quality floor tiles. Compared to the royal palaces it was rather underwhelming but the setting, amid trees with a view of mountains across water made for an above average location.

Art pointed out something to remind me what Ta Mok's finely located house had cost: the prison cages the Khmer Rouge had specialised in. About ten feet by ten feet, they didn't look that bad to me. Until Art made a disturbing mime, arms pressed to his sides, up on his toes, head tilted back and gasping for air. There wasn't a cage each; people were packed into these.

The forests around Ta Mok's house were a contrast to the bare, flat and then flatter miles we'd driven from Siem Reap. We were going up into the Dangrek mountains, a landscape that immediately made me hear the thuk thuk thuk of helicopter blades; sounds and images from Vietnam war movies.

The land flattened again, filled with line after line of identical small, stilted houses. Art told me they were for soldiers. The border with Thailand was close and there had been vicious fighting, currently at a pause, for control of the sacred site of Prasat Preah Vihar – where we were headed.

Built by Cambodian kings who lost it in a war, Prasat Preah Vihar had been ruled by Thailand for hundreds of years but the French gave it over to Cambodian control in 1907. The Thai military seized it in 1959 but King Sihanouk ran crying to The Hague and was given back control in 1962. In 1979 the Thai military pushed forty thousand Cambodian refugees over the border into land around the temple that was now thick with landmines. They were pushed into Khmer Rouge territory and many were maimed or killed by mines on the way. The Thai defence was they didn't want the Khmer Rouge coming in to their country pretending to be refugees and they didn't want to be bombed by the Vietnamese for harbouring possible Khmer Rouge...

The Khmer Rouge retook the temple area in 1998 as part of their last stand. Then they lost it again. The battle over the territory continued viciously until 2011. It has now been conceded to Thailand.

"Of course it is not Thailand," Sophea told me. "It was stolen but we are stronger in another way: we stop a war because we are better in soul."

Fine sentiment as this was, it seemed to me that the truth had more to do with Thailand's relative wealth and power than souls. But Sophea was sending me on an assignment.

"Take pictures, it is poisonous for Cambodians up there now. Our stolen history, or sold by our rulers from us. The naga will take it back for us. Please Annie, take pictures to show me the buildings are Khmer. And ask people in the area their opinion because if they are Khmer they will know the truth."

I agreed to do this. Although I didn't quite understand what the next phase would be. Sophea, myself and the naga on some Mission Impossible quest? But I wanted her distracted from grief and weariness.

Showing my passport and buying a ticket, I was closely supervised by Art, as if he was allowing me to do these grown-up things by myself but was ready to step in if I came unstuck. Then he told me, in several different ways, to stick to the paths when I was up there; they said all the mines and cluster bombs had been cleared but this was never certain.

I was approached by several men in the car park, asking if I wanted to take a moto to the top, or a jeep. A motorbike was five dollars, a jeep on my own would be twenty five. As the excursion was already proving an expensive day out – entrance ticket ten dollars, Art a hundred dollars – I thought I might risk the motorbike. Everyone agreed it was much too far and steep to walk.

"No moto, no motorbike, it is very dangerous and if you have accident Mr Kiri and Mr Ponleak will kill me. Kill me. Please, they will kill me."

When I saw how very high, steep and potholed the road was I was glad to have given in to Art's panic.

A tall, unfriendly driver, next in line for customers, seemed reluctant to let me have the jeep to myself. Most people went up in a group but the price was the same, so what was the matter with him? Did he just hate me for being, relatively, that rich? Would he miss out on tips if there weren't six passengers?

Art went away, pointing to the row of restaurants by the car park:

"I will be in first one. Very good place. Big bowls!"

The jeep driver very aggressively told me to get in. As he drove off he looked at me with contempt, then shouted something to the other drivers hanging around. I knew, and I knew he wanted me to know, that he was shouting something really unpleasant about me.

If I was to ask complicated questions about the politics of the area, I decided not to ask this man.

All along the road, soldiers were sitting on the kerb smoking, or lolling, surly, against rocks watching the jeep head upward. Them and their vaguely held armaments were not as unnerving as the waves of aggression and resentment coming from the driver. It was so unnerving I took out my little phone, held out of his view and pretended to be texting someone. Who would save me out here anyway? Stubby little Art? I didn't even have a phone number for him.

The driver, perhaps assisted by some of the soldiers when they learned how hateful I was, could haul me off into the woods and cut my throat. Perhaps they could throw me where they knew there was an unexploded land mine, pretend I was a crazy person who'd darted off the path. They'd tried to stop me but pow! Actually, then they'd get maimed in the explosion, so that plan to dispose of my body wasn't very good. Perhaps they could...

My imagination wasn't so frivolous at the time. The driver was big, muscular and scared me. Then the game changed. I let out an involuntary gasp as we turned a hairpin corner to face a slope of broken road as steep as a Swiss roof.

"Don't worry." The driver said with an alligator smile. "I've been driving this road for four years. In fact I can drive this easier than a flat road now."

There was a contempt in his grin that wanted me to know, I felt, that this was a tired patter for every journey up the mountain.

Four years. Before that this land was Cambodian. What had he been doing before? I was sure he'd been in the army but peace-time meant he was stuck with the likes of me.

Lifting his hand from the wheel for a moment, the driver pointed to a couple of plastic bags in the space between us.

"The people around here are really very poor. If you buy one of these bags for the soldiers it helps them a lot. There's coffee, biscuits, condensed milk and cigarettes, things they can't afford. Only seven dollars, nothing to you but a fortune to the poor soldiers."

Seven dollars? For friends of his? I shifted from uneasy to angry and just stared out of the window. As I knew he would, he drove faster.

At the drop off point, a car park among trees, full of jeeps, motorbikes and refreshment stalls I realised that I was hardly in an isolated or dangerous place, and that the opinions of such an angry man might be interesting. Of the people in the area he was probably one likely to speak frankly. I paused by the jeep, trying to formulate a good question.

"You want something? You want to buy the coffee? Give me a tip?" The driver barked at me.

I hadn't thought up any well formulated questions. I managed to say "no" to the driver's questions.

He barked on; "So you can go. GO. I'll wait here, car six, thanks, bye bye."

With a smirk he involved a couple of soldiers nearby, saying something to them in what was obviously the nastier tone of joke. They smiled but seemed to think what he'd said was too much. Meanwhile I felt very failed as an intrepid investigator. As I walked toward the temple complex I could see my driver, leaning against his bonnet now, regaling his fellow drivers with a spiteful humorous tale; maybe it wasn't about me. Maybe he had a whole repertoire of things he sneered at. I couldn't face a journey with him again anytime soon. And I had reconnaissance photos to take for Sophea.

There were also once-in-a-lifetime views out across Cambodia and Thailand….

Prasat Preah Vihar had been a place of pilgrimage, added to by seven successive Angkorian monarchs, from 889 to 1152. It was constructed to represent Mount Meru, sacred in the Hindu religion and dedicated to the god Shiva. Perhaps the pilgrimage intention, or the less evolved architecture and artistry at this pre-Angkorian site, made it very plain. No representations of royal glory, warriors, dancers...

The views had indeed been worth the worrying drive up but the place had a sour atmosphere. There were more soldiers around than tourists. Hundreds of people had died up here less than five years ago. I didn't explore for long.

In the car park there was no sign of my horrible driver. A man with a walkie-talkie asked what car I wanted. After some shouted enquiries into his machine he told me:

"Car six go down, come back ten minutes. Sit down please."

He pointed to a bench under trees. I sat a while but too many insects were biting me for me to stand it more than a second after ten minutes. I went back to the car supervisor. More shouting into the walkie-talkie.

"Sorry madam, ten more minutes."

I had a feeling this could go on for ages. The driver was probably waiting at the bottom to pick up more passengers and the longer I had to wait, the happier he'd be. Or he was just messing with me.

"Can't I go in another car?"

I saw a group of Japanese backpackers getting ready to leave. One of them had noticed my plight and said they had a spare seat.

The supervisor sighed and said it was OK but I might as well sit up front with the driver.

"To be more comfortable after inconvenience."

I did have a comfortable ride down, improved by seeing the horrible driver sitting on the kerb by a roadside kiosk. He glared at me; I glared at him.

"Car six." I said to my current driver.

"Yes." He said in an irritated tone. Irritated with car six, not me.

"What's wrong with him?"

The driver shrugged. "Maybe tired."

Maybe a psychopath.

I slept most of the two-hour drive back, occasionally waking when Art blared the horn at a suicidal dog, a runaway cow... Then somewhere in the flat nothingness, Art asked if we could call in on his uncle. Uncle was very poor and as Art was seldom up this way....

We pulled up at a scattering of wooden shacks. An exhausted looking woman came out of one that seemed to be a very basic car repair shop. Surprised to see me, she bowed and told Art his uncle was out helping pick up a car for repair. The woman was a neighbour and Art's uncle helped out with the car business because the woman's husband had been killed in a motorbike accident two months ago. Art gave the woman a couple of dollars with his condolences.

There had been some children in the dust around the houses. The woman had fallen on two dollars as a godsend. And this was peacetime up here, the good times.

It was almost sunset as we drove home through the edge of the Angkor park. On the grass people were settling, some with picnics, to watch the coming of night through the trees. Women selling tubes of sticky rice lined the roadsides and a group on a cycle tour came to a halt beside them. For what Art said was no reason at all a couple of fireworks went off in the distance, flowering in the sky. This was the Cambodia it was beautiful to live in, build spa hotels and charity schemes in. Only the tiniest trickle of this world reached the tiniest number of Cambodians.

The next morning, Sophea called.

When I told her I hadn't found out much because the driver made me nervous, she said: "Oh, you let me down Annie. You are supposed to have courage in your job and you don't even ask questions? OK but be stronger for the rest of our journey or the book will be very weak and no good."

She'd be back in a few days. I had missed her reassuring take on things.

In an attempt to strengthen my resolve, I asked Ponleak to drive me up to the Western Baray. Standing by the breezy waters, I watched a line of monks picking their way down the steps to go on a boat trip. Why was it whenever I saw monks they were being given gifts, or out on a treat?

I shopped around the Baray market for some white shirts for Sophea. I had a feeling she had to wear mourning white for a few months. I saw a children's clothes stall and thought about presents for Ponleak's children but he might be offended. However scruffy he was, however battered the tuk tuk, the children were always immaculate.

Looking out over the water again, monks setting sail now, I realised they weren't on a lark, they were headed for the Mebon temple dedicated to Vishnu, on an island in the centre of the water. There were probably prayers to be said, monk work to be done.

Ponleak was sitting in his tuk tuk under the trees. He had a present for me. A bag of water melon slices. One for me, one for himself. We sat, watched by a small hopeful dog as we ate fruit and listened to the flies in the air; the distant shouts of children splashing the water in inner tubes and the shouts of women up at the market trying to tempt foreigners:

"Try insect, try insect!"

When all the watermelon was gone, Ponleak went to the fruit stalls and brought back a jug of water for us to clean our hands.

I was glad I hadn't bought the clothes.

CHAPTER 17: NOT EXACTLY A MIRROR

You couldn't tell it was a wig and it made Sophea look like Audrey Hepburn. She danced a little less than she usually did, talked a little more, but that was the only indicator of what she had been through and how tired she was.

In the cool hotel library, a long candle burning at the back and bowls of perfect lotus buds around Sophea's small stage gave the sense of a sacred space. This was a discreetly appointed room, as if it was the very place where feng shui was invented. There were a few well-presented architectural studies on the shelves; the better quality of guide book and photography behind the soft slide of glass.

At most, the leather armchairs rearranged for the evening could accommodate an audience of a dozen people. This evening there were eight guests: two Japanese businessmen; two groomed Frenchmen who looked like a couple and a mixed French couple who were definitely a couple. Then there was an older American couple. He was in his mid-sixties, she perhaps a little younger but they both had no look of people who'd been born into money. If gruff had a visual, this tall big-knuckled man in his sixties would be it. A big-knuckled man who owned some kind of manly business that he'd built from scratch. All this was after his time in the military because I was jumping to the conclusion I always leapt at when I came across Americans his age in Cambodia: this was a war veteran doing some kind of penance. I also presumed that this man being in for a dance performance was to humour the wife. She was a practical-looking woman; I imagined she'd raised at least four children and, now they were grown, she was getting a chance to enjoy her husband's money, see some wonders. He had always wanted to come back to Cambodia, give donations to a hospital, an orphanage.... They were probably nothing like the people I'd decided they were. And when Sophea began speaking, I noticed that it was the American husband who leant forward, fascinated. When she faltered in her explanation of the sacred nature of the dance, saying:

"I apologise, my English..."

The American said: "No, no please, go on, you're doing great."

His wife nodded and smiled at her husband.

In the question section, he asked about the stories, the history, the music...

"The stories are from the Ramayana, from the life of Buddha. I don't learn the whole story as dance. Just my sections of the dance. But I know the story of Buddha's life because it is my belief."

"So you couldn't you choreograph your own dance?" The Frenchwoman asked. Sophea looked awkward. The American glared at the Frenchwoman.

Sophea said: "I could a little, I can pick a story of Buddha and make a dance. But the movements are like signals, they can't change, just the story. The flying, the flower, the angry movements, they are the same."

She demonstrated the gestures she spoke about. The American, transfixed, wanted to know if there was a history of the dance anywhere.

"There is some history with the queen mother, some old written history that was saved but very little was written anyway, it passed down, generation to generation. But if the teachers are not there, it will not pass down."

"Shouldn't the government do something about protecting the culture?"

Sophea smiled and bowed her head. The American understood that he hadn't said something tactful.

His wife asked how many different tunes were there?

"There are many songs. Some are written. More of the music has been saved, written down. But it is the dance that will be lost because to the young people, it's not interesting to them. They think it is for the past, the royal family and not for them."

One of the Japanese businessmen said young people were only interested in photographing themselves. Everyone laughed.

The American and his wife applauded deafeningly after the dance Sophea had announced as her last one. She did this with great charm.

"We will now have a final dance, then the music ends and we blow out the candle as the spirit leaves us. The dance is to say to the spirit 'goodbye', as it flies away and 'goodbye' to our guests when they fly home safe with the spirit to guide them."

The American couple lingered when the show was over.

"We were just looking at the programme of events, you won't be here again until Sunday after next?" The wife looked as though she might cry.

"It is the low season. Next month, December, January I will be here more often."

"Oh what a shame, that was so beautiful. And those carvings we saw in the temples, they'd have been doing the same dance as you?"

"We are the same."

The Americans praised her and thanked her again, wandering off into the poolside night.

Sophea, the musician and Sokha who danced the female role, packed up their things. Pale, round-faced Sokha, had been trained at the royal ballet school in Phnom Penh but moved to Siem Reap when her father's hotel management job demanded. Now, having performed with Sophea for three years, Sokha was getting married and wanted to leave the group.

Sophea knew the female role dances that plump, round-faced girls were chosen to do, simply because she'd always been keen to learn all the dances she could. She'd begun her demonstration show at the hotel on her own with a musician, why not carry on alone?

"Maybe I have to. But it does not look good. It is my dream to have a full troupe and soon again there will be only me and the musician. And he complains I don't pay him enough. No troupe, no school. All my dream is fall down."

I wanted to kick myself, I shouldn't have skulked on the side-lines. I should have barged in and told those Americans how desperate the situation was. When I apologised to Sophea for not having the gumption to do this, she looked horrified.

"Are you crazy? I will lose my job. We cannot ask guests for help like that."

"But if I talked to them?"

"Stop this, Annie. I have no time to think about the troupe now. I am too tired. Why me? Why doesn't somebody else care about the dance? I am too sad. I am too tired."

Grief and trauma and disappointment had probably overwhelmed Sophea long before I arrived. She didn't trust anything to work out, not really.

I could always get up and have another go at things because I knew what being lucky felt like. I was pushing her to do something that would take huge energy and confidence to achieve. Why should she have to carry on with her dance for the people dream, if it had become too exhausting to even think about?

Sophea just wanted to be left alone; be allowed to change her mind and live quietly. Resignation might not hurt as much as one more disappointment.

But then.

CHAPTER 18: YOUR FAULT. NO, YOURS.

"As for you, you in particular shouldn't waste a day."

I had thought eastern mystics were supposed to talk in gentle, elliptical ways and look fasted but here I had a fat, California-accented monk, wearing glasses that made him a dead ringer for Eric Morecambe, chuckling at me.

We were in the right place, sitting on a mat, under the trees in a Battambang monastery. Everything smelt jasminey, with incense wafting from somewhere and there was even distant chanting. This monk who had let us down last time, who had taught Sophea advanced level meditation and the sacredness in the dance, had been very welcoming and apologetic. But I had expected something more.... other-worldly.

I had expected to be going home.

I didn't feel there was a reason to stay on if Sophea was giving up on her dream. But then she'd almost crashed her bicycle into Mr Kiri she was in such an excited rush at the guesthouse and at me with her new idea.

"I don't sleep. We don't stop yet. We are tired and we are confused and we need help. I have telephoned to Battambang, you will come?"

So here we were, halfway through our consultation with Eric Morecambe the monk, and I still felt confused.

He had told Sophea she was welcome to come back to the monastery any time. He could help her meditate more deeply. She could learn more prayers to summon spirits to the dance, she was welcome to stay as long as she liked. Perhaps I could stay too; try to get in touch with my spiritual side, now I sensed my mortality.

Sophea had looked very happy. This was what she wanted. Would I stay, just for a little while? Wouldn't that be wonderful?

"We are the same, we don't fall down. You can write how you feel when you meditate and we get an idea for my dance."

But monk Eric Morecambe put his hands together and shook his head.
"Bong Sophea, excuse me, but isn't that escaping? Didn't you tell me years ago that the small pagoda near you had offered you a space for a class? Why can't you begin?"
"I have nothing. I am so tired. It's so much to organise. Where will I find funding?"
The monk looked at her, blunt and earthy as a bank manager.
"You can't do this for money. You find a way to do it. Maybe it even costs you money. That is the good karma, Bong Sophea."
Sophea must have felt her old acquaintance, disappointment, kick her in the gut. The monk had been this last, desperate hope for encouragement and he was adding to her burdens.
He smiled at her, softening, fond of her. "Just do what you can. That'll be enough."
That's when he told me to, I suppose, seize the day. I really had hoped for more – at least for the monk not to say things everyone said on Facebook.
Sophea parted from him polite and taut.
I asked her what she thought?
"Nothing. I think nothing. He is changed."

On the drive back from Battambang, I remembered sitting with Ponleak eating water melon slices. Ponleak lived in a village full of concrete toilet cubicles. He kept coloured singing birds. Kiri earned seventy dollars a month for working round the clock and he would like to see a classical ballet show. A big gruff American hadn't wanted Sophea's show to end.
She had something that was necessary.
I couldn't share the half-formed inspirations I was having with Sophea because she was silently staring out of the window on the other side of the packed share-taxi. All the other passengers were having a rowdy discussion that I assumed was political. I kept hearing the word yuon, the disparaging term for the Vietnamese. It meant foreigner. The Vietnamese called Cambodians tho, meaning coarse and rustic.

Ponleak with both his children and Sophea's friend, Chenda, came to collect us from the taxi stop. With a detour to buy groceries, we were soon in Sophea's house, eating. After food, I knew, was a better time to broach difficult subjects with Sophea. I didn't know what she would make of my idea but I was thinking of the village library project. Village children had no money, couldn't keep regular hours or travel far – but why shouldn't they have beautiful things?
Ponleak squinted at me when I explained: "She goes to villages to dance?"
"Not just like that, she'd have to go around on her moped and tell people what was happening, what time, make sure they know it is free..."

Sophea looked dubious: "With no music, just me?"
I reminded her of the little film we'd made. When we'd made that, she'd carried what she needed in one bag, and the film, short as it was, worked. Her dream of a group of poor children forming a troupe that would pay for itself, that was huge, and no reason why it might not happen, but wasn't my idea something she could do tomorrow? Something less overwhelming? Wasn't it what the monk had been telling her?
I realised I was on the verge of saying: "Let's do the show right here!"
Sophea translated for Chenda who smiled and pointed to Sophea's altar. Sophea looked sceptical. Ponleak looked sceptical.
"I say to Chenda, but this is not a job, how will I live? And she says just pray. There will be a solution."
"Well no one is saying you do it full-time. But, as the monk said, this is about karma."
Sophea watched Ponleak's children for a moment. Urged them to take more rice.
"I think you are blaming the monk but it is your idea. I will work for nothing and it is your fault."
"It's your fault I've had to spend tons of money dragging all the way back and forth to Cambodia."
As I'd hoped, she laughed.
"Oh yes, Europeans suffer very badly in Cambodia. They hate to be here."
She served a toffee she made from mangoes. The children had refused more rice because they'd spotted this heaven-wrapped-in-banana-leaf the moment they came in.
Outside in the road a man walked past carrying a very long bamboo pole. Quite often people in the countryside walked around carrying long poles. I wasn't sure if the poles were for fishing, or building, or if the pole-carrying was an end in itself.
I was going to ask about the poles when Sophea sat back on her heels decisively.
"In fact your idea is not stupid. Even if the children will never learn properly they will enjoy it when they come. Maybe one will get the idea to do it and fight to go forward, like me. For the rest, they'll just understand maybe a little how they can be close with Lord Buddha. Your idea is not stupid."
"Thanks."
"I will be old and be starving but it is for good karma."
I didn't see why there had to be actual starving involved. I hardly dared ask but...
"What about Henri, the restaurant?"
Both Chenda and Ponleak looked startled.
"No, no. I will help him if he asks me but if I take his money I feel bad. If I take nothing I am clean. I have my job at the hotel. Maybe I will sell the other

piece of land behind my house here. I feel excited. I am not scared. I told you this monk was good."

"Now it's a good idea it's the monk's idea?"

"Of course."

It was Sunday morning and our odd little expedition arrived at the pagoda half a mile from Sophea's house. It was small and shabby, on the edge of a poor part of Siem Reap. In the open-sided prayer hall, Sophea put down a mat, lit a candle and began to pray. With a couple of the monks who'd welcomed us, Chenda, Ponleak, his mother, the children and I sat to watch Sophea practise what she might do for the village children.

She spoke in Khmer but I knew she was explaining the costume, her jewellery, and then she showed the flying dance. She invited Maly to come and try some basic movement with her. Ponleak's son, Vibol, sucked his thumb and fell asleep against his grandmother. Grandmother listened to and watched Sophea, enthralled.

Discreetly, Ponleak slipped away; he had spotted two dirt-dipped children watching from behind a tree. As he approached, they ran. But we were only practising. Once the children understood they were welcome to be here with Maly, following Sophea's turns, trying to copy her hand movements, maybe they'd dare to come over.

Sophea showed Maly's little hands how to make the back-tilted flat hand for flight; the thumb and forefinger being joined to make a hand offering a flower; the hand up protesting; the hand pointing down in anger; the salute in humble attitude.

Not far away, some development was going up and their machinery thumped, clanked, with drills tearing into the ground. Somewhere further was traffic fighting itself. Here, just here was the jingle of Sophea's bracelets and giggling as Maly followed a dance that went back and back in time, summoning the spirits to bring harmony.... For us, an oddly assorted gathering, with our fights and fears waiting for us outside this moment, the dancing worked.

AFTERWORD

TWO days after Annie returned from Cambodia, she suffered a seizure.

I met her off the plane. Annie was exhilarated from the trip but tired and happy to be home. On the tube she confessed that she might have had some kind of tiny blackout in the bathroom of her hotel room, which she put down to overtiredness.

But she was absolutely fine now, she said, a little spacey; understandable after the 20 hour journey from Siem Reap.

Annie lost her hair from the cancer treatment. On this trip Sophea shaved her hair off as a mark of mourning following the death of her father.

They both went wig shopping. Annie had chosen one out of the hospital brochure, tried it on, out of sight of everyone, including me, then threw it in the corner of the bedroom, never to be worn again.

She went with Sophea to the market, where they bought a dark bob wig which made Sophea look like Audrey Hepburn.

There was another sad parallel in the lives of Annie and her Cambodian Twin.

On this trip Sophea's father died. Annie felt like an intruder, a tourist clumsily treading through Sophea's grief and this foreign way of death.

The day after Annie landed back in London her own father died.

We were packing bags to go up to Leicester to be with her mother. Annie started chatting, confused, making little sense, laughing.

I was ringing the Macmillan nurse for guidance when Annie keeled over on to the bed, shaking uncontrollably.

It is not uncommon for a patient with lung cancer to develop, even while in remission, a brain tumor. This is something I learned later that night, in a quiet corridor of the A & E department of the Charing Cross Hospital.

A few days later, a surgeon visited Annie's ward bed. Annie looked at me in despair.

"They want to take out a lump of my brain, Martin."

The fear went directly to the core of her. Would she still be able to have the same thoughts; the same creative processes? Would she still be able to make up jokes, write more plays and what about her book?

Again, a cancer specialist with the right words, at the right moment.

"You will still have the same thoughts, you will still make jokes, you will still be able to write, you will still be the same Annie, Annie."

The quiet, miraculous intuition of a physician who knows they need to treat the patient as comprehensively as they treat the disease.

On the day of the operation, a few days into the New Year, we taxied across to the Charing Cross Hospital. I sat with her on the ward as they administered pre-operation drugs and she became drowsy and was wheeled away to the operating room.

That night my mother, who had been ill, died in the Chelsea and Westminster.

In the morning, after visiting my mother's room on the Chelsea ward to say a prayer and my goodbyes, I went back to Charing Cross.

The surgeon was delighted. The operation had been a success.

Annie was very much awake and bad tempered. She wanted her laptop as she had to get back to writing her book. I couldn't tell her about my mother, not just yet.

So we were back home again; Annie convalescing, and writing.

The first seizure, after the operation, occurred in early spring.

It set us back. There is a place that goes beyond disappointment.

Still Annie continued working away on the Cambodia book, writing up the copious notes she made on her last trip, battling toward the end of the book.

A new round of laser radiotherapy fired directly at the tumor.

Then, to try to keep the seizures at bay, steadily increasing dosages of steroids, along with a bewildering clutch of other drugs.

Every seizure, every emergency trip to hospital, every increase in the medication made her weaker. But not so much that she couldn't write.

She would be sat up in bed, leaned on a wall of pillows, surrounded by piles of manuscript pages. In the bed would be at least half a dozen pens. I learned quickly that there was no point in giving Annie one pen. She would lose it in among the sheets and get frustrated. Surrounding her with a whole bunch of writing implements meant there was a decent chance she could reach out and locate one at the very moment she needed to make some crucial mark on paper.

She completed the manuscript and the edits over the summer.

Annie's mind turned to new projects. She couldn't type anymore so she would write outlines and ideas on an A4 pad. Her condition continued to deteriorate and so did her hand coordination. A page would now contain one large, incoherent sentence and then, a few weeks on, one word.

She hung onto the doctor's words like a mantra: "You will still be the same Annie, Annie."

One project in planning was a radio documentary about brain tumours and seizures. About how they have been viewed through history in literature, fables, movies and religion and what we know and still don't know about them today.

Annie, the intensely private writer, who would conceal her illness from so many of her friends but would lay it all out in her writing. She was looking forward to interviewing the surgeon who had opened her head and cut out a piece of her brain.

One thing still not present was self-pity. She could not allow herself the sin of feeling sorry for herself and she hated if anyone displayed an ounce of pity toward her.

There were unspoken but strictly observed rules for visitors. They were not there to mope or whine or ask about her condition. They were there to give her gossip about her enemies, entertain her with ludicrous stories about them and make her laugh.
All the time our narrative to each other was to fight on; to believe, with certainty, that Annie would beat this.
Until. Another Saturday night emergency call. Another ambulance. Annie strapped into a stretcher and me sat in the jump seat, clasping a small case. Experience taught me what was needed for these trips, some basic toiletries, nightgown, underwear, a full bag of Annie's medication, a box of the inhalators she was still using, even though we both gave up smoking more than ten years earlier, and her red medical progress book.
As we were driven, through busy weekend traffic, the short distance up to the hospital, the attendee asked how long me and Annie had been together.
"15 years."
She nodded slightly, turned her head back to the monitors, making herself busy, and said nothing.
At that moment I realized, finally, fully, that Annie was not going to recover.
It was confirmed a few weeks later, back in Dr Tom's office, me alone this time, no x-ray on the lightbox.
The tumour in Annie's brain had reappeared, and it was growing. The lung cancer was back, and spreading out across her body.
Even as I asked about further treatments I knew.
"My first duty Martin is to do no harm to my patients. Any more invasive treatment would likely kill Annie."
On his desk he had a photo Annie had taken at the Preah Vihar Temple, high up in the Dangek Mountains. She wanted to let Dr Tom know where he had got her.
"I like having it there," he said.
Dr Tom had been true to his word. Annie got back to Cambodia and finished her book, despite everything.
Certainly Annie believed working to complete this book had helped extend her life. It had given her the focus and drive that Dr Tom had sought to instil in her on that first meeting.

I will never forget how Annie looked up at me from the stretcher, a sad smile on her face, as the ambulance slowly delivered us across the Thames river to the hospice on the north side of Clapham Common. I knew she just wanted us to go home; to return to our small, eccentric, funny life together.
The hospice was well designed, non-clinical and clean; situated around a mature, well-tended and deceptively large garden with lots of paved walkways and quiet nooks.
Annie was too ill to visit the garden, but her room was on the lower ground floor and looked directly out to the lush English greenery, not yet turned by the autumn, and, on the rare sunny days, we would pull open the French windows and wheel her bed out onto the patio for lunch.
I am grateful for this tranquil place where she spent the last weeks of her life.

I am happy that the nursing staff would often come to close our door because the noise of loud, animated storytelling and raucous laughter from Annie and her visitors was disturbing the almost tomb like silence from the other rooms.
I take comfort that when we apologised for the racket, the nurses would tell us there was nothing to apologise for; that Annie's room was their favourite place because it was always full of life and love and laughter.
In her final weeks, Annie was surrounded by family and friends, people who truly loved her.
At the very end she was rarely conscious. We couldn't be sure that Annie could hear our stories, but we kept telling them to her anyway, as she lay in the bed, the slow drip of morphine keeping pain at bay.
And sometimes there would appear a smile on her lips and that was enough for us.

- **MM**

ABOUT THE AUTHOR

Annie Caulfield was a travel writer, dramatist and broadcaster.

Her travel books explore Australia, Benin, Jordan and her homeland, Northern Ireland. She published in newspapers and magazines, made documentaries for BBC Radio 4 and appeared regularly on From Our Own Correspondent and Crossing Continents.

Annie wrote many acclaimed plays for BBC Radio 3 and Radio 4, including Robeson, with Lenny Henry. After You've Gone, about the African-American singing duo Layton and Johnstone, received a race-in-the-media award. Dusty Won't Play, about Dusty Springfield's 1964 stand against apartheid, was a Tinniswood prize finalist.

Her stage work included Didn't Die for the Clean Break Theatre Company which won a Time Out magazine award.

Annie's children's book, Katie Milk Solves Crimes, was shortlisted for the Glen Dimplex award and longlisted for Ottakars' book awards. Annie created the Grim Tales children's series for Channel 4, script edited The Real McCoy comedy series and wrote episodes of the cult show This Life.

A BBC Radio Four play, also called My Cambodian Twin, about Annie's struggle to finish this book was broadcast in May 2019.

My Cambodian Twin was her last book.

Printed in Great Britain
by Amazon